Praise for *Where the Devil Ca...*

'A gripping reminder of h...
world around us'

VAL MCDERMID

'Anya Lipska's remarkable novel has been accruing considerable praise ... all of it justified'

The Good Book Guide

'A gripping, suspenseful, page-turner, spiced with humour and grit, with an addictive, charismatic, compelling, and excitingly different lead in Janusz Kiszka. RIP Nordic crime – here come the Poles'

EMLYN REES, author of *Hunted*

'Lipska's debut novel won't disappoint crime fiction fans ... keeps the plot twists coming at every turn'

We Love This Book

'A most unusual and exciting thriller with an immediacy and vividness that give it terrific appeal. It is a great read'
DAME JOAN BAKEWELL, broadcaster and author

'The moment I started reading this exciting thriller, I felt that thrill – the thrill of discovering a new favourite author'
MARK EDWARDS, author of *Catch Your Death*

'For those who like their thrillers with plots as convoluted as the inside of a snail's shell and with action that pulls no punches, it will be hard to put down'

The Tablet

'The story just flew off the page. An exciting new talent with a truly unique voice'

MARI HANNAH, author, the DCI Kate Daniels series

'It's not Anya Lipska's startling knowledge of police work that sets her apart: it's how cleverly she uses it to enhance the plot of this gripping thriller. A frighteningly good debut'

CHRIS SIMMS, author of *The Edge*

A DEVIL UNDER THE SKIN

By the same author

Where the Devil Can't Go
Death Can't Take a Joke

A DEVIL UNDER THE SKIN

ANYA LIPSKA

THE
FRIDAY
PROJECT

The Friday Project
An imprint of HarperCollins*Publishers*
1 London Bridge Street
London SE1 9GF
www.harpercollins.co.uk

First published by The Friday Project in 2015

ISBN: 978-0-00-810035-3

Printed and bound in Great Britain by
Clays Ltd, St Ives plc

MIX
Paper from
responsible sources
FSC™ C007454

For my brothers, Chris and Nick

He prays, but has a devil under the skin

Polish proverb

Prologue

PC Natalie Kershaw gripped the wheel as she steered the armed response vehicle around the Green Man round-about, the scream of the two-tone scything a path through the rush-hour traffic.

'Third exit. Left, left,' said Matt from the passenger seat, sending her a grin. She smiled back, breathing fast, her pulse marking a purposeful beat, yet feeling totally focused. This was what she'd spent eight weeks training for, and from what they'd been told about the shout, it was no false alarm this time – no kid poking a toy gun out of his bedroom window. Her brain noted the comforting cocoon of the body armour flattening her breasts, forcing her to sit upright, and the reassuring pressure of the Glock in its pancake holster against her thigh.

She felt … *safe*.

'It's the Maccy D's on Leytonstone High Street, right?' she asked, her voice sounding to her ears as tight and high as the engine of the BMW. She knew where they were going, obviously, but saying it out loud made it feel more real.

The gravelled voice of the Silver Commander came over the radio: 'Control room to Trojan 3. Latest we have is the suspect is in the toilets. Staff have been instructed to stay clear.'

The Sarge leaned in from the back seat, his face impassive. 'Pull up beyond the curry house, Natalie,' he said, as calmly as if they were about to pop in for a biryani. A restless knot of rubberneckers had gathered on the pavement outside the McDonald's. 'No borough uniforms,' he noted, with just the ghost of a sigh. 'Natalie, you cover the front exit and manage the MOPs, okay?' Although still conversational, his tone brooked no objection.

'Sarge.' She knew her place in the trio: she was the newbie, just a couple of months out of firearms training – still learning the ropes. *No problem.*

Matt and the Sarge approached the glass door of the McDonald's at a crabbing run, cradling their weapons, while Kershaw radioed in an update. After signing off, she left the ARV and took a few steps towards the onlookers. 'Armed police!' she shouted, one hand on the MP5 carbine slung from her shoulder, the other gesturing south down the high street. 'Move away *now*!'

Most of them scurried off sharpish, either at her tone or the sight of the gun. But one guy stood his ground, ignoring her command. 'What's going on?' he asked in that '*I know my rights*' tone that always made her heart sink.

She threw a look back at the Maccy D's – wondering if the boys had immobilised the suspect yet. *Where the fuck were the local uniforms?*

'*Sir*, will you just ...' She didn't finish the sentence. Registered instead the sudden widening of his eyes, fixed over her shoulder. Heard the Sarge bellow 'Natalie!' *His voice not cool any more.*

She spun round. In the car park, jogging towards her from behind a parked van was a young guy. Not very big or threatening to look at. *Mousy*, you might call him. Except for the thing he whirled in a great flashing arc out to one side. Something that made a rushing noise as it carved a passage through the air.

A giant samurai sword.

One

'This one is nice, no?' Kasia leaned over to look at the pricetag. 'Janek?'

Janusz Kiszka dragged his gaze from the black-denimed curve of his girlfriend's rear to squint at yet another sofa, no doubt called something like Dipstykk or Kolon by some marketing executive in Stockholm.

He shrugged. 'Yeah, it's ... nice.'

Tucking a lock of auburn hair behind one ear, Kasia shot him a mock-reproachful look. 'You're not taking this seriously, Janek! It's your apartment we're talking about here, you know.'

'Your apartment, too, in a few days' time,' he told her, feeling the corner of his mouth tug upward. He and Kasia might have been lovers for almost three years but now, standing on the brink of this new chapter in their lives, he kept experiencing a return of that fizzing, heady feeling that had accompanied the affair's early days.

Kasia regarded him sideways along her long lovely eyes, a dent in one cheek betraying a fugitive smile, before frowning down at the sofa again. She raked a long black-painted nail along its arm before giving a decisive nod. '*Tak.* I liked the tweedy one but leather is more hard-wearing, which is important with that cat of yours.'

Women, thought Janusz amiably. *So ... implacably practical. How the hell did men come to be labelled the unromantic sex?*

As they queued to pay under the fluorescent glare of the IKEA exit hangar, he glanced over at another couple, also in their forties, in the neighbouring line. The woman looked purposeful, contented, but the guy had the air of someone who'd been shot with a tranquilliser dart before being handcuffed to the overloaded trolley he was steering. The men exchanged a comradely look. It lasted no more than a second but it summed up everything Janusz knew he was about to lose – and gain – by giving up his bachelor lifestyle.

Later, back at his apartment in a Highbury mansion block, Janusz knelt on the living room floor trying to assemble a bedside cabinet, while Kasia tidied around him, her movements quicksilver. She bent to retrieve an ashtray overflowing with cigar butts from under the sofa, wrinkling her nose – after giving up smoking a few weeks earlier she could no longer stand the smell of stale tobacco – before moving to the wide bay window, where she tried to straighten the collapsing ramparts of *New Scientist* magazines stacked against the radiator.

'I'll find another home for them,' he promised, grinning up at her. She was still looking a little drawn and preoccupied, as she had for the last couple of weeks, but whenever he brought it up she just waved off his concern.

He reminded himself that it must be a stressful time for her.

She paused for a moment, gazing out of the window over the soft green ellipse of Highbury Fields, marshalled on its eastern side by a phalanx of Georgian terraces. 'Such a fantastic location,' she said. 'It must be worth a fortune these days. Have you never been tempted to move, buy something bigger a bit further out?'

Janusz had bought the place off his landlord for a song back in the eighties, the deposit hard earned by toil on a dozen building sites. Since then the cars parked around the Fields had grown sleeker and glossier by the year, the windowsills of the houses sprouting boxes of conifers so manicured they looked artificial. Only one of his original neighbours in the block remained – a cantankerous sitting tenant called Ron; the rest were junior investment bankers, or something in branding. Whenever Janusz bumped into one of them, he relished their evident confusion and shock at finding a big Polish guy in a shabby greatcoat, here in their exclusive block.

Abandoning his attempt to locate the elusive lug A, a critical component of the cabinet, he went to join Kasia at the window. Threading his arms around her waist he noticed that the first leaf buds were emerging on the plane tree outside. '*Nie, kotku,*' he said. 'Practically all my work is in the East End, and from here I can be there in twenty minutes.'

He was looking forward to playing house with Kasia, especially the novelty of sleeping together every night and waking up next to her, but some things were non-negotiable. He'd be wearing an oak overcoat before he'd consider relocating to some suburban hellhole in Zone 6.

'*Nie, nie*, I love it here!' she said. 'And only ten minutes to get into the West End!' She turned her head up to him, eyes wide. 'We could join the National Film Theatre!'

'Sure. Why not?' Janusz smiled to see her excitement. In her youth, Kasia had graduated from Lodz Film School, whose alumni included world class directors like Kieslowski and Wajda, but since Janusz had known her she rarely expressed any interest in film, and if he tried to bring up the subject, her manner seemed to say it was all a piece of a long-lost youthful foolishness.

Taking her hand, his fingers encountered her wedding band. She tugged at it. 'I can't get it off,' she told him, 'not even with oil.'

He sensed tears at the edge of her voice – most unlike Kasia.

'I have a bolt cutter, if you want me to ...?'

There was a tiny pause, before she said, 'Okay. But not now. Next time I come, *misiu*.'

He kissed the nape of her neck, where wisps of hair had escaped the ponytail she'd put it in to do the cleaning. Leaning back into him, she turned her face up to his. Their kiss was just getting interesting when the entryphone buzzer shattered the mood. She arched an enquiring eyebrow.

'It's probably Oskar,' murmured Janusz. 'We're going over to his place, to pick up the bathroom tiles.' Kasia hadn't asked for many improvements to his admittedly down-at-heel apartment, but on one score she'd been resolute: the vintage avocado bathroom suite and mould-streaked tiles had to go. Women were fussy about things like that.

8

Thirty seconds later, the barrel-shaped form of Janusz's lifelong mate Oskar burst through the door. 'Put your pantyhose on, ladyboy, I'm on a single yellow ...' He stopped in mid-flow. 'Oh, *przepraszam*, Kasia, I didn't know you were here.' They kissed three times on alternate cheeks in the Polish manner, but – not for the first time – Janusz wondered if he didn't detect a certain ... reserve in Oskar's body language. Had it always been there and he'd simply not noticed before, or was it a new development?

'You boys go ahead,' said Kasia. 'I've got to get back to the nail bar anyway. Saturday afternoons are always busy.'

'You haven't eaten anything all day!' Janusz chided; her lack of appetite was clearly another sign of the strain she was under. 'Have a couple of *pierogi* at least, before you go?'

'No time!' she said, picking up her coat. 'I'll grab something in Stratford.'

'I could manage a few *pierogi*,' offered Oskar, before clocking the meaningful look Janusz sent him. '*Dobrze*. I'll go and wait in the van, Janek, head off any traffic wardens. They're like sharks round here.' And with a lubricious wink at his mate, he disappeared.

Janusz drew Kasia to him by her coat lapels, getting a waft of the cinnamony scent he'd bought her for Christmas. She was tall, for a girl, but the top of her head only came to his nose. 'Are you sure it's a good idea to go back to the flat tonight?' he asked.

'*Tak*, why not?' She lifted one shoulder.

'Well, you said you're not sure whether Steve really believes it yet – that you're leaving?' His voice darkened.

'I don't want him giving you any trouble.' In the past, during domestic arguments, Kasia's husband had been known to compensate for the poverty of his vocabulary by resorting to his fists.

'Don't worry. I told you, he hasn't laid a finger on me in years.' She reached up to set her hands on his shoulders. 'Listen, I promised I'd stay for his birthday and I won't go back on that. He says there's something important he wants my advice on.'

Janusz didn't like the sound of that. 'Like what?!'

'I don't know – he won't say. It's probably just one of his business ideas.'

'And what if he tries to talk you out of leaving?' Janusz scowled at the floor, appalled at how needy the words made him sound.

'Janek, *kochanie*. He knows I'm moving out Monday evening. I already booked the cab to bring my things. I know I've talked about leaving before, but you have to believe me.' She cupped his jaw in her hand, let her seaweed-green eyes linger on his. 'This time it's different.'

After she'd left, he went over to the bay window so he could watch her crossing the Fields. Her figure, while no longer girlish, was still slender, and her brisk and hopeful walk gave her the look of a woman on the cusp of a great adventure. He craned to keep her in sight until the last possible moment before turning away, a lop-sided grin twisting his big jaw.

Had Janusz been able to keep Kasia in view for another twenty or thirty metres he would have seen something else: the outline of a black-clad figure hurrying across the park towards her.

TWO

'I made three and a half grand off the last shipment, and I can barely keep up with the orders!' Oskar was in high spirits as the Transit van sped off Highbury Corner roundabout. The two men were heading east to Oskar's lock-up garage, to collect the tiles Kasia had chosen for the bathroom.

Janusz grunted. Importing ceramic tiles from Poland, where they cost a fraction of the London price, was the latest in Oskar's long line of moneymaking ventures and, even allowing for the inevitable exaggeration, it did sound like it might prove his most lucrative yet.

'The tile factory's in Torun, so I've been able to see Gosia and the girls twice in the last month.' Oskar's round face was flushed with excitement – or perhaps from the half-drunk can of Tyskie sitting in the cup holder between them. 'I'm thinking I might hire a bigger van for the next run.'

When Janusz and Oskar had left Poland in the eighties, its economy had been flatlining, decimated by decades of

Communist rule and the ideological inanities of a state-run economy. Nowadays, the rationing and queues for flour were ancient history, but like so many of their compatriots who'd arrived in the UK more recently, Oskar still couldn't earn a decent income back home to support himself and his family – wife Gosia and two girls under ten.

'*Kurwa*, Janek! I said, does that mate of yours in Hackney still have a Luton van?' Janusz had been gazing out of the window, lost in thoughts of Kasia. 'You should see your face!' crowed Oskar, making loud kissing noises. 'You look like a schoolgirl just back from her first date!' Janusz rearranged his face into a scowl but it was too late – Oskar was on a roll. 'What's she got you doing next, loverboy, after the new bathroom? New carpets? Flowery curtains maybe? Mind you, that would be right up your street.'

'If I need any advice on patterns I'll give you a call,' growled Janusz, digging in his pocket for his smokes – despite all his attempts to cut down he still got through a tin a day of the small slim cigars he'd smoked for twenty-odd years. 'Anyway' – he sent Oskar a broad grin – 'whatever she wants, it'll be a small price to pay for having her between my sheets every night of the week.'

Oskar roared with laughter. 'Don't tell me! After she moves in, you think it's going to be pussy on demand?!' He slapped the steering wheel. 'You wait, sisterfucker. After a few weeks, she'll be spending all her time and energy scrubbing the kitchen floor – when she's not kicking your *dupe* because the place is a pigsty.'

The wind-up was to be expected, but this all-too-plausible picture triggered a flicker of disquiet in Janusz nonetheless. He hadn't lived with a woman since his brief and disastrous marriage to Marta back in Communist Poland, a lifetime ago. Was he kidding himself that he could adjust so late in life to the inevitable compromises it would require of him?

'We'd better grab a few beers before your prison door slams shut,' said Oskar, draining the contents of his can. 'I expect you lovebirds will be having a big romantic dinner tonight.'

Janusz wound the window down a few centimetres, tapped out some cigar ash. 'She's not moving in till Monday night.'

'Why not?' Oskar sounded mystified.

Janusz shifted in his seat. 'It's Steve's fortieth birthday tomorrow. He begged her to stay till then.'

Oskar tapped his fingers on the wheel, fallen uncharacteristically silent.

Janusz studied his mate out of the tail of his eye. They'd first met on national service, a pair of green and gawky nineteen-year-olds, but even now – more than a quarter-century later – Oskar hadn't got any better at hiding his feelings. He remembered the awkwardness he'd picked up in his body language towards Kasia, back at the apartment.

'Spit it out, Oskar,' he sighed.

'I just don't want to see you disappointed, Janek,' he said – a wary expression on his chubby features. 'After all, she's talked about leaving him before, hasn't she? Before some priest or other talked her out of it.'

Janusz fought down a spurt of fury, telling himself that Oskar only had his interests at heart. 'It's different this time,' he said, hearing the pathetic cry of the eternally hopeful lover. *Might Oskar be right – was he being a fool to believe her?*

It was true that, up until the last few months – despite her clear disillusionment with her husband – Kasia had been adamant on one score: as a devout Catholic the idea of abandoning her marriage was *niemozliwe*. Impossible.

Steve Fisher was a loudmouthed Cockney who, in two decades of marriage, had never held down a proper job for any length of time. From what Janusz could gather, he was the type who was permanently on the brink of some get-rich-quick scheme or other, none of which ever came to fruition. Then, as Kasia was approaching forty, she suddenly announced she was starting her own business, opening a nail bar with a friend. Perhaps the venture's subsequent success had given her confidence, or perhaps the milestone of her birthday had forced her to stare down the barrel of another four decades yoked to her useless *kutas* of a husband. Whatever the reason, a couple of weeks ago she'd indicated to Janusz that if he'd still have her, she was prepared to risk her mortal soul for the chance of earthly happiness.

Janusz threw his spent cigar stub out of the window. 'She says the pair of them grew up together, reckons she owes him something.' When Oskar didn't respond he went on, 'Listen, *kolego*, I know Kasia. Once she's made her mind up about something it would take a thermonuclear device to change it. I can wait a couple more days.'

Oskar heaved a theatrical sigh. 'It's your life, Janek. I just never thought you'd go to such extreme lengths to protect your cover story.'

Janusz frowned in incomprehension.

14

'Moving in with a woman, just to pretend you're heterosexual.'

Janusz was spared a further onslaught by a piercing whistled ditty – the unbearably chirpy ringtone of Oskar's new mobile. While he took the call, Janusz retrieved a crumpled newspaper from the footwell.

It was yesterday's copy of the *Evening Standard*, with a front-page headline that screamed: '*GIRL COP WHO SHOT SWORD MAN CLEARED*'. Inside, Janusz found the full story, which covered an inquest into the death of some nutjob who'd gone berserk with a samurai sword in Leytonstone McDonald's the previous year – an incident which, not surprisingly, had left swordboy with three police bullets in the chest. Janusz dimly recalled there had been a great fuss in the media about it all when the story first broke.

To protect her identity, the female firearms cop who'd shot the guy was referred to solely by her codename, and yet as Janusz read on, it dawned on him that he knew exactly who officer V71 was. *Natalie Kershaw*. The girl *detektyw* who'd crossed his path more than once, most recently when she'd investigated the murder of one of his dearest friends – an investigation that had led to her being brutally stabbed. According to the report, V71 was the only female member of the armed response unit based at Walthamstow. Hadn't she told him, the last time they'd met, eighteen months back, that she was about to become Walthamstow's first female firearms officer?

The inquest verdict was 'lawful killing', but a senior officer at the Met was quoted as saying that V71 would have to undergo 'extensive psychological assessment' to decide whether she was fit to return to operational duties.

Janusz closed the paper, a frown corrugating his brow. 'You remember that girl cop, Natalia?' he said, after Oskar had hung up.

'Blondie, you mean? The one who tried to get you arrested once?'

'Yeah, that's her. I think she's the one who shot that guy in Leytonstone, outside McDonald's, last year.'

'*Naprawde?*' said Oskar. 'Still, what do they expect, handing guns out to girls? She probably had a row with her boyfriend at breakfast, then some poor *kutas* looks at her the wrong way.' Holding the steering wheel steady with his knees, he used both hands to aim an imaginary gun at Janusz. '*Boum!*'

'*Oskar!*' Janusz pressed himself back into his seat as the van veered to the left. 'Anyway, this guy had it coming – he went for her with a samurai sword.'

'*Kurwa mac!*' Oskar gave an appreciative whistle. 'The girl's got bigger *jaja* than you, *kolego*!'

'Yeah, and in any sane country they'd give the girl a medal, but here she'll probably get a big black mark on her record.'

'It's "health and safety gone mad",' said Oskar. It was one of his favourite English phrases and one he used often, even when it signally failed to fit the circumstances.

Janusz stared at the front-page headline. The girl might have threatened him with arrest in the past, it was true, but she'd also saved his life once, and he'd grown to respect her uncompromising stance, her determination to nail the bad guys. He wondered if he should call her. *And say what, exactly?* That shooting the fruitcake had clearly been the right thing to do? As though his opinion on the subject would mean anything to her.

The last time he'd seen her, in a Walthamstow pub, she'd been recovering from the knifing, an attack that he still felt responsible for. He remembered sensing a change in her then, a feeling that beneath her usual tough girl bravado she was as raw as a freshly skinned blister.

Three

'Perhaps I can turn the question around. Why do *you* think you're here?' The sunlight streaming through the window bounced off the letterbox specs of the lady shrink, making it impossible for PC Natalie Kershaw to make out the expression in her eyes.

Kershaw picked at a loose thread that had escaped the inside seam of her jacket sleeve. 'Because I shot a paranoid schizophrenic who was about to disembowel me on Leytonstone High Street.'

The shrink didn't respond, but as Kershaw was already learning, Pamela – *or was it Paula?* – had the disconcerting ability to fill even her silences with meaning. She risked a sideways glance at the wall clock: barely twenty minutes into her first session of psych assessment and already she felt like chewing her own arm off. In the eleven months since she'd shot Kyle Furnell, every tiny detail of her actions on that day had already been picked apart, first by internal investigators, then by counsel at the inquest – and now she had to go through it all over again. She swallowed a sigh, hearing again her old Sarge and confidant, DS 'Streaky' Bacon, telling her to play the game and get it over with so she could get back to operational duties.

'I totally understand it's a big deal when somebody gets shot,' said Kershaw, trying for a more conciliatory tone. 'But like I told everyone from the start, when I pulled the trigger, I honestly believed there was an immediate threat to my life.'

Pamela/Paula bestowed a half-smile of what could be encouragement but still said nothing.

Christ on a bike.

'The inquest did exonerate me,' Kershaw went on, feeling sweat prickle on her scalp – *it was stifling in here.* 'The coroner said it was wholly understandable, in the circumstances, for me to shoot him.' She remembered his summing-up, and how he'd described Furnell as a 'profoundly disturbed young man'. He'd gone on to remind the jury what Furnell had ingested that day, in the hours leading up to his fateful realisation that the staff at Leytonstone Maccy D's were secret members of a cult bent on eliminating the citizens of E11 – presumably by poisoning their Chicken McNuggets. The list had included Temazepam, Ketamine, a four-pack of Special Brew and a bottle of Night Nurse, the last item prompting a few titters from the public benches. On hearing the coroner's words, a great wave of relief had engulfed Kershaw as she sensed which way the verdict would go.

When she'd watched the TV coverage of the inquest at home that night, well on her way through the evening's first bottle of red wine, it had stirred more complex emotions. The family's solicitor – all sharp suit and professional outrage – did most of the talking on the court steps after the verdict, but it was the figure standing alongside him whom Kershaw's eyes kept being drawn back to. *Furnell's mum.*

Tanya Furnell was a shapeless lump of a woman in a shabby fake fur jacket with badly dyed red hair. She looked nearer fifty than her actual age of thirty-eight – and yet she held herself ramrod-straight on those steps, her expression defiant yet dignified. When the reporter asked for her response to the verdict, she said that all she'd ever wanted was some word of regret from the Met about the way her son had died. *Dream on,* Kershaw had thought, not unsympathetically. That just wasn't gonna happen – not after the Met had won the case.

Almost a year on, Kershaw could barely remember the shooting itself beyond a series of blurred freeze-frame images, but for some reason, the look on Tanya Furnell's face in the news report – that had burned itself indelibly into her memory.

She pulled at the errant thread on her sleeve again, before snapping it clean off.

'Are you sure you wouldn't be more comfortable taking your jacket off?' asked the shrink.

'I'm fine, thanks,' Kershaw bared her teeth in a facsimile of a grin. She'd never been on the wrong end of an interrogation before and she wasn't enjoying the experience.

The therapist checked something in the file she had open on her knee. 'The coroner did also say, didn't he, that a more experienced officer would probably have reached for their Taser, rather than the, um ...'

'Glock 17.'

Oops. Now she was looking at Kershaw like she just said something really interesting.

'And the other weapon you were carrying?'

'A Heckler and Koch MP5.'

'How would you describe that to a lay person?'

Kershaw shrugged, looked at the floor. 'It's a 9mm semi-automatic carbine, set to single fire.'

'Carrying lethal weapons like that, I'd imagine it must give you a great feeling of power?'

'Not really. It's not like we go out planning to use them.'

The shrink's face was arranged in a caring expression but behind the glasses, her gaze was unblinking. 'It would be understandable though, to imagine shooting someone who was about to do you great harm.'

'Well I never have,' she lied.

'Let's go back a bit, to when you first applied to become an Authorised Firearms Officer.' Pamela/Paula looked down at the file on her lap. 'I'm sure it must have crossed your mind that being armed might have saved you from the very serious assault you'd suffered, just a few months earlier?'

Kershaw froze, her throat tightening. *The cry of a seagull. The sight of the Thames far below, through a plate glass window. A bloody handprint on white paint.* Mentally batting away the other images, she gripped the armrests of her chair, fighting the sudden swoop of vertigo.

'What's that got to do with anything?' she said, abandoning all efforts to keep the anger out of her voice. 'It had nothing to do with my decision to go into SCO19!'

Paula – *yes, Paula, that was her name* – fell silent again, but her gaze flickered down, just for a millisecond.

Kershaw realised that her right hand had gone to her side, and was cradling the spot where she'd been stabbed. Feeling the warmth of her skin through her shirt, she pictured the line of stitches: they looked like the backbone of a swordfish, fading to silver now but still there to greet her every time she caught an unwitting glimpse of herself naked in the mirror. The place where her spleen had once nestled, thinking itself safe behind the bones of her ribcage; the place where sometimes she'd swear she could still feel an ... absence.

She remembered what Streaky had drummed into her, years ago when she'd started in CID, his golden rule when interrogating suspects. *Take control.*

She cleared her throat. 'If I could ask a question?'

Paula nodded.

'I appreciate that it's important to assess an AFO after there's been ... a fatal shooting,' she said, choosing her words uber-carefully, 'but I'd be really grateful if you could give me an idea of how long you expect ... all this to take? It's just, well, it cost a shedload of taxpayers' money to train me up as a firearms officer and I think it's my responsibility to get back to work as quickly as possible.'

Paula gave her a long, intent look. 'I think your sense of responsibility is to be admired.' Kershaw scanned her expression, but couldn't find any sarcasm there. 'You're an intelligent woman, Natalie, so I'll tell you frankly what I think. In my view, it was ... unusual, to say the least, that you were accepted for firearms training so soon after suffering such a serious assault. It makes the process we have to go through now a more complex and potentially lengthy one. Because it's *my* responsibility to ensure that

22

officers are not returned to firearms duty unless I am one hundred per cent sure it is safe and prudent to do so.'

Smiling at Kershaw, she closed the file on her knee. 'Time's up for today. Please book another appointment at reception on your way out.'

As the door clicked shut behind her, Kershaw was struck by an infuriating realisation. For the entirety of their forty-five-minute encounter, it had been the shrink, and not her, who'd been in complete control.

Four

On Monday morning, as Janusz climbed the long up-escalator at Wanstead tube – a station so far east on the Central line it could make your ears bleed – he reflected that the new contract with the insurance company couldn't have come at a better time.

His work as a private investigator, which largely involved chasing bad debts and missing persons for clients from East London's Polish community, tended to follow the feast-or-famine model. Most years, it produced more than enough for a single man to live on, but with Kasia moving in he needed something more *solidne* – even if she was a successful businesswoman in her own right. *Or perhaps because she was*, he allowed, with a wry grin. An old-fashioned outlook perhaps, but that was how he'd been brought up – and at his age he wasn't likely to suddenly come over all metrosexual.

Then there was Bobek, his son back in Poland, to think about. The boy might have been fathered in a single misjudged night of reunion with ex-wife Marta, but from the moment Janusz had laid eyes on the shockingly vulnerable scrap of humanity in the maternity ward crib, he'd loved him beyond reason. He made it a point of principle never to miss a single month's maintenance cheque, even when times had been tough. And now Bobek was fifteen, would be sixteen in a couple of months – *Mother of God! Incredible to think he was almost a man* – there would be new expenses, university fees for one, to think about.

Five minutes' walk from the tube, Janusz found the place he was looking for – the St Francis of Assisi Residential Home. Even with half the facade obscured by a lattice of builders' scaffolding, the place was an imposing chunk of nineteenth-century Gothic, its pillared entrance so reminiscent of a church that Janusz had to check an impulse to make the sign of the cross as he stepped over the threshold. Having braced himself for the familiar undernote of old piss and Dettol he'd encountered in old people's homes, he was pleasantly surprised to find that the only smell was the lavender whiff of furniture polish. Sure, the faded floral carpet and striped wallpaper hadn't been in fashion since the eighties, but the double height lobby bisected by an old oak staircase made the place feel pleasingly airy and bright.

'I have an appointment to see Mr Raczynski,' Janusz told the apricot-cheeked girl on reception. 'On behalf of Haven Insurance.' She was no more than twenty, and clearly Polish, judging by her accent – not to mention a level of grooming rarely seen among English girls of that age. She started dialling a number but before she'd even finished, Janusz heard a gravelly voice close by his ear.

'I just saw Wojtek going into the conservatory, Beata – why don't I take our guest through?'

Janusz turned to see the beaky profile of an elderly man, tall in spite of his advanced age, if somewhat stooped.

Beata nodded, smiling. *'Dziekuje bardzo*, Panie Kasparek.'

'English, please, Beata, English.' As the old guy wagged a skinny finger at her, the tableau formed by the pair of them put Janusz in mind of some medieval engraving – Death warning Youth of the brevity of Life, perhaps.

He turned his gaze on Janusz – eyes dark as a sparrow's and alive with intelligence – and in a sibilant whisper that could have been heard fifty metres away told him, *'Integration*. That's the way to get on. No point coming to London and behaving like you're still in fucking Poznan.'

Janusz grinned. 'I agree.' He put out his hand. 'Janusz Kiszka. Pleased to make your acquaintance.'

'I'm forgetting my manners. Stefan Kasparek. *Enchanté.*' The old man's hand felt bony but his grip was a match for Janusz's meaty fist, nonetheless. 'You'll need a guide – I'm afraid the place is an absolute rabbit warren.' His English sounded unmistakably upper class, with only the trace of a Polish accent, and he was well turned out in a tweed jacket and tie, although Janusz couldn't help noticing the worn elbows of the jacket, the shirt collar fraying at the edges.

'Onward,' said Kasparek. He grasped the younger man's arm with the unembarrassed pragmatism of the old and they set out, Janusz adjusting his step to his companion's determined – if somewhat lurching – gait.

26

'Lost the kneecap, to a Boche sniper, in '44,' said Stefan, succinctly. 'The son of a whore.'

Along the way, they encountered several residents making their dogged way to and fro, Stefan handing out greetings and advice like some cheerful early pontiff dispensing indulgences. 'Bohuslaw!' he cried, spying a shuffling bald man with a pronounced pot belly. 'I'm going to the bookmakers later, if you'd like me to place a wager for you?' Bohuslaw raised a shaky thumbs-up. 'Used to shag anything that moved,' Stefan confided, in his penetrating sotto voce, once he'd passed. 'But now he's down to one testicle, he sticks to the four-legged fillies.'

'Is everyone here Polish?' Janusz asked.

'No, no,' Stefan shook his head, 'there's a good few Irish and English here, too. Some Catholic do-gooder started the place back in the eighties, so there tend to be a lot of left-footers, but I'm reliably informed that a belief in the Virgin Birth isn't compulsory.'

At a set of French doors, he paused to kiss the hand of an etiolated woman, who must have been a great beauty in her youth. Now, her well-cut frock seemed to mock her flat chest and wasted flanks. She smiled vaguely, in another world, until Stefan stooped to whisper something in her ear, making her laugh and returning the ghost of a blush to her once-pretty cheeks.

'You should see pictures of her as a girl,' sighed Stefan. 'She'd have given Maureen O'Hara a run for her money.'

'I can imagine,' said Janusz. 'You seem to know everyone. Have you been here long?'

'Oh for ever,' said Stefan with a dismissive wave. 'As billets go, it's not bad – but there's no time off for good behaviour and when you do leave, it's a one-way voyage to the boneyard.' He pronounced *'voyage'* in the French way.

In the conservatory, Stefan steered him to a rattan sofa overlooking the garden where a chubby man in his eighties sat eating biscuits, a mug of tea in his hand. 'Ah, here he is,' said Stefan. 'Wojtek! You have a visitor, you lucky dog.'

After Stefan's acerbic intelligence, Janusz found the interview uphill work. Wojtek Raczynski was a jolly soul, a little like a clean-shaven Father Christmas, but all too easily sidetracked onto the subject of his great-grandchildren, who he believed were learning *okropne* habits – swearing and cheeking their elders – from their comprehensive school in Leyton.

According to Tomek Morski, Janusz's contact at Haven Insurance, the firm paid Wojtek a £25,000 annual pension, funded by an annuity he'd bought some twelve years earlier, and since they'd be shelling out till he dropped off the twig, they wanted to make sure he hadn't done so already. Apparently, it wasn't uncommon for family members to 'forget' to tell the insurance company to halt payments after their loved one had departed this life.

Janusz had been hired to run spot checks on a random selection of their Polish-speaking annuitants: with getting on for a million Poles in the UK, there was a growing demand for investigators who spoke the language and had a nose for anything fishy. As much as it grieved him to admit it, the scale of the recent influx of his compatriots had inevitably brought with it a number of scam artists and criminals. According to

Tomek, if Janusz did a good job on this first round of work for them, he'd be up for a slice of the insurance fraud pie – fake whiplash claims, staged car accidents, and the like – cases whose complexity could make them highly lucrative.

Wojtek's case promised to be child's play by comparison. He was demonstrably alive and – judging by the number of biscuits he demolished during their half-hour interview – in robust health for a man of eighty-eight. The only hitch was that Janusz needed to see photographic ID to confirm beyond doubt that Wojtek was who he said he was – but he didn't have anything to hand. Janusz arranged to return to check the old boy's passport, which his daughter looked after for him, in a few days' time.

Half an hour later, Janusz emerged between the Corinthian columns that framed the front porch into a surprisingly spring-like March day, with a powerfully positive impression of life at St Francis. He'd always thought he'd rather die than go into an old people's home, but he had to admit that seeing out your final days at a place like this one mightn't be the ordeal he'd feared, after all.

He'd just reached the street and was about to light a cigar when he heard a voice behind him calling his name. It was Stefan, one skinny arm raised as though hailing a taxi, the other leaning on a walking stick.

'What a splendid day!' he said, on reaching Janusz. 'Walk with me to the High Street,' he added, brandishing his stick like a battle standard. Suppressing a smile at the old boy's imperious manner, Janusz fell into step alongside him.

At the corner of the High Street, he turned to bid Stefan farewell, but the old guy said, 'Let me buy you a cup of tea. It isn't often I get the opportunity to converse with someone still in possession of a full set of marbles.'

Janusz barely paused before bowing his head in acceptance: he wasn't in a rush, and anyway, he enjoyed the company of old people. It wasn't far to what was clearly Stefan's regular café, judging by the effusive welcome he received from the Turkish guys behind the counter.

'When I first came to London, in '45, all the greasy spoons were run by Eyeties,' said Stefan, in a whisper loud enough to turn heads as they made for a window table. 'Now, it's Turks. Next year, who knows!' His chuckle sounded like a rusted iron door being wrenched open.

Sitting opposite each other, Janusz got his first proper look at his companion. Age had sculpted what remained of the flesh on Stefan's face into dramatic folds and fissures, but he still had a luxuriant head of white hair, swept back from a pronounced widow's peak in a style that had last enjoyed popularity in the fifties or early sixties. And yet there was something about his darting gaze and ever-changing expression that gave him an air of irrepressible youth, making it hard for Janusz to guess his age. *Late seventies, perhaps?*

The bird-like eyes caught Janusz's gaze. 'You're wondering how old I am' – an age-spotted hand waved away his polite murmur of protest – 'Don't worry. I'm used to it. Paradoxically, I find it's always the young who are the most obsessed with age.'

He poured a stream of sugar into his black tea – Janusz noting, approvingly, that his commitment to integration stopped short of polluting the brew with milk – and stirred it briskly. 'I was born in Lwow, which I believe the Ukrainians now call Lviv – in 1923.'

Kurwa! Janusz did the sums: the old boy must be ninety. He appeared in astonishingly good shape for his age – as well as being sharp as a tack. 'You don't look it,' he said; the automatic response to learning the age of anyone over thirty, although this time, sincerely meant.

Stefan straightened his back. 'My father lived to 101, God Rest his Soul. Never missed a day in his vegetable garden, and dropped dead hoeing the asparagus bed.'

'So ... were you in Lwow when the Russians invaded?'

'Indeed I was. The tanks arrived the day after my seventeenth birthday. As a boy scout, I naturally took part in the defence of the city – until the generals *kapitulowali*.' It was the first time he'd slipped into Polish, as if such a shameful event could only properly be named in their mother tongue.

The waiter delivered Stefan's bacon sandwich but instead of starting to eat, he lifted off the top layer of bread and set it aside.

'I ended up in Kolyma, in the camps, mining gold for Stalin.' As Stefan talked, he retrieved a plastic bag from his breast pocket, and produced a pair of nail scissors, before starting to snip the fatty rind from a rasher, apparently oblivious to Janusz's mystified look. 'Mining!' he chuckled. 'That's a fancy word for hacking lumps out of permafrost with a fucking pickaxe.'

After dropping the spiral of bacon rind into his plastic bag, he was just starting surgery on a second rasher when he noticed Janusz's expression. 'I have to watch my figure, you know,' he said, patting his trim midriff. 'The

31

birdies are the beneficiaries. Waste not, want not –
Kolyma taught me that.'

Once the bacon had been denuded of all its fat, Stefan
cleaned his scissors on a paper napkin, continuing in a
matter of fact tone, 'It was minus 50 the first winter. Men
died like snowflakes on a hot stove. I was young. I
survived.' Bracing his shoulders, he took a surprisingly
large bite of his sandwich.

'How long were you there?'

Stefan took his time finishing his mouthful, before
dabbing his lips with a napkin. 'They let me out in '42 to
join Anders' Army – the Allies were desperate for young
men by that time. So I exchanged Siberia for *la bella
Italia*.'

'You fought in Italy?' Janusz was impressed: General
Anders' Second Polish Corps had played a decisive role in
the Allied push through Italy, earning renown for their
bravery at the Battle of Monte Cassino. 'Yes. That was
where I mislaid my kneecap, just outside Ancona.'

Janusz struggled to think of something to say that
wouldn't be a platitude: he always felt overawed to hear
of the bravery and sacrifice made by the wartime generation of his fellow Poles. Stefan would have grown up
under the Second Republic, when Poland had been one
of the great European powers – until its invasion by the
Nazis from one side, and the Red Army from the other.
Then, to have survived Kolyma – the most brutal place in
the entire gulag, graveyard to hundreds of thousands of
Poles and countless other 'enemies of socialism' – to fight
as an Allied soldier … and for what? To see America and
Britain deliver his country into the arms of Stalin and
decades of Soviet rule.

Stefan was frowning down at his stick-like wrists as if they belonged to someone else. 'I was built like a bull, then, though you wouldn't believe it now.' Suddenly he flapped his free hand. 'Anyway, that's all ancient history, old men's war stories. What about you? I take it you're some kind of insurance investigator?'

Janusz paused. Put like that, he wasn't at all sure he liked the sound of his new role. Private investigator was one thing, 'insurance investigator' summoned up something more corporate and somehow less ... *honorowy* – especially when measured alongside Stefan's life. He realised he felt something close to envy for the old man's generation. He would never experience an existential fight, never be part of a band of brothers. He remembered something someone had once said on the subject that had always stuck in his mind: 'War exists so that men can experience unconditional love.'

He laid out the bare bones of what he was doing for Haven – avoiding any confidential details – while making it plain that most of his work as a private investigator was carried out not for corporations but on behalf of fellow Poles.

The opening bars of a Chopin polka sounded from Stefan's pocket. Setting down his sandwich, he pulled out an iPhone – Janusz was amused to see it was the latest model – and using a stylus device, tapped in his passcode.

'Forgive me,' he said, squinting at the screen, 'I'm playing chess with someone in Kiev and the bastard has just threatened my queen.'

While Stefan decided his next move, Janusz took the opportunity to check his own phone. He wanted to find out what time Kasia would be arriving at the flat with her stuff that evening, but the two texts he'd sent since they parted on Saturday had so far gone unanswered.

Still nothing. There was, however, a missed call from Barbara, her partner in the nail bar.

'Janek,' she said, her voice strung as tight as piano wire. 'Please call me the minute you get this. It's urgent.'

Five

Kershaw swiped her card at the entrance of the SCO19 office, trying to ignore the sour churning in her gut – which wasn't entirely down to the bottle of Shiraz followed by Metaxa chasers she'd put away the previous night while watching some forgettable DVD box-set.

Throughout the long months of the internal inquiry, then the inquest, she'd convinced herself that once she'd been exonerated – and she'd never seriously considered the alternative – she'd be out on shouts within a few weeks. Yesterday's session with the shrink had upended a bucket of cold water over that idea. She cursed her own naivety: she should have known they'd make her jump through hoops before she got back her firearms authorisation – if only for the benefit of the media.

'Here she is,' said a friendly voice. It was Matt, her fellow crewmate in the ARV on the day that Kyle Furnell had got shot. He set a mug of tea down on her desk. 'Saw you parking up, so I made you a brew.'

35

'That's very thoughtful of you, Matt,' she said, raising a quizzical eyebrow. 'You're not working up to a proposal of marriage, are you?'

He pretended to consider the idea, before shaking his head. 'Nah. No offence, Nat, but I've set my heart on having kids who'll grow up bigger than hobbits.'

With the routine hostilities out of the way, Matt sat down at his desk, opposite hers. 'You all right?' he asked – concern softening his features. She pulled a half shrug, half nod. 'You did get my message, after the inquest?'

'Yeah, thanks for that, Matt. Sorry I didn't reply. I decided to have a quiet weekend, you know, after all the hoo-hah last week.' She'd almost taken Matt up on his suggestion of a few jars down the local to celebrate the result, but after seeing the news report with Kyle Furnell's mum, she just hadn't felt like it.

He nodded. 'I can imagine. I just wanted you to know that everyone here was made up for you, after the coroner gave you the all-clear?'

'Ah, bless them,' she said. A year ago, after the shooting, when she'd got back to the unit, all the guys had made a point of coming over to tell her they'd have done exactly the same thing in her situation. *Well, nearly all the guys.* 'What about Lee Carver?' she asked, eyebrows raised. They both knew there would be a few in SCO19 who'd be revelling in her recent troubles, older guys who still had a visceral reaction to the idea of a woman carrying – aka armed. Lee Carver, a firearms training instructor in his fifties, was one of them.

'Well, maybe not him.' Matt sank his head into his shoulders and deepened his voice to an inarticulate growl. *'The only thing I want to see a female carrying is my dinner – on a fucking tray.'*

They both laughed – but Kershaw's heart wasn't really in it.

During her first week of firearms training, Carver had more or less blanked her – pointedly avoiding eye contact and only addressing her when it was absolutely necessary. Then, out on the range one day, just as she was lining up on a target, he'd dropped to a crouch alongside her. 'Help me out would you, Kershaw?' he murmured close by her ear, all friendly curiosity.

'Yes, Skipper?' *Men like Carver loved being called Skipper.*

'You *are* a woman, right?' He let his eyes flick down to her breasts, once – as if they puzzled him.

'Yes, Skipper.'

'That's what I thought.' She could still see his hot blue eyes, inches from her face, and smell the gusts of his notoriously rank breath. 'So what exactly are you doing here – on my fucking range?'

Pretty much everyone on the course – all of them guys her age or a few years older – thought Carver was a knuckle-dragging gobshite. And if Kershaw had reported his outburst, he'd have been chin-deep in shit. But that wasn't her way: never had been, in all the four and a half years she'd been in the Job. *No.* Her response was to memorise the instruction manual and use every second of the target practice on offer, as well as doubling the hours she spent in the gym. Marksmanship was only half the story: you had to be superfit, too, especially when it came to the fiendish 'run and shoot' exercise. *Sprint for 100 metres, adopt shoot position shouted by instructor, one shot at target. Miss and you fail. Exceed 45 seconds and you fail.*

After five or six weeks, Kershaw was hitting body mass on the bad-guy-shaped target, 46, sometimes 48, times out of a possible 50.

By the last day, of the sixteen who'd started, only Kershaw and seven others had gone the distance and qualified – and she'd risen to become the second best shooter of her intake. Later, when everyone was down the local celebrating, she'd picked her moment to collar Lee Carver at the bar. 'If it hadn't been for you, Skipper,' she said, smiling up at him, 'I probably would have packed it in after the first week.' He stared down at her, confusion and three pints of Stella narrowing his eyes. 'So … I got you a thank-you pressie,' she said, handing him a Boots bag. Left him staring at a bottle of Listerine.

The thought of Lee Carver and his kind getting off on her current predicament did have one positive, though: it iron-plated her resolve to get her firearms authorisation back and prove them all wrong.

Taking a gulp of tea, Kershaw started to go through her email inbox, but found her thoughts drifting back to the day she'd qualified, almost a year ago. At the moment the chief instructor had handed her the little red book that was her authorisation to carry, she'd fizzed like a freshly popped bottle of champagne. But on the heels of the elation came a deep sadness. She'd convinced herself, wrongly as it turned out, that such a big life landmark would bring the return of something she had lost.

Because the worst legacy of getting stabbed hadn't been the loss of her spleen, but the disappearance of something she valued far more: her dad's voice. After he'd died of cancer nearly five years ago, she would still hear him popping into her head with one of his sayings or daft gags – his East End drawl, always on the brink of a chuckle, sounding as clear and real as if he was standing next to her. He usually appeared just when she most needed a word of consolation or encouragement – or even, now and again, a telling-off.

But ever since the stabbing – even at the moment she'd won her spurs as a firearms officer – *silence*. Just when she'd needed him most, his voice had disappeared. *Like Scotch mist.*

'Nat? Are you all right?'

Looking up to find Matt's worried eyes on her, she realised she must have said the phrase – one of her dad's – out loud.

'Sorry. Must be going bonkers.'

'Good job you're seeing a shrink, then.' He raised an eyebrow. 'How's that working out for you by the way?'

'Like having a root canal and a bikini wax at the same time.'

The phone on her desk trilled. After a brief exchange she hung up, blowing out an exasperated breath.

'What's up?' asked Matt.

'Guess what I'm gonna be doing the rest of the day?'

Matt shrugged.

'Cleaning weapons in the armoury. Five years as a cop, two as a detective, all that grief getting my ticket to carry? And now I've literally been demoted to oily rag.'

Six

The nail bar business that Kasia co-owned with Barbara stood in one of the farthest reaches of Stratford's old shopping centre. Built in the early seventies, when poured concrete was the building material of choice for the trend-conscious architect, the mall squatted sulkily in the midst of Stratford's one-way system, ugly sister to the glittering new towers of Westfield Stratford City across the way.

In fact, Janusz had always preferred the older, shabbier development over the flashy new pretender. For starters, it still housed an old-fashioned market on weekdays that – alongside the familiar ranks of anaemic Dutch tomatoes and golden delicious – now also boasted a Lithuanian stall selling passable *kielbasa* and decent pickles.

As he pushed open the door of Elegant Nailz, he was hit by a vaporous wave of solvent that made his eyes water. The place was more of a glorified kiosk than a proper shop, the original premises having been split down the middle to create two shop fronts, the other housing a shoe repairers run by a family from Hong Kong. There was barely enough room for three nail tables, but Kasia and Barbara did a brisk enough trade in acrylic and gel extensions to keep them busy past 7 p.m. most evenings.

Barbara was working on the nails of a pretty black girl with long straightened hair. Turning on the tabletop fan, she left her client drying her talons under the air stream and came over to the minuscule reception desk, to embrace him.

'I kept getting your voicemail,' he said. 'So I came straight over. What's up?'

'Have you heard anything from Kasia?' Her anxious eyes scanned his face.

'*Nie.* Not for a couple of days.' Seeing Barbara's pretty features crumple at his response, Janusz felt a physical sense of dread – as if someone just blasted his gut full of quick-setting cement.

'I haven't seen her since Saturday,' Barbara went on. 'When she didn't turn up this morning I wasn't too worried – Monday mornings are always quiet so she often works from home on the website, or following up email queries. You know me, I am a *katastrofa* with computers. But she missed three appointments this afternoon and her phone is going straight to voicemail – Kasia's *never* done that before.'

After disgorging this rush of information, Barbara glanced over her shoulder and managed a smile at the black girl, still playing an invisible piano beneath the fan dryer. The girl returned the smile – she could see there was some drama unfolding between nail-lady and the big guy in the old-school army-style coat but since they were

41

speaking Polish there was very little point in trying to earwig on their conversation.

Seeing how jittery Barbara was, Janusz took her hands in his and spoke quietly, reassuringly. '*Dobrze*. So she came in on Saturday afternoon, right?' – as he said it, he saw again Kasia trotting across Highbury Fields, her hair glinting in the sunshine.

'*Tak*. Around 4 p.m., in time for the late appointments. She left at seven.'

'And you've had no contact since then?' He kept his voice low and his eyes locked on hers.

'*Zero*.'

'And … Steve?'

'I can't raise him either.' Barbara's voice fell to a whisper. 'It's as if they both dropped off the face of the earth.'

'I am sure there's a perfectly reasonable explanation.' Janusz dredged up a comforting grin. 'Maybe she's sick and Steve was meant to call you to let you know. You know what he's like.'

She looked doubtful.

'Look, I'm going to head over to the flat,' he said. 'Just to make sure everything's okay.'

'*Dobrze*,' she sighed, twisting a bangle on her wrist. 'I hope it's the right thing to do.' She met his gaze, before looking away, embarrassed. 'You might run into Steve.' As Kasia's closest friend, Barbara knew all about their three-year affair, and – no doubt – the fact she was finally leaving Steve.

Barbara took a breath and for a moment seemed on the brink of saying more, but instead gave a tiny shake of her head. 'Just be careful.'

42

He patted her hand. 'Don't you worry, Barbara, I can handle Steve.'

Twenty minutes later, he was approaching the Victorian terrace within sight of the Olympic stadium where Kasia and Steve lived, wondering what he'd say if he did encounter her husband. Their paths had crossed once before, after Kasia had turned up to meet Janusz sporting a black eye that make-up couldn't quite conceal. After Janusz had coaxed out of her what had happened, he'd paid Steve a surprise visit, pretending to be Kasia's cousin over from Poland, and given the *chuj* a taste of what it felt like to be on the wrong end of a fist. It seemed the encounter had achieved the intended effect – according to Kasia, he'd never raised his hand to her again.

It suddenly occurred to him that Kasia's impending departure might have changed that. Was Kasia lying in a darkened room, ashamed to go out, wearing the souvenirs of her husband's ungovernable rage? As that image rose before him, Janusz knocked on the front door of their maisonette louder than was really necessary. Far from being worried about bumping into Steve, he was starting to look forward to it.

When, after a second knock, it was clear that there was nobody home, Janusz pulled out the bump key he always carried with him. Twenty seconds of jiggling later and he was inside.

'Kasia?' he tried. 'Steve?' *Nothing.*

It was strange to be back here. The woodwork had been painted in one of those dreary heritage colours that Kasia liked – and she'd probably done the graft, too, no doubt while Steve was down the pub talking up his latest moneymaking scheme.

43

The place was as clean as a teardrop – even the skirting boards betrayed not a speck of dust – and the citrus smell of cleaning product sang in the air. The only sound was the discreet burble of the fridge freezer in the kitchen, where he found nothing out of place but for a single upended coffee cup in a rack on the draining board. He checked the fridge, which held a cling-filmed plateful of *pierogi*, a pint of fresh milk missing an inch, and a chiller drawer full of plastic wrapped vegetables, with use-by dates a couple of days hence.

So far, his professionalism had allowed Janusz to case the joint as if this were just another investigation, but he was finding it hard to fight down a yawing sensation in the pit of his stomach. *Where was Kasia? And Steve? What the fuck was going on?*

He realised he'd been putting off checking the bedroom till last. *Grow up*, he growled to himself as he opened the door.

Still, seeing the double bed, it was hard not to visualise Kasia lying there beside her husband. Janusz shut his eyes, trying to retrieve something she had said to him one night, early on in their relationship. *How had she put it?* Something like 'the physical side of the marriage died a long time ago'.

The bedside tables bore no sign of any of the paraphernalia of illness – no water glass, no box of tissues. He tried the drawers of one, finding nothing more exciting than a Bible in Polish, a pair of women's sunglasses he recognised as Kasia's and a few female bits and bobs. Then he tried Steve's side. Some survival book by an ex-SAS man, a few old lottery scratch cards (all losers – *just like the fucker who bought them*, he thought savagely) and a tatty photo of Kasia and Steve holding ice-cream cones, which looked like it had been taken ages ago, on holiday somewhere.

They were both smiling, and Kasia's hair was blonde, as it had been when he'd first met her. Seeing the sprinkle of youthful freckles across her nose he felt a tugging sensation in his chest. Folding the picture carefully so that Steve disappeared, he pocketed it, before starting to leaf through the SAS survival guide, a look of scorn growing on his face. A look that dissolved at what he found, tucked towards the back of the book.

It was a printout of a booking confirmation made out to Steven Fisher, for two seats on flight AM47 from Luton to Alicante. The second passenger name: Kasia Fisher. Janusz checked the departure details. The flight had left at 11.30 that morning.

Oskar paused in the act of conveying a forkload of *gulasz* to his mouth. 'It's simple science, Janek. As long as you eat according to your blood group, the excess weight will just fall off naturally!'

The two friends were having a late lunch in their favourite café, the *Polska Kuchnia* in Maryland, and Oskar was keen to proselytise about his latest fad diet.

'You see. This is protein.' Oskar gestured towards his plate with a professorial air. 'So being blood type B, I can eat as much of it as I like.' There was a moment's silence while he dispatched the forkful, following it down with a swallow of beer that made his throat bulge.

'Because of your blood group.'

'*Dobrze*. Type B dates from the time when man was nomadic, so I can eat most things and still lose weight.'

He spoke with the modesty of a man disinclined to boast of his good fortune.

'Right. And this is all based on your ancestors having a varied diet – because they travelled around a lot.'

If Oskar detected any sarcasm, he ignored it. 'That's right. I just have to avoid hydrocarbons.'

'Carbohydrates.'

'*Tak*, like I said.'

Watching Oskar take a glug of beer, Janusz toyed with the idea of explaining nutrition to him, or indeed the fundamentals of evolution, but he knew he'd only be doing it to put off the moment when he'd have to broach the Kasia situation. Pushing aside the meal he had barely touched, he told him the news.

'*Kurwa mac*, Janek!' Oskar wiped his mouth with a balled napkin. 'You should have said before!'

Janusz felt his chest tighten at the distress on his mate's chubby face. He might not be the brightest bulb in the chandelier, but since Janusz's mother and father died, many years ago, Oskar was the closest thing to family he had.

'I know how it looks,' said Janusz. 'But I don't believe for one minute she's gone off to Spain with Steve.'

'But what about the flights?'

'I don't think she went on any flight. Her favourite sunglasses were still in the flat. Anyway, she's not the type who'd leave a fridgeful of food to rot.'

Oskar popped another can of Tyskie, his face furrowed, and topped up their glasses, avoiding Janusz's eyes. 'You don't think … Is it not possible …'

'That she had second thoughts about moving in with me?' Janusz growled. 'No. I mean, of course it's possible.

But I know there's no way she'd go without telling me – she's not a coward. And she wouldn't leave Barbara hanging like that, either.'

'So what do you think happened, Janek?'

Janusz stared at the ceiling, trying to visualise for the hundredth time what might have happened between Saturday afternoon, when Kasia had left his apartment, and now.

'I think he's taken her somewhere.' Voicing this unwelcome thought, he recalled how preoccupied she'd seemed recently. Had she been frightened – despite all her denials – about what Steve might be driven to do as her departure became a reality?

'You mean taken against her will?' asked Oskar, eyes wide.

'*Tak*. I think he tricked her into going somewhere out of town with him. I don't know – told her he'd booked something to celebrate his birthday? Maybe he hoped that from there, he could persuade her to go to Spain with him.'

'And when she refused, he wouldn't let her go?'

Janusz gave a grim nod. 'If he's hurt her in any way ...' Realising that his hands were clenched into fists he made a conscious effort to unball them.

'What are you going to do?'

'I'm going to find her. Find both of them.'

Oskar nodded. 'If anyone can do it, *kolego*, you can.'

Janusz didn't tell Oskar the thing that had been troubling him the most since his visit to the flat that afternoon. The tickets to Alicante Steve had booked for himself and Kasia had been one-way. Whatever the worthless *skurwysyn* had been planning, it hadn't involved either of them coming back.

Seven

The Pineapple, which Janusz knew to be Steve Fisher's local, was a rain-stained one-storey building of eighties vintage marooned in the midst of a Stratford council estate. Its car park stood empty but for an old torn sofa, contents bulging like entrails, but by the time Janusz pushed open the door at around 6 p.m., the place was already pretty busy, most eyes trained on the huge TV screen which showed three pundits warming up for the Arsenal v. West Ham match. It was the kind of pub where people came to spend their benefit or pension cheque on cheap lager and enjoy a bit of free heating and Sky Sports.

Janusz tried to ignore the smell of stale beer and old vomit, the unpleasant sensation of the carpet adhering to the underside of his boots. He clocked the flag of St George hanging above the bar with a wary eye – in his experience it sometimes signalled a less than warm welcome for someone sporting a foreign accent, which might hinder his intelligence gathering.

48

So it was a relief when the woman behind the bar – the landlady, judging by her proprietorial demeanour – greeted him in a brisk but not unfriendly manner. After ordering a drink, Janusz pulled up a bar stool and asked, 'Steve Fisher been in today?' – sending her a grin that suggested he and Steve went way back.

Uncapping his bottle of beer, she shook her head. 'Nah. Haven't seen him since Saturday. You meant to be meeting him?'

Janusz's gaze flickered over her face but he decided she was just making small talk. In her early sixties, she was surprisingly well groomed for such a rat-shit boozer, he thought – her hair looked professionally coloured and her preternaturally even tan said spray-job or sunbed rather than recent holiday.

'No. I just popped in on the off-chance.'

After she'd given him his change, he turned to scope the pub over the rim of his glass. A knot of lads – plasterers judging by the state of their boots – laughed quietly over their drinks in one corner. *Polish*, he decided, as much from their self-effacing manner as the half-discerned rhythms of their speech. His gaze slid over a noisier cluster of youngsters wearing Arsenal shirts, and the usual scatter of old guys drinking solo, before coming to rest on a group who sat separately in a raised area by the back wall. Six or seven white men in their forties and fifties, they made a morose huddle, paying no attention to the TV screen and barely talking, despite a forest of empties on their table.

They looked like the sort of working-class men Janusz had worked alongside on building sites back in the eighties and nineties, the kind who'd left the inner city in droves long ago for suburbs like Enfield or Romford – an exodus often disparagingly described as 'white flight'. The ones left behind were largely the unskilled rump, a forgotten minority, routinely despised – in his experience, often unfairly – for their presumed xenophobic attitudes.

Fixing his gaze on the football coverage, Janusz settled down to wait. Ten minutes later, his strategy bore fruit when one of the men came up to the bar.

'Five pints of Stella with whisky chasers, Kath, love.' He was a big guy in his fifties with a despondent air, wearing a suit jacket that had fitted him, once, before he'd started the really serious work on his beer gut.

'Singles or doubles?'

He popped his cheeks, blew out a breath. 'Go on then, make 'em doubles.'

The Stella foamed up while the landlady was pulling the first pint and, as she disappeared to put a new barrel on, Janusz seized the chance to strike up a conversation. 'Who do you fancy for tonight then?' he asked, nodding at the screen.

The guy frowned up at the screen. 'Wenger's lot. So long as they keep their heads this time.' He examined the big Pole with frank but friendly curiosity. 'What about you?'

'I think you're right,' Janusz said. '2-0 to Arsenal.'

'You Polish, I'm guessing?'

Janusz tipped his head in assent.

The man lodged one buttock on the nearest bar stool, taking the weight off. He had a pouchy, lugubrious face, which a badly trimmed moustache did nothing to cheer up. 'My first job was crewing on the container ships – we went all over the Baltic. Whereabouts in Poland you from?'

'Gdansk.'

'You're having a laugh?!' he chuckled. 'If I sailed into Gdynia once I must have done it a hundred times!'

The guy introduced himself as Bill Boyce and soon the two of them were swapping stories about some of the Baltic seaboard's least salubrious nightspots, memories that evidently recalled happier times for the older man.

'What line of work are you in now?' asked Janusz.

'Chippie,' he said. 'Not that I get a lot of work these days. Last job I had was a month ago, fitting a front door for an old girl I know.' He grinned, baring a set of disturbingly white dentures. 'I blame your lot, pricing us honest English tradesmen out of business.'

Janusz made a rueful face: there was some truth in Bill's point. Twenty, thirty years ago, when he'd worked on building sites, Poles were a rarity and he was welcomed as an exotic breed – but the arrival of so many of his countrymen over the last decade had inevitably depressed wage levels and stirred resentment. But he wasn't here to discuss the downside of globalisation and the free movement of labour.

He nodded over at Bill's table. 'Your friends, they don't seem very interested in the footie?'

Bill stared at the floor, his face crumpling even more. 'We had a bit of bad news this morning.'

'Oh?'

'Yeah. We just heard that one of our muckers upped and died.'

'I'm sorry to hear that.' Janusz left a respectful pause. 'Elderly gent, was he?'

'No. *Forty-three*.'

Janusz made the kind of shocked noises that were appropriate to the death of someone so young, albeit a stranger.

Bill shook his head. 'Yeah. He was bit of a scallywag, was Jared, but a good mate. I've known him twenty-odd years – we met on a building site down by Royal Docks.'

'What happened?'

Bill hesitated, but the compulsion to talk won out. 'It was a freak accident, happened yesterday they think. He was found in his flat, electrocuted.'

'Christ!'

'Yeah. They say he drilled into a live cable, putting up a shelf or something.' Perplexity creased his face – either at Jared's stupidity, or perhaps at the cosmic lottery of sudden, unexpected death.

'Jared ...' mused Janusz, before taking a slug of beer. 'That's an unusual name. What's his surname?'

'Bateman.'

'Yeah, I think my mate Steve might have mentioned him once or twice.' *A total fabrication, of course, but worth a punt.*

'Steve Fisher, you mean? Yeah, him and Jared were as thick as thieves.' Bill's look suggested that in their case, the expression might be more than just a turn of phrase.

Before Janusz had a chance to probe further, the landlady reappeared looking harassed. 'Sorry, Bill love, but I just couldn't get that barrel on. You'll have to have something else, I'm afraid.'

'You must be out of practice, Kath,' said Bill with a grin. 'Make it four pints of Foster's then.'

He turned back to Janusz. 'I've been trying to get hold of Steve, as it happens, ever since we heard about Jared. But he isn't answering his phone. You wouldn't be seeing him soon, I suppose?'

'Yeah, I might be, later on,' Janusz lied. 'Shall I get him to call you?'

As they exchanged phone numbers, one of Bill's friends came over to help him carry the drinks. Although he was shorter than Janusz, his muscled neck and broad shoulders gave him the look of a bull mastiff – and one that might bite at the smallest provocation. The guy, who Janusz gathered was called Simeon, smiled readily enough but his eyes sized Janusz up as though he were a second-hand car with no service history. He had a high-pitched voice, which sounded incongruous coming out of that stocky frame.

Deciding not to expose himself to further scrutiny, Janusz made a show of checking his watch and drank up. As he headed for the door, the sticky carpet sucked at the soles of his feet as though reluctant to let him go.

That night, Janusz stayed up cooking till the early hours. He made some *barszcz*, followed by a batch of pork meatballs stuffed with mushrooms, and a loaf of half-rye bread, not because he felt like eating, but because cooking always cleared his head, helping him to puzzle out conundrums. And because focusing on the facts of the case was the only way of keeping at bay the images that lurked at the periphery of his vision, images of what might be happening to Kasia, *right that minute*.

By 2 a.m., he had enough food for a week but no bolt-of-lightning revelations about where Steve might have taken Kasia. It would have to be somewhere remote, where she couldn't escape or raise the alarm – but Steve was a Londoner, bred and buttered, hardly the type to have access to some rural bolthole. As for the death-by-DIY of Steve's electrician mate, Jared: Janusz had turned it over in his mind, but could discern no plausible connection to the couple's disappearance. *No*. The law of Occam's Razor told him the simplest solution was the most likely: Steve had lured Kasia away somewhere, and after she refused to go along with his idea of moving to Spain, starting afresh, was holding her there against her will.

The question was, *where?* And was she in imminent danger? Janusz sent up a fervent prayer: that Kasia would say – and do – whatever she needed to in order to keep Steve sweet, until he could track her down.

Slumping onto the sofa with a bottle of beer he barely noticed the cat, Copetka, jumping onto his lap. What seemed like moments later he woke with a sudden shudder, blinking open his eyes to find himself lying at full stretch, sunlight streaming through the open curtains. The cat, which now lay on his chest, yawned companionably in his face and started to purr.

Janusz realised that while he slept, he'd reached a decision.

'Copetka?' he growled into the cat's face. 'You've never heard me say it before. But I think I'm going to have to call the police.'

54

Eight

'I'm putting you on sick leave from today.'

'But, Sarge!'

'No arguments. I don't want to see your face anywhere in the unit for the next two weeks.'

Kershaw stared at the floor. She'd known she was in for a bollocking, of course, but even being on non-operational duties was preferable to this ... *exile*. What the fuck was she going to do with herself for two weeks? *Drink, probably*, replied a sarcastic voice in her head.

'*Natalie*. Is that understood?'

She gave a mulish nod. She'd never heard the Sarge sound so angry before: Toby Greenacre was legendary for his cool throughout the unit.

His expression softened. 'Listen, Natalie. Just count your blessings that the guy didn't want to make something of it, or you'd be up before Divisional Standards.'

Kershaw had to concede that it probably hadn't been a good idea to stay on drinking in the pub on her own last night. It had been sweet of Matt to take her out for a post-work jar, when he'd seen how down she was after a ten-hour shift spent cleaning guns, checking equipment, updating the armoury's records. But later, after Matt had gone home to his fiancee in Chingford, and she'd put away a couple more glasses of red wine, she'd started to get properly pissed off at the thought of how many more months of this purgatory she'd have to endure. She'd done nothing wrong and yet it felt as if she was sitting in the waiting room of her own life.

So, when some drunken lowlife started mouthing off at the girl behind the bar while Kershaw stood behind him waiting to order, it had been a monumentally bad accident of timing.

'The guy was bang out of order,' she told the Sarge, sticking her chin out. 'He called her a "useless fucking slag" – because she forgot to put ice in his JD and coke. She couldn't have been more than eighteen!'

She had tapped the guy on the shoulder, and politely told him to apologise. He threw a look backwards, clocked a five-foot-two-inch blonde girl, and *laughed*. Looking back, she thought it might have turned out differently if he'd sworn at her. It was the way he'd *dismissed* her in a glance – that was what had really pulled her trigger. *Bang*. Before she even knew what she was doing, she had his arm yanked up tight between his shoulder blades – all that upper body strength training paying off – and was reading him his rights.

'I don't think I need to remind you about the rules governing the behaviour of an off-duty officer, Natalie,' the Sarge was saying. 'Especially since you were visibly the worse for drink, according to the officer who got dragged in to sort things out.'

Kershaw knew she should just keep *schtum* but there was no stopping herself. 'Are we supposed just to ignore it then, Sarge, when someone behaves like that?'

He fixed her with his calm brown eyes. 'Do you think your intervention made the situation better or worse for the barmaid?'

She pictured the girl's weary face throughout the hour-long drama that had played out in the street outside, as the local cops questioned all three of them. A drama that had ended with 'no complaint' by the girl and without so much as a ticking-off for the loudmouth. 'I'm not going to caution him,' she recalled the older uniform confiding to her, not unkindly. 'If we do, he'll only make trouble for you.'

'And how do you think it would have played in the *Standard*,' the Sarge went on, 'if it had come out that the officer involved in the Kyle Furnell shooting got herself into a pub scrap?'

Christ. She had to admit that scenario had never even occurred to her.

The Sarge regarded her in silence for a long moment, the look on his face suggesting he was waiting for an apology. She just stared at the floor. Finally, he stood up behind his desk, indicating the interview was over, and walked her to the door.

'Speaking of the Furnell business – now the inquest is over, I hope you're cracking on with your psych assessment?'

'I've had the first session, Sarge.' *No point mentioning she hadn't got round to booking another one yet.*

'I suggest you use the time off to go every day. The quicker you get the sign-off, Natalie, the quicker we can have you back on ops, where you belong. Okay?'

As Kershaw descended the stairs, she decided that the worst thing about the bollocking had been the expression in the Sarge's eyes at the end. A few years ago, Sergeant Toby Greenacre had been in charge of a nasty hostage situation: a standoff that had ended with him slotting a man who was holding a shotgun to the head of his pregnant wife. The look he'd given her said that he'd been there – that he knew what it was like to be under the microscope for so long, waiting for normal life to restart.

She'd turned her mobile off for the bollocking. Switching it back on, she saw she'd missed a call. There was a text, too. It said simply: *'Call me. Janusz Kiszka.'*

Nine

Kershaw was the first to arrive in the Rochester, the Walthamstow gastropub where she'd arranged to meet Kiszka. Standing at the bar, it struck her that although it was only eighteen months since they'd last met here, a couple of weeks after the stabbing, it seemed like a memory from a distant era. Back then, she'd yet to trade her detective's badge for an MP5, and was still debating whether she and Ben, her then-boyfriend, might still have a future together.

She pictured again the look in Ben's Bournville-dark eyes, when she'd finally told him it was over. *Had she done the right thing?* It was a question to which her mind returned periodically, only to deliver the never-changing answer. *Probably.* Staying with Ben just hadn't been an option, not after the way he'd let her down. She took a slug of her wine. *Now what have I got to look forward to?* She was thirty years old, boyfriend-less, and with her new career in firearms on hold before it had even properly got started.

Then she saw the rangy, unmistakable outline of Janusz Kiszka looming through the etched glass of the pub doors, and felt her spirits rise.

After insisting on buying her another glass of wine – which she made no more than a token effort to decline – he sat down opposite her, his big frame comically too large for the pub chair.

'How are you?' From the look he sent her under his brows the enquiry was more than just the routine social formula.

'Oh, I'm fine. Fully recovered.'

'So you got into the firearms unit, just as you wanted to?'

'Yep.'

'Congratulations.' Despite looking a bit on the thin side, she was still an attractive little thing, Janusz decided – the kind of girl you'd definitely look twice at in the street. 'I read about the crazy guy who got himself shot,' he said frowning into his beer. 'That was you, right?'

She nodded, her expression betraying no pride, but no regret either, before knocking back half a glass of wine. Janusz recalled that she'd been drinking for England the last time they met and, judging by the red veins clustered at the corners of her eyes and the bruised look beneath them, she still was. It stirred in him memories of dark times, long ago in Poland, when he'd sought the comforting blankness that only strong drink could bring.

'You did the right thing,' he growled. 'Did it get you into trouble?'

'Not in theory,' she said. 'But I'm still NAC ... sorry, not authorised to carry. And I've got to confess my deepest, darkest feelings to a shrink before they'll give me my gun back.'

The thought of her being subjected to the perambulations and circumlocutions of a trick cyclist made Janusz grin. 'I bet that's fun.' She returned the smile, reminding him how much prettier she looked without the perpetual frown stitched between her brows.

'Anyway. You wanted to see me about something?' she asked. 'Or was it just a social call?'

Janusz hesitated. Growing up under a totalitarian regime had instilled in him a profound distrust of authority of any kind – especially the police. In the Poland where he'd grown up you didn't turn to the *milicja* to sort out your problems: you looked to family, to the community, or to your own devices. Even now, decades later, the idea of asking a cop for help still made him feel queasy.

'My girlfriend ... Kasia. She was meant to be moving in with me this week – but she's gone missing.' He stared at the table. 'I think her husband may have abducted her.'

'Because she told him she was leaving?' asked Kershaw. He opened those big shovel-like hands in assent. 'Have you considered that she might just have had second thoughts? People do – especially at the last minute.'

He met her gaze. 'Not without a word to me. And she hasn't turned up at work either.'

'Maybe she's pulled a sickie.'

Janusz bridled. 'She runs her own business,' he said. 'Anyway, I checked their flat – there's no sign of either of them.'

'Right.' Kershaw hesitated, trying to find a diplomatic way of telling him that ninety-nine per cent of missing

61

persons cases turned out to be people disappearing of their own free will. *Then there was the other one per cent.* 'Tell me a bit more about her – and this husband of hers.'

Janusz related how back home in Poland, Kasia had worked two jobs to help fund her studies at Lodz Film School, arriving in nineties London with a hundred pounds and a single goal: to get into the film industry. Instead, while working in a Polish bakery in Ealing, she'd met Steve – someone in whom she thought she saw an enterprising spirit to match her own. Three months later they were married.

'And her directing ambitions?'

'Soon went out of the window.' He shrugged. 'She discovered that Steve's talk was just that. Talk. His business schemes were fantasy. He did the odd cash-in-hand job on building sites but she ended up being the main breadwinner, working in bars, mostly.' Out of respect for Kasia, he didn't mention her brief stint as a pole dancer in a Soho club – telling himself it could hardly have any relevance to her disappearance.

'Marry in haste, repent at leisure, as my nan used to say,' said Kershaw. 'So why did she stick with him all this time?'

'The Church,' he said, with a wry grimace.

Kershaw rotated her glass on the table, thinking. 'So she's a devout Catholic, who puts up with him for what, twenty years, because she doesn't believe in divorce.' She frowned up at him. 'Why the sudden change of heart?'

As the girl's unblinking gaze skewered Janusz he was reminded of the time she'd interrogated him about a murder, the first time they'd met. He shifted about in the narrow chair. Why *had* Kasia changed her mind about leaving Steve? The milestone of her recent fortieth birthday suddenly struck him as an inadequate motive for such a momentous volte-face.

To change the subject, he told her about the one-way tickets to Alicante Steve had booked, and his conviction that the couple were still in the UK.

Kershaw chewed at a nail. 'So you think he strung her a line about a birthday dinner or something to get her somewhere quiet, then sprung the idea of this trip on her?'

'Yeah. He's a fantasist. He probably thought he could change her mind with some story about starting a new life in Spain.'

She nodded, that made sense. 'What kind of guy is he? If your theory's right, do you think she could be in danger?'

He paused, wondering how much to tell her. 'He has hit her, a couple of times. I had to have a word with him once.'

She raised an eyebrow, imagining the one-sided nature of that discussion.

Janusz narrowed his eyes, recalling the impression of Steve he'd got from that single face-to-face encounter. Skinny and unprepossessing to look at, yet full of himself, Steve had alternated between braggadocio and aggrieved self-pity. 'I think he's a lazy lowlife with a big mouth, but I never thought he'd have it in him … to really hurt her. Not till now, anyway.'

'Once a wife beater, always a wife beater, in my experience,' she said, regretting her glib words when she saw his jaw clench in a spasm of distress.

She felt torn. The likeliest explanation was probably the most obvious one – that Kasia had got cold feet about going to live with Kiszka. His caveman looks, the edge of danger about him would no doubt be attractive to some girls, but as life partner material? On the other hand, she couldn't help feeling intrigued by the story – especially since she knew what a big deal it must have been for Kiszka to ask for help from a cop.

'Why are you asking me to get involved? Why not just report her missing?'

He lifted one shoulder. 'Because the police would just assume I was a jilted boyfriend. Even if they did believe me, they're hardly going to invest serious resources in finding yet another missing person, are they?'

'Fair point.'

'So … will you help?' He drained the rest of his pint, avoiding her eyes.

Kershaw suddenly realised that her pulse was beating a little faster than when she'd first walked in the pub. It seemed that the mystery of Kiszka's missing girlfriend had got under her skin. She'd need to tread carefully, of course: the last thing she needed was to get herself in any more trouble at work.

'I'll do what I can,' she told him.

Janusz bared his teeth in a grin. 'Another one of those?' he asked, pointing at her empty wine glass.

After he'd gone to the bar, having waved away her attempt to buy a round, Kershaw realised that there was another reason she'd agreed to help, the return of a feeling she'd almost forgotten. There was something about being around Janusz Kiszka that somehow made her feel more alive.

Ten

At Walthamstow Central tube station, heading home to Highbury, Janusz found himself in the midst of a deepening crush on the southbound Victoria line platform, the muffled drone of the announcer overhead saying something about signal problems. Luckily, Walthamstow was the line's northernmost terminus, so when a train finally did arrive it emptied completely, allowing him to bag a seat. The journey was slow, punctuated by long stops in tunnels, and the fresh influx of rush-hour humanity that squeezed itself onto the packed train at Tottenham Hale triggered a very English symphony of muted *tuts*.

Right under Janusz's nose, a guy in his twenties wearing a too-tight suit all but body-blocked an older woman carrying shopping bags to capture a just-vacated seat opposite. Seeking eye contact to establish whether the lady might take offence – an advisable step in London, he had long ago discovered – Janusz wordlessly offered her his seat, and when she smiled her thanks, stood to make way for her. Taking hold of the overhead passenger rail with both hands, he proceeded to direct an unblinking stare down on the discourteous *kutas* in the suit, who grew increasingly fidgety during the long wait in the next tunnel, before unaccountably deciding to get off at the next stop. *Claustrophobic, probably*, thought Janusz with an inward grin.

Minutes later, as the train lurched to a halt yet again, Janusz idly scanned the faces of the passengers either side of him, each immured within their own private citadel. A head-scarfed Asian girl, eyes elongated with kohl, playing a game on her phone, a man intently reading an article on London house prices in the *Standard*, and a white girl with dreadlocks, tinny music spilling out of her head-phones. He let his eyes drift back to the man reading the paper. He remembered noticing the same guy amid the crush on the packed platform at Walthamstow. And he'd been reading the same page of the paper then.

No one was that slow a reader. Janusz squinted at the tube map just above his eye level, relying on his peripheral vision to build a picture of the guy. Reddened, pock-marked skin, like someone who'd spent too many years in the sun – or in extreme cold. Forty-five, or there-abouts, around Janusz's age. Close-cropped hair, balding at the temples. Expensive-looking bomber jacket.

Maybe he was just being paranoid, but Janusz had long ago learned a valuable lesson: in his line of work, a little paranoia could seriously boost your life expectancy. So when the train reached Highbury, he made sure he was first up the short flight of stairs from the platform and into the exit tunnel. Rounding a sharp bend which meant he couldn't be seen from behind, he broke into a jog, and didn't slow down when he reached the escalator, climbing it two steps at a time, the metal treads flashing beneath his boots. Highbury was one of the network's deepest stations and by the time he neared the top, his breathing was sawing like an old tree in a high wind. He slapped his Oyster card on the reader – praying it would work first time – and the gates parted to release him.

Outside, twilight was descending, and Janusz ducked into the pub next to the station where he sometimes had a homecoming beer, positioning himself by a window with a view of the station exit. Twenty or thirty seconds later, he spotted bomber jacket cutting a path through the seething tide of homeward-bound passengers, scoping his surroundings with an alert yet casual gaze. For a heart-stopping moment his eyes lingered on the pub, before he disappeared from view towards the main road.

The guy's body language appeared unhurried. But his watchful air, the purposefulness of that measured stride – all said professional tail. Suspecting that his new-found friend might double back at any moment to check out the pub, Janusz headed out back towards the lavatories. Down a corridor and past the door marked *Gents* he found what he was looking for: an emergency exit he occasionally used to nip out for a cigar. It gave onto a quiet back-street that bore west towards Liverpool Road, the opposite direction to his apartment.

He pushed the bar – and a deafening two-tone wail split the air.

Kurwa mac! When did the officious bastards get the door alarmed? Janusz took off running down the street. No point hoping that bomber jacket would fail to notice the ear-piercing racket – you could probably hear it a mile away. All he could do was put as much distance as possible between the two of them while he still had the chance.

After fifty or sixty metres, he shot a glance over his shoulder. And saw the man burst out of the emergency exit like a human cannonball. Despite his short and stocky build, he ran like a pro, head down, arms tucked into his sides, gaze fixed laser-like on his target.

The sight sent adrenaline rushing through Janusz's veins. He could swear he felt his heart inflating, vascular system dilating to deliver blood to his muscles, the pavement becoming a blur beneath his pounding feet. Realising that the street's lack of bends would make him an easy target should his pursuer have a gun, he took a last-minute decision to swerve sharp left into a side turning, his right ankle sending a memo of protest to his brain. Then left again into a narrow cobbled alleyway, its high walls distilling the darkness. Knowing the geography of the area was a big advantage: every turn he made bought precious seconds, forcing bomber jacket to work out the route his quarry had taken.

A hipster with a portfolio pressed himself against the wall, open-mouthed, as the big guy barrelled past, his greatcoat flapping either side of him. Janusz could see the traffic on the busy main road at the end of the alleyway now, the headlights of vehicles coming on as the sky darkened. He risked another look back, hoping against hope he might have shaken off his tail. Saw the guy skidding to a halt at the mouth of the alleyway, close enough for Janusz to make out his lips working in a silent curse.

On reaching Upper Street, he found his progress slowed by knots of straggling pedestrians and baby buggies, and decided to cut across the road. The traffic

slowed here as it approached Highbury Corner roundabout but he still had to employ a jinking jog and a raised
palm, which did nothing to quell the cacophony of horns
or the angry gestures of drivers. On the other side stood
a double decker bus, pulled up at a stop. As Janusz
rounded its rear, he saw a last passenger boarding and put
on a determined spurt. The bus hid him momentarily
from view – and, with luck, would whisk him away
before bomber jacket had even worked out where he'd
gone.

Janusz reached the front of the bus, his lungs burning
– just as the doors sighed shut. Tapping politely on the
glass, he caught the driver's eye and – abandoning all
dignity – pantomimed a hopeful *'Please?'* Nearly three
decades in London made the driver's responding shrug
depressingly easy to decipher. It said *'Not my problem,
sunshine.'*

With a consumptive wheeze of its air brakes, the bus
trundled away – leaving Janusz feeling brutally exposed.
He looked back across Upper Street – and straight into the
face of the man in the bomber jacket, standing on the
kerb opposite. Seeing his vulpine half-smile, Janusz realised what a sorry picture he must make – one arm flung
round the bus stop for support, gasping like a landed
carp. As Janusz gathered up his last vestiges of energy to
run, bomber jacket threw a look to his left and stepped
off the kerb towards him.

There came the shriek of rubber on tarmac, a horn
blast – and a bang. Janusz squinted through the traffic,
trying to make sense of what just happened. The scene
came into focus: a red mail van skewed across the lane
blocking the traffic, a scatter of mirror fragments in the

gutter behind it. And bomber jacket on all fours, in the road, a solicitous cluster of passers-by forming around him. He was shaking his head as if trying, unsuccessfully, to clear it.

Janusz allowed himself a grin before limping off into the thickening dusk.

After putting some distance between himself and his erstwhile pursuer he lit a cigar, dragging the reviving smoke deep into his lungs, but it was still five minutes or more before his pulse rate returned to normal and he was able to think clearly. *Why on earth should anyone want to follow him? There couldn't be any connection with Kasia and Steve's disappearing act – could there?* An all too plausible scenario occurred to him: if Steve had been driven into a murderous rage by the prospect of Kasia leaving him, then Janusz would be the obvious target for his revenge. He recalled Kasia complaining more than once that her husband had some questionable friends – including one who'd been in jail – so taking out a hit on his rival might not overly stretch his skillset.

Replaying the chase with bomber jacket in his mind, Janusz came to a sudden halt in the middle of the pavement. His pursuer had looked to the left before stepping out into the traffic. From which Janusz deduced that he either had the road sense of a four-year-old – or had recently arrived from a country where they drove on the right.

Whoever the guy was, Janusz had to admit the incident had left him rattled. Not because he feared for his own safety – he could look after himself. But if Steve really was crazy enough to take out a contract on him, then what did it say about the danger Kasia was in?

Just as this terrible thought entered his head, he saw the pale spire of St Stanislaus up ahead. He decided to pay Father Pietruski a visit: Kasia had been going to confession at St Stan's for the last year, so there was just a chance that the priest might be able to offer some clue as to her whereabouts.

Hearing the deep clunk of the church door closing, Father Piotr Pietruski looked up from the altar where he was setting out wine and communion wafers, and peered into the gloom.

His expression brightened as he saw who his visitor was – although his tone sounded as caustic as ever. 'Ah! Look what the wind blew in. I was thinking only today how long it had been since you had graced us with your presence.' The old man bustled down the stairs from the altar, holding on to the rail. 'I would hear your *konfesja*, but it will no doubt take some time, and as you can see, I am preparing for Holy Mass ...'

'I haven't come to make confession, *prosze pana*. I need to talk to you about Kasia Fisher.'

Father Pietruski dropped his gaze, but not before Janusz saw his face sag in disappointment – and something else. *Disapproval.* Unlike Janusz, Kasia made her confession once a week without fail, so the old boy knew all about their affair, and since he steadfastly refused to recognise even Janusz's two-decades-old divorce, in his eyes they were both committed and unrepentant adulterers.

'Come into the vestry,' he said. Janusz followed him through a side door, noting with a pang how stooped the old guy was getting, and how the sparse silver combover barely covered his age-spotted scalp.

Pietruski lowered himself into one of two dilapidated leather armchairs and waved at the other. '*Siadaj*. Sit. You'd better tell me what all this is about.'

Janusz sketched out what he knew about Kasia's disappearance, her failure to show up at work and the couple's empty flat. When he mentioned that she'd been due to move into his apartment, Pietruski didn't look happy, but he didn't betray any surprise either.

Janusz felt his spirits lift. The fact that Kasia had got up the courage to tell her priest she was leaving the marriage dissipated any last whisper of doubt he might have had about her changing her mind.

'Perhaps she realised the terrible sin she was about to commit in betraying her marriage vows,' said Pietruski, sending Janusz a reproachful look. 'A sin you seem determined to encourage her in, despite being a married man yourself.' He plucked distractedly at the embroidered cover on the arm of his chair.

Janusz tried to tell himself that he was immune to the old man's disapproval, but he knew that wasn't true. Pietruski had saved him from self-annihilation when he first arrived from Poland, a skinny nineteen-year-old fleeing a disastrous marriage. He'd wed Marta just weeks after his girlfriend Iza died at a demonstration against the Communist regime – a tragedy for which he held himself responsible. Father Pietruski – still in possession of a full head of hair back then – had found him sprawled across the steps of this very church, insensible with *wodka*. He had given Janusz a meal and found him somewhere to sleep, later introducing him to the Irish building contractor who gave him his first labouring job.

Janusz shifted about in the armchair – its high leather sides made it narrow and too deep for comfort, and an errant spring in the base pressed insistently into the back of his thigh. 'I respect your views on how we should conduct our lives, Father,' he said, making an effort to keep his temper. 'But the fact remains that Kasia is an adult woman, free to do as she sees fit.'

'The modern-day doctrine of "please oneself", you mean? Which has brought people nothing but unhappiness, it seems to me. You do realise, that if she does leave, you can never marry, *naturalnie*?' The look in Pietruski's eyes was one of profound compassion.

The marriage question meant next to nothing to Janusz – his faith was a hazy affair, grounded more in nostalgia and respect for tradition than in any profound supernatural belief – although he knew what it would cost Kasia to live in sin for the rest of their days together, denied the sacrament of communion.

'I'm not here to debate doctrine. And I don't think Kasia has gone missing because she's suddenly seen the light – I think her husband has abducted her.'

Pietruski blinked rapidly. 'Surely not? Might they not simply have gone away to celebrate his birthday?'

Janusz stared at him for a moment. 'It was you who persuaded her to stay till his birthday, wasn't it?'

The old man lifted his chin. 'You know very well that I cannot divulge what is said within the sacred confines of the confessional,' he said – as good as confirming Janusz's hunch – 'but I would never apologise for doing everything within my power to preserve the sacrament of marriage.'

Janusz imagined the guilt trip the priest would have laid on Kasia about her plan to leave her husband. He could practically hear the scheming old bastard murmuring through the grille of the confession box: *'Stay until his birthday, at least. Surely you owe him that?'*

Abandoning himself to a surge of rage, Janusz jackknifed out of the chair, freeing himself from its imprisoning embrace.

'You care so much about her soul that you never considered she might be in danger of her life,' he growled. 'You, who must surely know of his violence towards her?'

'A man striking a woman is an evil I would never ...'

Janusz didn't let him finish. 'If she has come to harm because of your interference, I shall never forgive you.'

The words were out of his mouth before he even knew he'd said them, ringing around the stone walls of the vestry like a curse.

As he strode up the aisle of the empty church, he could still see the stricken expression on the face of his father confessor as if it were branded on his brain.

Eleven

While Janusz was quizzing Father Pietruski at St Stanislaus, Kershaw was back home in her flat on the blower to her cousin Jason in Special Branch for the second time that day.

'Any joy?' she asked.

'Yep. It's actually one of the easier things you've asked for.'

Kershaw had called Jason right after she'd left Kiszka, to see if he could get hold of the passenger manifest for flight AM47 to Alicante, the one Steve had booked himself and Kasia onto. Jason wasn't supposed to run checks without signed documentation, of course, but since she was godmother – and occasional babysitter – to his two increasingly boisterous boys, he'd been happy to do her the favour.

'You won't get into any trouble, will you?' she asked.

'Nah. We're always asking the airlines for stuff like that. Anyway, the girl there fancies me.'

75

'Who can blame her?'

'Exactly.'

'So, were they on the flight or what?'

'Nope. They were both marked down as no-shows.'

She felt a little buzz of excitement. Kiszka had been right about one thing: *Steve and his wife hadn't boarded the flight.* 'Thanks, Jason. I appreciate it.'

'No worries. When are you coming over anyway? The boys would love to see their Auntie Nat – and Kirsty was saying the other day we haven't seen you in ages.'

Together with Jason's mum, her Auntie Carol, they were the only family Kershaw had left and yet it must be a year at least, she realised, since she'd been out to Billericay to visit. Since the shooting – in fact, even since she got stabbed – she'd become a bit of a hermit, her life distilling down to a cycle of *work, drink, sleep*: her only social life the occasional after-work drink or visit to the gym.

Before hanging up, she promised Jason that once spring finally arrived, she'd come out for a family barbecue.

Kershaw reached for the last bottle of Argentinian Malbec in the rack, before switching the kettle on instead – she needed a clear head to think things through. Obviously, it was still a major leap from a missed flight to believing that Steve was holed up somewhere, holding Kasia against her will, but she wondered whether she should just play it safe and report Kasia Fisher missing to Walthamstow CID. Coming from her, they might be persuaded to take it seriously. But by the time the kettle had boiled she'd concluded that it would still sit in someone's inbox for days before any action would be taken.

Meanwhile, she was sitting around on her arse with her brain on standby.

She decided there was only one sensible course of action: do the initial spadework herself, and if she found any solid leads on Kasia's whereabouts, hand the case over to her old boss, DS 'Streaky' Bacon. Congratulating herself on having made the right decision, she opened the cupboard and awarded herself a chocolate biscuit.

Twelve

The following day, Janusz found himself once again passing through the pillared portico of St Francis of Assisi Residential Home. He'd been hyper-vigilant during the journey from Highbury – but had seen no evidence of anyone tailing him. He'd even considered postponing today's appointment to check Wojtek Raczynski's passport, before deciding that it was better to stay busy, if only to try to keep his mind off the Kasia situation. What good would it do her, after all, if he let himself go to pieces?

Sunk in his thoughts, he suddenly found himself at the reception desk – and did a double-take. Instead of the creamy cheeks of the young Polish receptionist, the face that looked up at him from behind the computer monitor was as brown and corrugated as an Arabian wadi.

'Sorry to disappoint you,' said Stefan, peering over his reading specs. 'Beata asked me to look at her computer. It's got more viruses than a clap clinic waiting room.'

'And you ... can fix it?' Janusz was having a job concealing his disbelief.

'Heavens, no.' He chuckled. 'But I know people who work in IT who are up to speed on these things. I'm just emailing over some details.' He tapped the keyboard. 'There, I think that's gone. Now, I'm guessing you're here for Wojtek?'

Janusz found his own way to the conservatory, where Wojtek was waiting for him. He had resigned himself to another lengthy bulletin on the doings of his wayward grandchildren, but this time, the old fellow barely said a word, sitting quietly as Janusz copied his passport details into a notebook. The passport was the old pre-EU kind, its midnight blue cover bearing the cruel profile of the Polish eagle above outstretched wings.

'Haven't seen one of these in a while,' said Janusz.

Wojtek shrugged, failing to take the conversational bait, and took a sip of his tea – no biscuits today – spilling a little down his chin.

Janusz sneaked a look at him out of the corner of his eye. The papers were full of scandals about the maltreatment of old people in residential homes – stories that filled him with a vision-darkening rage. What kind of *skurwysyn* would harm a helpless old person? St Francis's seemed a happy enough place on the surface, but he knew that wherever the strong held sway over the weak, there was the ever-present risk of abuse. What was it somebody once said? *Man makes evil like a bee makes honey.*

He hesitated, then took the plunge. 'They do treat you all right here, do they?'

Wojtek looked flustered. '*Tak, tak! Dobrze*, it's a good place.'

'I'm glad to hear it.' Janusz handed him a card – the one with his private number – and pocketing the notebook, stood to go. 'But if you do ever have any problem, then you tell your daughter to call me, okay?'

As he bade Wojtek farewell, Janusz made a decision to assess the place with a more critical eye. Making his way out of the conservatory, he noticed a staff member playing Scrabble with two old girls. One of the ladies had just spelled out *ARSE* and they were all laughing like naughty children – the staffer included. En route back to reception, he paused to check out a room in which a gaggle of residents were singing along to a piano. The singing was ragged and out of tune, but they all seemed happy enough.

Seeing that Beata was back at the reception desk, he paused to admire her complexion – and to ask if Stefan was around. She dipped her head apologetically. *'Przepraszam pana*, but I think I saw Pan Kasparek going out for lunch.'

Having established that his likeliest luncheon venue was the Wetherspoons opposite the tube station, Janusz was on his way there to ask if he could explain Wojtek's changed manner, when he saw a missed call on his phone.

It was from Bill Boyce, the guy he'd chatted to at Steve's local.

Bill picked up on the first ring and, after a cursory greeting, asked: 'Did you see Steve that night, after we met?' He sounded jittery.

'No ...' said Janusz, improvising. 'He called to say he couldn't make it.'

'He's still not answering his phone.' There was a moment's silence. 'Do you think you can get a message to him for me?'

'Sure, what's the message?'

'I'm not being funny, but I'd rather give it you face to face.'

'Okay …Shall we meet at the Pineapple?'

'No. Come to my gaff, in an hour.' Bill gave him an address. 'And look, I know it sounds daft, but don't tell anyone we're meeting, okay?'

Janusz navigated his way across two lines of moving traffic towards Wanstead tube, deaf to the hoots of motorists, in the grip of the rushing sensation that sometimes came over him during an investigation: an awareness of wheels and cogs starting to turn faster, unstoppable forces set in motion.

He found Bill's apartment on the third floor of a shabby redbrick fifties council block with a view of Leytonstone High Road. The red Meccano jumble of the ArcelorMittal Orbit could be glimpsed over the rooftops, barely half a mile away, although the tide of money poured into the area for London's staging of the Olympics had apparently petered out before making landfall at this end of Stratford.

After climbing the dank stairs to the third floor's outside walkway, Janusz knocked at Bill's door, but was met only with silence. Shading his eyes, he peered in through the single window, but couldn't see anything through the crack in the grimy curtains. Recalling how paranoid Bill had sounded on the phone, he bent to push open the letterbox.

'Bill, it's Janusz,' he said, speaking awkwardly through the gap. No response came from the empty hallway beyond. Eyeing the mortice lock beneath the Yale, he cursed under his breath – if the door were double locked, then nothing short of a drill or a monkey wrench would do the job. But he was in luck, and forty seconds later he was stepping over the threshold, pocketing his trusty bump key.

In the tiny hallway, the acrid whiff of burned bacon cut through the unwashed socks smell of a man living alone, but the place was silent: the only sound the muffled shouts of the kids he had passed playing football in the courtyard outside. In the kitchen, touching the back of his hand to the kettle, he found it still warm, recently boiled, and on the worktop a thin blue carrier bag spilled a packet of Bourbon biscuits – no doubt bought in his honour. In the living room, the door onto the balcony hung ajar, and he risked a quick look over the parapet – for a wild moment half expecting to see Bill sprawled below. He checked out the rest of the apartment, a faint yet insistent feeling of dread building in his gut. Finally, there was only the bathroom still unchecked. He stood irresolute for a moment before the half-open door, hearing the blood swish-swishing in his ears, before pushing it open with the toe of his boot.

Bill was a big man, easily 220, 230 pounds, Janusz would guess. Which would explain why the shower rail from which he hung was deeply bowed and kinked at the point where the belt was tied.

The protruding eyes, half-open as though he had just woken from slumber, and the tongue protruding through those brilliant white dentures told a pretty conclusive story, but Janusz set two fingers against Bill's throat below the tight-stretched leather, just to make sure. Already cooling, his skin felt waxy and there was no pulse.

Kurwa mac! Janusz sat on the toilet more heavily than he'd intended, and tried to steady the whirl and clatter of his thoughts. Bill had died on the point of giving him a message for Steve, a message too important to pass on over the phone. The idea that he'd arranged their rendez-vous, even popping out to buy biscuits, only to change his mind and top himself instead, was laughable. He forced himself to look at the body again. Bill's knees were bent, with his feet touching the floor, and no way could that bowed rail have been strong enough to carry his weight long enough to asphyxiate him. *Nie.* He'd been strangled before being strung up – a hasty cover-up job that wouldn't survive even the most cursory examination by the cops.

Realising that a swift exit would be the better part of valour, Janusz stood to go. Casting a last glance at Bill's pouched and sorrowful features, he pictured him in better times, a brawny seaman striding the deck of a container ship, full of vigour and a young man's plans and dreams.

Seemingly of their own volition, the words of the prayer for the dead rose to his lips. *'By Thy resurrection from the dead, O Christ, death no longer hath dominion over those who die in holiness ...'*

By the time Janusz reached the Pineapple, he'd smoked his way through two cigars and his heart rate was almost back to normal. He approached the place cautiously, checking out the bar through a side-window before venturing inside, but found it near empty today, the only customers two old men nursing pints at opposite ends of the bar. He wondered how it survived. Old-style no-frills boozers no longer served the shifting demographic of the inner city: the white working-class drinkers had largely left, to be replaced by Muslims – and, more recently, by middle-class types who preferred a nice gastropub.

There was no sign of any of the party whom Bill had been drinking with on Janusz's first visit, and when he asked the young girl behind the bar if she'd seen Simeon – Bill's stocky mate with the suspicious stare – she shook her head, her expression as blank as a plate.

After the shock of finding Bill's body, he was sorely tempted to have a drink, but decided against. Hanging around on the off-chance of learning something was unlikely to be productive – and might even prove dangerous, especially since the cops would soon find their way to Bill's local to ask who he'd been talking to recently.

Thinking about the cops reminded Janusz of the girl *detektyw*, and her promise to help him find Kasia. The gratitude he felt towards her presented him with an uncomfortable dilemma. He seriously considered telling her what had happened – the mystery call from Bill, finding him strung up in his bathroom like the Christmas goose – before dismissing the idea. Until he'd found out what, if any, connection Steve might have to Bill's murder, he could see nothing to gain by having a load of nosy cops trampling over his investigation in their size tens. And since Natalia would feel compelled to report his discovery of the body and their recent conversation, that might put her in an awkward position.

Naprawde, when you looked at it like that, he was doing her a favour.

Thirteen

PC Natalie Kershaw had tucked her Ford Ka into a poorly lit corner of the armed response unit's car park – a spot that still allowed her a partial view of the only entrance. Shivering in the night air, she was finally rewarded, at 22.10, by the sight of Sergeant Toby Greenacre strolling out through the door. She hunkered down in the driver's seat, but he didn't so much as glance in her direction before disappearing round the side of the building. Seconds later, she saw his people carrier pause at the security barrier before pulling out into the street. It was a lucky escape: when Kershaw first arrived around an hour earlier she'd almost waltzed straight into the office – before remembering just in time that the Sarge was on late turn till the end of the week.

It wasn't until she reached the front door that another thought struck her: would her access card still work? It was a relief to hear the soft click as the lock snapped open, although she also had to suppress a pang of guilt:

it clearly hadn't even occurred to the Sarge that she might break the terms of her banishment.

Breezing in like she had every right to be there, she made straight for her desk, and fired up the computer. It felt weird to be sitting there in her civilian clobber – wearing her uniform while officially off duty would have really been asking for trouble – but if anyone challenged her, she had her story down pat. She'd lost her phone and with it the contact details of the police shrink everyone knew she was seeing. The place seemed deserted, anyway – the night shift boys must be out on a shout – and with a bit of luck she'd be gone before they got back.

Kershaw's first job was to send an email from her Met address to Transport for London. Officially, requests for customers' Oyster card records had to be accompanied by a form signed by a sergeant or above, and submitted via head office, but she had a TfL contact from her time at Walthamstow murder squad. Terry was the kind of guy who liked hanging out with cops, so he was usually happy to shortcut the bureaucracy in the interests of nailing the bad guys.

She asked him to check recent activity on any Oyster card registered to Kasia and Steven Fisher, tapping out the address and postcode Kiszka had given her, before finishing with: '*I'm out and about tomorrow, so could you do me a favour and send the info to my home email? As you know, The System won't let us log in remotely …*' – capitalising 'the system' was a nice touch, she thought – '*Thanks, Terry, I owe you a pint or three next time you're down the Moon. Cheers – Nat.*' Her finger hovered briefly over the 'X' key but in the end she just pressed 'send' – better to stay on the right side of professional.

Next, she needed to access the Police National Computer. After typing in her password, she hesitated, chewing at the side of a fingernail. If anyone should ever decide to check her PNC search history, she could face some very awkward questions.

She pressed 'enter' with a flourish.

Fourteen

In Janusz's Highbury apartment, Oskar had already put away two bowls of the *barszcz* that Janusz had made during his marathon cooking session, and was now making short work of a plateful of mushroom and pork meatballs with buckwheat. Finally, he collapsed back onto the sofa with a groan.

'*Kurwa*, Janusz, you made me break my diet!' he complained, running chubby hands over his domed stomach.

'Nobody made you, Oskar. You could have just had the soup,' pointed out Janusz. He set his own plate aside, having managed only a couple of the *kotlety*. It wasn't just the memory of poor dead Bill's mournful face that was spoiling his appetite, but a new and troubling puzzle. *What – if anything – did the murder have to do with Steve's abduction of Kasia?*

Blowing out a windy sigh, Oskar reached for a fresh can of Tyskie. 'Maybe I just need to accept that I'm naturally big boned.'

'*Dobrze*. Especially around the ribs.'

Oskar nodded towards Janusz's half-eaten meal. 'You need to eat, Janek, keep your strength up.' He leaned forward, seeking his friend's gaze. 'How's the investigation going, anyway? Any clues yet about where Kasia might be?'

Janusz rubbed his unshaven jaw. '*Nie*. But I know that neither of them flew to Alicante.'

'*Naprawde?*' Oskar's eyebrows shot up, his face a comic roundel of surprise. 'How do you know?'

Visualising the text Natalia had sent him, Janusz wondered whether to tell his mate about the bit of free-lance policing she was doing on his behalf. The impulse lasted about half a second. 'Never mind how I know. I just do,' he said, before taking a deep swig of his beer. Although he loved Oskar like a – somewhat exasperating – kid brother, he had discovered long ago that entrusting him with a secret was like giving a toddler a Fabergé egg to play with.

Oskar sat up. 'Oh, I nearly forgot, I asked some of my contacts about that guy, the one with the *komiczne* name ...?'

'Jared Bateman.'

'*Tak*.' Oskar chuckled. '"Jar-head."'

'Well? Any joy?' asked Janusz. After two years spent working as a foreman on the Olympics build, Oskar had amassed a vast network of East End construction contacts, and had agreed to put the word out – see if anyone knew Steve's best mate. Janusz knew it was a long shot but then he had scarcely anything to go on.

'Somebody texted me back this morning.' Digging into the pocket of his work overalls, Oskar retrieved his phone and flourished it dramatically.

'Get on with it, Oskar,' growled Janusz.

After a few moments of scrolling, he said, 'Here it is. A contractor called Dermot I used to work with. Says he remembers hiring someone called "Jarhead Bateman" on a big refit job two or three months ago.'

'Whereabouts?'

'In Docklands.'

'And has he worked with him since?'

'*Nie.*'

'Did Dermot ever hear him talk about his best mate Steve? Does he have any idea where he's been working lately?' Janusz was aware of sounding increasingly testy.

Occupied with draining his can of beer, Oskar could only shake his head.

Janusz dragged both hands through his hair. *What had he expected anyway*, he asked himself, *from such a slender lead?* Reaching for a fresh can of Tyskie, he worked his fingertip under the ring pull. 'What job did he hire Jared to do, on site?'

'Chief spark.'

A jet of beer foamed out of the can and all over the rug.

Kurwa mac! How did someone who'd worked as chief electrician on a building site manage to electrocute himself doing Mickey Mouse DIY?

Janusz pictured again the puzzlement on Bill's lugubrious face as he'd related Jared's unexpected demise. At the time, Janusz assumed he was simply struggling with the haphazard nature of life and sudden death. Now, he realised that wasn't it at all. Bill had been trying to work out how an experienced spark could do something so suicidally inept as to drill into a live cable.

Oskar, who had leaned forward to tap him on the knee, interrupted his train of thought.

'Janek,' he said, a serious look on his face. 'Did you say there was cheesecake?'

Later, after Oskar had gone, Janusz sat up for hours trying to work out a plausible connection between recent events. Steve had abducted Kasia to stop her leaving, that much he was confident of. Bill had been murdered while trying to get in touch with Steve. And then there was the 'accidental' death of Jared – one of Steve's best mates – which now looked deeply suspicious, too. And, at some point during his investigation, somebody had had Janusz followed.

It was hardly rocket science to work out that the common thread in all this was one Steven Fisher; but it was starting to look to Janusz that he might be involved in something even more sinister and far-reaching than kidnapping his faithless wife.

Kasia

That's strange, thought Kasia. I'm underwater and yet I can still breathe.

She could see the silvery string of bubbles streaming from her mouth as she hung there in the aquamarine water. She laughed, delighted by the discovery. Euphoria enveloped her, a little like the sensation a shot of cold vodka on an empty stomach could produce, but multiplied many times over. Rolling and stretching in the water, she luxuriated in the feeling of weightlessness, all her worries dissipating like the air bubbles into the infinite, limitless blue – the same colour as Mary's robe in the big window above the altar when Mama took her to church.

Something changed. The water around her was turning a paler blue. She realised that she was floating gently upward, and saw something glittering overhead that filled her with a sudden foreboding. A glass ceiling. The surface. Twisting her body, she flung out her arms and kicked with her legs, trying to swim back down, desperate to return to the peaceful turquoise depths, away from what awaited her above.

But she was still gliding up, up through the water – ever faster. Squeezing her eyes shut, she tried to block out the light above her, which was growing painfully bright. She could hear a sound like the roar of surf drumming in her ears, and a dull pain booming against her skull.

She crash-landed into the air, light spearing her eyes. She blinked rapidly. When things came into focus there was no aquamarine water, no surf – just a stained blue mattress beneath her cheek. Trying to gulp air, she found her mouth taped shut. From behind the barrier of her lips, she shouted for Janusz, over and over.

All that remained of her dream was the smell of chlorine.

Fifteen

'Listen, I found some stuff out last night, can I come over?'

Since this wasn't preceded by 'good morning', or any of the other standard courtesies, it took Janusz's sleep-fuddled brain a moment or two to process who had just catapulted him out of a deep and dreamless sleep.

Natalia. The girl *detektyw.*

'Sure,' he grunted. 'I'll put the coffee on.' It was only after she'd hung up that he squinted at his old wind-up alarm clock and discovered it wasn't even 7 a.m. yet.

Half an hour later, he was pouring a treacle-black stream of coffee from a stovetop pot into porcelain cups so delicate that they glowed translucent in the morning sunlight.

After taking a cautious sip, Kershaw added a generous slug of milk to hers. 'This is new,' she said, running an appreciative hand along the blonde wood grain of the kitchen table – a major improvement on the battered, orange pine version she recalled from her last visit – and the walls had been recently painted, too, in a soft shade

of sage. Kiszka didn't exactly strike her as the Farrow &
Ball type. 'I like the new colour scheme. Is the makeover
down to Kasia?' At the mention of his girlfriend's name,
he dropped his gaze, but not before she'd caught the
heaviness in his eyes. He looked as big and burly as ever
– the china cup cradled in one of his mitts looking as if it
came from a doll's tea set – but for the first time she
sensed a fragility about him.

'You said you found something,' grunted Janusz. If she
were a man he would have said *Get to the fucking point*.

'Okay,' she got out her notebook. 'I'm still waiting to
hear back about Oyster card records but I did find out a
bit more about Steven Fisher. Did you know he's got a
criminal record?'

Janusz lifted one shoulder: a gesture that said he hadn't
known but that it didn't exactly come as a surprise.

'We're not talking Premier league villainy,' she went
on. 'Handling stolen goods … a common assault in a
kebab shop … two counts of twoccing.' Seeing his frown,
she explained: 'Taking without the owner's consent – car
theft, in other words.'

'Are you saying he's been in *prison*?'

Kershaw made a dismissive noise. 'You've got to do
more than that to get banged up these days. No, he's got
off with probation and a couple of community service
orders so far. Any of this ring any bells?' He shook his
head. 'So Kasia never mentioned anything about Steve
being in trouble with the law?'

Despite her studiedly neutral expression, Janusz picked
up the sceptical undertone. 'She would have been too
ashamed to tell me about it,' he growled. 'Maybe an
English person wouldn't understand.'

Ignoring the implied insult, Kershaw flipped over a page in her notebook. 'Then there's Jared Bateman.' Her gaze flicked up to his face but he showed no sign of recognition. 'He was Steve's co-defendant in a case last year. The pair of them were flogging stolen iPads down the pub ...'

'The Pineapple?'

'No ... The Bird in Hand, in Barking. Why d'you ask?'

As her eyes, the colour of steel seen through seawater, locked onto his Janusz berated himself for the slip-up. Evidently, the girl had yet to learn of Jared's death – or indeed Bill's – but when she did, the Pineapple would surely come up as the dead men's local. He could only pray that the pub's perma-tanned landlady had forgotten the big Pole who'd had a nice long chinwag with Bill Boyce, two days before his murder.

'No reason,' he said. 'Kasia mentioned it as a boozer he sometimes drinks at, that's all.'

'Well, anyway,' she went on, apparently accepting his explanation, 'they were doing a roaring trade by all accounts – but unfortunately for them, one of their customers was an off-duty traffic cop.'

They shared a dry smile.

'It turned out the iPads came from an armed robbery – a gang hijacked a freight lorry just off the boat at Felixstowe, got away with more than half a million quid's worth.'

Janusz whistled. 'Big job.'

'And a nasty one. When the driver refused to open up, they shot him. The bullet severed his spinal cord – left him paralysed from the neck down.'

'Bastards.'

'Yeah. When it came to court, Steve and Jared gave some fairytale about buying the gear in a lay-by from a bunch of travellers, and got off with a charge of handling stolen goods.'

'Were they thought to be involved, in the actual robbery, I mean?'

The perennial line between her eyebrows deepened. 'Probably not. They only had a few dozen of the iPads and their alibis were solid.'

'So they were just fencing the gear?'

She nodded slowly. 'I can't see anyone hiring them for something that big. Guys like Steve and Jared, they're bottom feeders – they get to hoover up the crumbs drifting down from the big kills overhead.'

Janusz delved into his pocket for his tin of cigars. 'Do you mind if I …?' He lit up, a scenario that had been taking shape in his mind since he'd found Bill's body beginning to gel. 'So Steve and Jared are small fry, hanging on the coat tails of the serious criminals. Did you get any other names – of bad guys that they might hang around with?'

'No one else who's mentioned on his record. And I can't access the police intelligence system without special permission.'

Janusz stood to retrieve an ashtray from one of the kitchen cupboards. 'What do you think is going on?'

'I think maybe the pair of them were starting to get more ambitious.'

'They're tired of playing second fiddle so they decide to pull a job of their own, you mean.'

'Possibly.'

'And that's why Steve disappears – because he's lying low somewhere.' As hard as it was for Janusz to picture

Steve as any kind of criminal mastermind, he'd reached more or less the same conclusion. 'But he's forty years old – it's a bit late in life to join the big boys, isn't it?' He levelled a look at her. 'And anyway, how would all this fit in with him kidnapping Kasia?'

There was a moment's awkward silence. Kershaw repositioned her spoon in its saucer, hunting for a diplomatic way to voice her suspicions. 'Maybe he hoped that if he finally made some money it might help to persuade Kasia not to leave him?' *Or maybe she didn't take much persuading,* she thought. Kiszka was clearly too nuts about his girlfriend to see it, but the likeliest scenario was that after Steve hit the criminal jackpot, Kasia – his wife of twenty years – had simply done a bunk with him.

Janusz knew what the girl *detektyw* was thinking: why would Steve even embark on such a dramatic course of action unless his wife was on board? She wasn't to know that Steve was a dim-witted fantasist who'd watched too many Hollywood heist movies. He'd probably been directing the final scene in his head for months: the one where he flings open a suitcase full of fifties, Kasia falls into his arms, and they jet off to a glamorous new life together.

Kershaw watched as he picked a flake of tobacco off his lip – a curiously fastidious gesture in such a big man – but couldn't decipher his expression.

'In this ... scenario of yours, how do you explain the fact that they didn't take the Alicante flight?' he asked.

'It might have been a diversion – to put their names onto one flight manifest while disappearing via some other route.' Luton had always struck her as an odd departure airport for anyone travelling from East London – Stansted or City being the more logical choices.

Janusz fought down an impulse to protest that whatever criminal enterprise Steve might have got himself embroiled in, there was no way that Kasia would ever be involved – but he knew how it would sound.

Kershaw eyed him – the mulish set of that big jaw a familiar sign of displeasure. 'It's all just a theory, of course,' she said.

Her mobile buzzed and she snatched it up.

'My contact at the tube says Steve didn't own a registered Oyster card,' she said, scrolling through a message. But then her frown gave way to a look of quiet excitement. 'But Kasia did. And the last time it was used was 0840 hours on Monday morning.'

'Monday?' *The day she was meant to be moving in with him.* 'Where the fuck did she go?'

'Epping. The last stop on the Central line.'

99

Sixteen

Janusz stood at the sink washing up the Opole porcelain coffee cups, reflecting on his latest encounter with Natalia Kershaw. It was clear that she suspected Kasia, at best, of making a mercenary calculation to stay with her husband; at worst, of being some kind of gangster's moll, up to her neck in his criminal activities. But then she *was* a cop, which, in his experience, came with a certain tendency to see things in black and white.

They were in agreement about one thing: that Steve was lying low after committing some robbery, a theory that could only be bolstered by Janusz's recent grim discoveries. Bill's murder, together with Jared's bizarre death-by-national-grid, looked like a storyline straight out of a heist movie. The gang of robbers who fall out after a big job; one of them deciding to bump off his partners in crime. *Why?* For the usual reason, Janusz supposed: to keep all the *szmalec* for himself. And since Steve was the one who'd pulled a vanishing act that made him the likeliest culprit.

Until now, he'd never have put Steve down as the murdering type, but the more he thought about it, the more sense it made. A lowlife and a wife beater who'd seen his every venture fail, and who now faced the worst failure of all: his wife leaving him for another man. Janusz was aware that, far from the powerful and super-intelligent figure of modern mythology, the typical killer was more often than not a self-pitying, lifetime loser.

None of it altered *ani o jote* his conviction that Steve had abducted Kasia and was holding her prisoner. At least he had a lead now: her mysterious tube journey out to Epping. Had Steve lured her out there on a pretext – perhaps claiming to be in some kind of trouble? That was plausible: even when it had become clear the marriage was over, Janusz sometimes still sensed an exasperated protectiveness in the way Kasia spoke of her husband. Screwing his eyes shut, he pictured her arriving in a quiet station car park, being bundled into a waiting van by Steve …

Janusz decided to head down to the nail bar to catch up with Barbara, see if she could shed any light on Kasia's trip to Essex.

But just as he was leaving, Tomek Morski, his contact at Haven Insurance, called.

'Look, Janek. I'm getting some stick from above about those annuitant security checks. Are you anywhere near finishing the paperwork yet?'

Kurwa! 'A thousand apologies, Tomek. I've been tied up doing some … unexpected work on a case.' What else could he say? That his girlfriend had been abducted by her psycho husband, and now he had dead Cockneys piling up all around him?

'Understood. How quickly can you turn around the files?'

Janusz did a swift calculation. 'I'll send you the ones I've already checked out later today. Then I might just need another couple of days on the last file.' The final Haven beneficiary he had yet to complete the paperwork for was Wojtek Raczynski.

'That sounds good. Shall we say next Monday as a final deadline then?' There was a delicate pause before he went on. 'We're going to be handing out a lot of work soon and I want to be able to tell the bosses that you deliver on time.'

Tomek's tone was as friendly as ever, but Janusz knew that the latitude afforded by their shared heritage only went so far: the guy had a job to do. And once he'd found Kasia, and this interruption to their life together was over, the Haven contract would be a solid foundation for the future.

After hanging up, Janusz got out his laptop and pulled up Wojtek's file.

He was tempted simply to sign off on his section of the form, but instead found himself staring at the photocopy of Wojtek's passport photo. He recalled how nervous he had seemed when he last saw him, and found himself wondering again what could have happened to cause such a change from the jolly, garrulous old boy of his first visit.

Just at that moment, Copetka jumped up on the table.

'*Kurwa*, Copetka! You nearly gave me a heart attack!' Planting his backside in the middle of the keyboard, the cat gazed up at him, purring like a well-tuned Merc – which could only mean one thing.

'*Dobrze, dobrze.* Did I forget your lunch, *moj tygrysku*?'

Bending to clatter dried food onto the little tiger's plate, Janusz said 'We're out of tinned food, so you'll have to make do with *biszkopty*.' And felt the hairs of his forearms crackle upright. It took a second for his frontal cortex to catch up, to put into words what his subconscious thought processes were telling him.

'Biscuits!' he said out loud.

Returning to Wojtek's file on the computer screen, he went straight to the section headed 'Medical History'.

After reading it through twice, he leaned back in his chair, a speculative look spreading across his face.

Seventeen

Kershaw had decided on a radically different approach for her second visit to the police psychotherapist. She had a suspicion that she might have come across as passive aggressive, or even obstructive-slash-hostile, during that first session, and since the whole charade would drag on until the shrink decreed that she was once again safe to carry a gun, she was going to take her old boss Streaky's advice. Which had been, more or less, *'Drop the bolshy tone, suck it up, talk the talk, and you'll be out of there in no time.'*

Surprised to feel her heart hammering, she settled herself into the easy chair, set at 45 degrees to Paula's own. A box of tissues placed within reach on a side table looked like a warning. *Or a challenge.*

'How are you?' asked Paula.

Kershaw eyed her. In any other setting, it would be the world's most banal question. A non-question. Here, it came freighted with hidden meaning.

'Fine. I mean, well, not fine, missing work, but yeah, you know, functioning.' *Well done, Natalie*, she told herself darkly. *Keep up these levels of personal insight and you'll still be coming here at Christmas.*

Paula offered only a blandly encouraging smile.

Bollocks.

'So I've been thinking about the shooting ... obviously. I think that although on the face of it, it wasn't my fault, I mean the guy *was* swinging a massive sword around, but yeah, I think I have to stand up and take responsibility for it.' She gave a decisive nod. 'It's a human life after all. It's a big deal. Yeah.'

'What does it mean, to you, "to take responsibility"?'

Jesus wept.

'Um.' Kershaw looked at the ceiling. 'Well, to accept that I did it. It was my decision to pull the trigger, however spur of the moment. And I knew he was gonna end up dead.'

Paula tipped her head to one side, as if to say *go on.*

She quelled a sigh. 'I think Joe Public has some cosy idea that we can stop someone non-lethally – you know, hit them in the arm or shoulder, like you see on the telly.'

'And that's a misunderstanding?'

'Yeah. If there's an immediate threat to life you shoot to stop. Which means you aim for the biggest target, the central body mass' – she hovered a spread hand across her chest and abdomen – 'and you keep shooting till the threat is neutralised.' Aware that this had all come out in a rush, she folded her arms. 'What I'm saying is, I accept that I killed him, deliberately. I hate it when terrorists lay their crimes at other people's doors. You know, strap a kilo of Semtex to a teenage suicide bomber and then blame the deaths of the innocent victims on some politician thousands of miles away?'

'You think that's disingenuous?'

'Yes. People should take responsibility for their actions, and say, "I did that – right or wrong – no one else." And it's got nothing to do with having a difficult childhood either.'

Another achingly long pause, while Kershaw kicked herself for the childhood reference, which just made her sound snarky.

Finally, Paula broke the silence. 'And who was responsible for the incident in which *you* were stabbed?'

I was, thought Kershaw. *Stupidity, bad policing, reading the signs wrong, failing to take my Airwaves out on a call ...*

'The person who stabbed me, obviously.' She spoke a bit too fast, her words tumbling into each other.

'Because sometimes it's easier to blame ourselves for things, don't you think?' said Paula. 'To tell ourselves we're unlucky, or cursed in some way.'

Kershaw bit the inside of her lip so hard she could taste the rusty tang of blood.

'You've not exactly had an easy time, the last few years,' she went on. Kershaw met her gaze, and seeing kindness there, looked away. 'Losing your dad – especially since he was the sole parent for much of your childhood – that must have been really tough.'

A sarcastic response leapt to her lips but an image of Streaky's stern gaze cut it off. *Suck it up, talk the talk ...*

Like a swimmer poised to dive into unknown waters, she took a deep breath and started to talk.

106

Eighteen

It was Janusz's third visit to the St Francis of Assisi Residential Home, but the first occasion on which he'd actually been in possession of the full facts regarding Haven Insurance annuitant Wojtek Raczynski.

A middle-aged woman in a smart suit, evidently one of the managers, greeted him today. She directed him up the oak staircase to Wojtek's room on the first floor, Janusz having requested that their final meeting – to 'tidy up a couple of loose ends', as he'd put it on the phone – take place in private. The moment he stepped through the door marked '3', he experienced a sharp-sweet pang of nostalgia, so strongly did the place remind him of his childhood. For although its wide bay window and high ceiling with ornate cornicing were unmistakably Victorian, there was something about the place that took him right back to his grandfather's study in the ramshackle old farmhouse on the outskirts of Gdansk where he'd spent a good part of his school holidays.

The room was large enough to accommodate a small sitting room area where Wojtek sat in one of those complicated-looking adjustable armchairs that looked like it could double as an instrument of torture. The walls were hung with prints of Polish landscape paintings in the nineteenth-century style – just like those in his *dziadzia*'s den. There was even a carved wooden clock with doors above its face, out of which, Janusz recalled, an old man and lady in traditional dress – one carrying a baton, the other a cymbal – would emerge to strike the hour.

In spite of Janusz's protests, the old boy struggled to his feet to greet him. His normally ruddy features looked grey, and he seemed, if anything, even more agitated than he had at their last meeting. The difference today was that Janusz had a pretty good idea what was worrying him, and it wasn't any unkindness on the part of the home's staff. After they'd exchanged the usual courtesies, Janusz produced his file of documents, which Wojtek eyed like a condemned man getting his first glimpse of the executioner's axe.

'Just a few questions, Pan Raczynski,' said Janusz, steeling himself for the task ahead. 'According to the medical records your GP, Dr Garrett, provided to Haven, you'd suffered some very serious medical conditions before buying your annuity in 2004.'

'*Tak*.' Nodding, Wojtek tried to steeple his fingers in front of him but they were shaking so much he set them back down on the chair arms.

Janusz ran his finger down the printout. 'In 1994 you were diagnosed with angina ... in 1997, diabetes; 1999, lung cancer ... All of them life-threatening conditions.'

'Thanks be to God, I was lucky to survive,' said Wojtek, trying to raise the smile of a man grateful for his good fortune.

'The problem I have is this, *prosze pana*.' Janusz shifted in his armchair, having identified what gave the room its potent nostalgic charge: the smell of the pipe tobacco that honeyed the air was the same brand his *dziadzia* used to smoke. 'You were treated for all these ailments back home in Lublin, which might explain why the records appear somewhat sketchy ... But when I checked with the hospital in Lublin directly, they were unable to find *any* details of treatment for you, nor any record of the many follow-up appointments one might expect to find considering the gravity of your conditions.'

'*Naprawde?*' said Wojtek. 'Maybe they lost my details. Everything is *skomputeryzowane* now. In my day, everything was properly recorded, ink on paper, and mark my words, there were many fewer mistakes.'

It was a brave rally, but from the way Wojtek's right hand was pawing at the arm of the chair, it was clear he could sense the game approaching its end stage. Just at that moment, Janusz heard a door squeak behind him. He saw Stefan emerging from the en-suite bathroom, his leathery features wearing an expression that was at once sardonic and rueful.

As Wojtek opened his mouth to say something, Stefan shushed him with a soothing gesture, before laying a hand on Janusz's shoulder. 'Good morning, Mr Kiszka,' he said. 'Forgive my resorting to the somewhat ... *Shakespearean* stratagem, but Wojtek asked me to be discreetly on hand should he need assistance.'

Janusz stared at him. *Mother of God! Was there anything round here the guy didn't have his bony beak in?* 'I'm afraid I'm not authorised to discuss Pan Raczynski's affairs with any third party,' he said, with an inward wince at the bureaucratic cant.

Stefan's grip on his shoulder tightened just a fraction and his tone became authoritative. 'Wojtek has granted me power of attorney over his affairs, so it's all quite above board, I assure you.' As Janusz hesitated, he added, 'Why don't you and I go somewhere to talk things through? I think Wojtek could do with a little rest.' When Janusz looked to Wojtek for permission the old boy nodded, clearly grateful that his ordeal was over – at least for now.

Outside in the gardens, Stefan ushered Janusz to an old ironwork bench, moving briskly despite his reliance on a walking stick. They sat under a canopy of fruit trees just coming into bud, overlooking the back of the home. Although the pale spring sunshine had burned off the morning chill, Janusz was still glad of his greatcoat; Stefan on the other hand looked perfectly comfortable in just a flannel shirt and his insubstantial-looking tweed jacket.

'What is it that makes you suspicious of my old friend Wojtek's medical history?' he asked, fixing those black-bird eyes on him. 'You know what Poland was like, even after the *Kommies* were chucked out. The public records were in chaos for years.'

'Nonetheless, doesn't he strike you as remarkably hale and hearty for a man who's survived heart disease *and* cancer?' Janusz recalled his eureka moment, while feeding Copetka, which had brought something about Wojtek's behaviour into sharp focus. 'For someone with a history of type-2 diabetes, he certainly makes short work of a packet of biscuits.'

Stefan gave a worldly shrug. 'I have castigated him for his imprudent diet, but people will persist in habits that are bad for their health.'

'He doesn't even appear to receive any medication from his GP for the condition. According to his medical records, he sees a private doctor for it.' Janusz raised a sceptical eyebrow.

'So what are you saying exactly? That Wojtek has fabricated all his ailments?' Stefan's beetling eyebrows came together to confer. 'Why in God's name would he do such a thing?'

Reaching for his tin of cigars, Janusz lit one. 'If you buy an annuity, the insurance company has to pay you a monthly amount for ever, guaranteed, until you die.' In order to work for Haven, he'd been required to attend an interminable weekend of lectures inducting him into the black arts of the annuity business. 'The better shape you're in, the less they pay you, because you're more likely to live to be a hundred. But people with a *bad* medical history get more, because the stats say they probably won't last long. It's the only insurance product which treats a poor life expectancy as a plus.'

'You're saying that Wojtek benefits financially from having these conditions?'

'Yes. He gets thousands of pounds a year more than someone with a good health record.'

Stefan whistled, impressed. 'And that's why the insurers wanted to check him out?'

Janusz shook his head. 'No. That was just a random ID check. They'd have no reason to question the medical report provided by his GP. The idea that someone could alter his medical records – I doubt that's even on the insurers' radar.' He wondered again how it might have been done. Had Wojtek bribed someone – a doctor or administrator – in Lublin Hospital, perhaps? Or the GP himself? One heard about such things, these days.

'What will you do?'

'I shall have to inform the insurance company of my suspicions.' Janusz shrugged. 'I imagine they'll mount a full investigation.'

Stefan levelled his beady gaze at Janusz. 'Wojtek is an intelligent man,' he said, after a moment. 'But I very much doubt he'd have the skills to devise such a sophisticated fraud, all on his own.' His expression was deadpan – like that of a chess player mounting a risky queen swap manoeuvre.

'You ... you know all about it, don't you?' said Janusz, feeling a total *glupek*.

In reply, Stefan simply sighed, before nodding at Janusz's cigar. 'Might I trouble you for one of those?' Taking one from the tin he leaned in to get a light. 'Can we speak in total confidence, on your word as a gentleman?'

Janusz shook his head. 'You know I can't promise that.'

Stefan gave a philosophical shrug, as if to say *'It was worth a try.'* His eyes followed the cigar smoke as it drifted up into the branches overhead. 'What if I told you that it was I who ... *modified* Wojtek's NHS records?'

'Really ...' said Janusz, trying to keep from smirking. 'And how did you do that exactly?'

'You don't believe an old codger like me could have pulled it off.'

112

Janusz raised his eyebrows. 'No offence, but breaking into the NHS system? Even if it were possible, which I doubt, that would take some serious hacking skills.'

Stefan smiled. 'I can see I shall have to tell you a little more about my history.' He took a cautious draw on his cigar. 'After the war, I couldn't go home – I didn't fancy another extended holiday in Siberia.'

Janusz gave a little nod: after fighting alongside the Allies, thousands of Polish ex-combatants had returned home only to face brutal persecution by a Stalinist regime which saw them as dangerous opponents of the new socialist order.

'For we Poles,' Stefan went on, 'the war continued – only the enemy and the methods changed. Luckily, I'd won medals for mathematics at school, which persuaded London University to offer me a place. After managing to win a first, I offered my services to the War Office, who kindly gave me a job.'

Janusz frowned, working it out. 'You worked as a code breaker? For *MI6*?'

'For sixteen happy years. I've never had so much sex in my life.' Stefan grinned, revealing pointy teeth. 'But I digress. I liked the work, but loathed the civil service politics, so when computing took off in the sixties, I left to join IBM as a programmer.'

'But you must have retired *decades* ago.'

'Of course, but I try to stay abreast of the developments in coding – I confess I spend far too much time online, chatting to some very bright young people. Still, it all helps to keep the brain ticking over.' He aimed a bony finger at Janusz. 'Mark my words: an idle mind is the fastest route to the boneyard.'

Janusz eyed the old rogue, still not convinced. 'But surely NHS security must be cast iron?'

Stefan gave a rusty chuckle. 'I'm afraid not,' he said.

'Look, if you expect me to believe that you hacked Wojtek's medical records, you'll have to explain exactly how you did it.'

'Very well. The first step is to acquire a GP's username and password – which I'm afraid is all too easy to extract over the telephone from the busy ladies on reception.'

'Really? How?'

'By posing as Josh, from the IT department, who's trying to fix a problem with the server.'

Janusz thought about it. Scamming people for security information was a tried and tested method, which he'd used himself in the course of investigations, and he knew that plenty of people kept their username and password on a Post-it note stuck to their computer. Nonetheless, Stefan would sound far too old to impersonate an IT worker convincingly.

'I'm guessing that *"Josh from IT"* is played by one of your young hacking friends?'

Stefan inclined his head in assent.

'Okay,' said Janusz. 'But then what? You're saying you can simply alter someone's medical history?'

'Every system needs to allow corrections and additions. Of course, if anyone who knew their way round the system actually went looking, they'd soon find a record of suspicious alterations to the database – but nobody ever does.'

Janusz stared at him. He was still trying to reconcile the image conjured up by the word 'hacker' with this ancient war veteran in a tweed jacket – and yet, he seemed to be telling the truth.

Realising his cigar had gone out, he paused to re-light it. 'Okay. So you add life-shortening conditions to Wojtek's medical history. They end up in the report that's sent to Haven. He gets a bigger annuity payment. What did you get out of it?'

'Not a penny. I still have my IBM shares and a decent pension.' He gestured with his stick towards St Francis's, its red brick glowing in the sunshine. 'You know, if this were a private concern it would cost eight hundred pounds a week to stay here, or possibly more. Since it's a charitable trust, they do keep the fees as low as humanly possible, but even so, this quality of care doesn't come cheap.'

'I fail to see how this is relevant to you and Wojtek conspiring to defraud Haven Insurance,' growled Janusz, trying to regain control of the situation.

'The residents aren't wealthy people. They paid every spare penny into pension schemes all their lives, only to find that the annuities they planned to live on in their old age were set to pay out peanuts.'

Kurwa! Janusz almost dropped his cigar, which had burned right down to his fingers. 'Are you saying you pulled this NHS records scam for everyone here?!'

'Not everyone,' said Stefan. 'Some bought annuities before they arrived, more's the pity.' He looked intently at Janusz, his expression serious. 'As you know, insurance companies pool information among themselves. If you file a report, I'm afraid there's little doubt it would trigger a full investigation – and that would mean fraud charges, not just against me, but against a number of residents.'

115

'If it ever came to that, I am sure the courts would be lenient towards elderly people,' said Janusz.

'Perhaps,' the old boy shrugged. 'But they could no longer afford to stay here. And the resulting scandal might even close the home.'

Janusz cast him a sideways look: Stefan's profile looked like some ancient desert monument, blasted over the aeons by innumerable sandstorms. He knew what the old bastard was up to: he was trying to take advantage of his natural sympathy and respect for vulnerable old people.

Unfortunately, it was working.

'So you see, if you turn us in to the insurance company, the consequences for the residents could be *katastrofalne*.' Stefan's habitual air of sardonic amusement had disappeared, leaving him sounding old and defeated.

Recalling the residents he'd met, and Wojtek's homely room, Janusz suddenly saw an image of the red tin his *dziadzia*'s pipe tobacco had come in. *The chiselled profile of a handsome naval* kapitan *smoking a pipe, the backswept lines of a warship behind him*. He'd loved that tin, as a boy – had clamoured to be allowed to fill his grandfather's pipe from it.

Janusz ground out his dead cigar underfoot, lost for words. After a moment, he got to his feet. 'I've got to go. I'll … be in touch.'

He didn't have long to dwell on the dilemma that Stefan had left him with. A text message from Barbara at the nail bar sent him racing the three stops west on the Central line to Stratford.

There, a square of fresh plywood replacing the glass panel in the nail bar door told a familiar story.

'When was the break-in?' Janusz asked Barbara, before they'd even embraced.

'Last night,' she said, lifting one shoulder – a gesture that reminded Janusz so vividly of Kasia that for a moment, it stole his breath. 'Our insurance premiums will go up now, of course. And we don't even keep any cash here.'

'Why didn't you let me know sooner? I would have come straight down.'

'Bless you, Janek. You have enough to do looking for poor dear Kasia.' Locking the door behind them she ushered him inside. 'Is there any news?'

He shook his head. 'Did they take anything?'

'Nothing seems to be missing. They broke this open' – she indicated a drawer in the desk at reception, its leading edge splintered – 'but all we keep inside are the spare keys. I'm having the locks changed, *naturalnie*. And the police were here this morning taking fingerprints.'

'*Dobrze*,' he patted her hand. 'You're doing all the right things.'

Her eyes scanned his face. 'You don't think it's got anything to do with Kasia?'

'*Nie, nie*.' Break-ins were hardly a rarity in this part of London and Janusz saw no point in frightening her when he had no proof that this was any more than a random burglary – the most likely perpetrator some junkie looking for petty cash. Still, it set his brain buzzing. If Steve had been involved in some kind of heist, and was now falling out with his fellow thieves in murderous fashion, then the break-in could be related. Did one of Steve's crew suspect him of hiding the proceeds of the job in his wife's workplace? Whatever the 'burglars' had

117

been looking for – having failed to find it, they had no reason to return.

'Listen, Barbara. Do you know if Kasia had any friends in Epping? Did she ever talk about going to visit someone out there?'

'Epp-ing?' Barbara split the unfamiliar English word into separate syllables. 'No ... I don't think so. Is it important?'

'Maybe. You said that on Monday mornings she worked from home, on the website, following up emails?'

'*Tak.*'

'She didn't mention anything about having to go to Essex on Monday, before coming to work? Something to do with Steve, maybe?'

'Nothing I can think of, Janek. Did you look on her laptop ...?'

'I searched the flat but I couldn't find it.' Janusz took her hand. 'Barbara, think hard now, what might take her out of town into Essex?'

Barbara shook her head, distress clouding her face. 'Sometimes she would go to meet new suppliers ... but I don't think she ever mentioned Epp-ing.'

Pulling out his phone, Janusz punched Epping into Google Maps. 'Sawbridgeworth, Abridge, Nazeing ...' he read out place names that looked within easy reach of the station.

'What's that?' She pointed over his shoulder at the great green swathe to the south.

'Epping Forest,' he said. He and Kasia had been there last autumn picking *boletas* – he still had the last two strings of them, dried, their bosky aroma perfuming his pantry.

118

'*Las … Las …*' she said, musingly, before taking off to the back of the shop. Janusz could see her peering at bits of paper pinned up on a corkboard, still murmuring to herself. When she came back, she was wearing an excited expression and carrying a pink Post-it note.

Seeing Kasia's familiar hand made his chest contract. What she had scrawled, evidently in haste, were the words *Sanktuarium Lasu*, and a postcode starting CM16. 'Forest Sanctuary,' he read.

'*To prawda!*' said Barbara, excitement raising the pitch of her voice. 'Some kind of spa hotel. When you said "forest" I suddenly remembered Kasia mentioning it a few days ago.'

CM could stand for Chelmsford. The nearest big town to Epping.

Janusz tapped the name and postcode into his phone and up popped a website. *The Forest Sanctuary and Spa Hotel, Epping Magna.* Bingo.

The Forest Sanctuary Hotel had once been a golf club, but its greens had been 'lovingly landscaped' into gardens, and ladies in towelling bathrobes had taken the place of crusty old men wearing club ties. When guests tired of the pool, steam room and sauna, they could take a variety of what the website grandly called 'treatments'. Janusz clicked through the picture gallery with a mystified expression, marvelling, not for the first time, at the apparently limitless ways in which women could be separated from their hard-earned cash – or that of their husbands. *Why, in the Name of all the Saints, would anyone pay good money to have hot rocks piled on their back?*

'This Forest place telephoned here?' Barbara nodded. 'And did Kasia say what they wanted?'

'We were very busy when they called.' Her shrug was apologetic. 'But I think they wanted to talk about offering a nail extension service, for their guests.'

'But who would run it? You two couldn't leave the shop?'

'Kasia always said we could easily train someone up if we wanted to expand. She was so clever about business.'

He nodded, it was just like Kasia – even on the day she was moving house – to race out to Epping on a new business enquiry.

A stricken look creased Barbara's face. 'I should have remembered all this before! It's just she never mentioned it again, Janek, never said she was going there.'

'*Nie*, don't worry, Barbara,' he soothed.

But to his alarm, her eyes filled with tears.

'Barbara! Please don't upset yourself. I'll check the place out, but it probably has nothing to do with her disappearing.'

She looked up at him, her eyes like those of a woman drowning, shaking her head. 'Janek, I hope you can forgive me. There's something else.'

The 'something else' that burst out of Kasia's best friend on a flood of tears and self-recrimination left him staggering like a teenage boxer who's taken his first knockout punch.

Kasia had been keeping a secret.

Nineteen

Kershaw didn't think anything of it when her old boss DS 'Streaky' Bacon called to suggest a drink that evening: after the stabbing, when she'd left murder squad to train as a firearms officer, he'd made a point of keeping in touch.

They arranged to meet in 'The Moon' on Hoe Street, Walthamstow nick's favourite watering hole. Officially called the Dog and Duck, the nickname was a reference to its absence of any detectable atmosphere. The drinks, however, were what Streaky liked to call 'reassuringly inexpensive'.

'How are your sessions with the head doctor going?' he asked, licking foam from his gingery moustache.

'Oh you know,' Kershaw rolled her eyes, 'raking over my childhood, all that old cobblers.' Then, clocking his look, '*I know* ... talk the talk. I am doing, Sarge, honest.' In fact, she was surprised to feel a little twinge of guilt at dissing the shrink, Paula. She was only doing her job, after all.

'I'm glad to hear it. The more of a struggle you put up, the longer it'll drag on. Who are you seeing, anyway?'

'Paula Reeve.'

'Any good?'

'She seems nice enough, but I don't think she's got the first idea what it's like, being in the Job.'

A smile twitched at Streaky's lips. After pausing to dispatch a third of his pint in one epic swallow, he asked, '"How many psychologists does it take to change a light bulb?"'

She shook her head as protocol demanded.

'"Only one, but it takes twelve visits."'

He split open a packet of crisps on the tabletop to form a foil platter, then sprinkled the contents of a bag of salted peanuts carefully on top, before inviting Kershaw to share the feast with a gracious gesture.

'So do you still think you made the right decision?' he asked, through a mouthful of crisp-and-nut. 'Giving up a proper career as a detective to join the boys with toys brigade?'

'Yeah. I feel at home in SCO19.' She rolled her eyes. 'Or I will once they give me my weapon back and trust me not to blow someone's head off.'

Streaky snorted. 'Trust you to use it, more like.'

Kershaw stared at him: she'd always assumed the whole shrink thing was to find out whether the experi- ence of being attacked outside the Maccy D's might make her trigger-happy, next time she was out on an op. Now she realised it was just as much about ensuring that – if the situation arose – she wouldn't hesitate to shoot to kill again.

'Because, much as it pains me to say it, you were a good detective,' he said, using a dampened finger to pick up the crisp crumbs.

'Thanks, Sarge.'

'For a woman,' he added.

After buying the next round, she'd just sat down again when Streaky dropped his little stink-bomb.

'So what's your interest in Steven Fisher?'

What the fuck? Streaky's pale blue eyes looked guileless enough, but it occurred to her that the last half-hour's chit-chat might have been all about putting her at ease – just like he'd taught her to do when interviewing a suspect.

'Steven Fisher ...?' She frowned into her Sauvignon, like the name rang a distant bell, giving herself a moment to think. Decided that the only way Streaky could possibly know about her interest in Fisher was because he'd seen the trail she'd left while searching the database for his criminal record. 'Oh yeah ...' she said. 'He's a distant contact of some guy we've got under surveillance.' *That sounded all right.* SCO19 did occasionally get involved in surveillance when they had advance intel on armed robberies and the like. 'I ran a PNC search on him.' Always good to offer more than was necessary – something she'd learned from the smarter breed of scumbag she'd interrogated over the years.

'Did you come up with anything?'

'Nah. He's pretty small beer, isn't he?' Her eyes wide over the rim of her glass.

'Has been up till now,' said Streaky. 'But his name's come up in connection with a murder.'

'Murder?' It was all she could do to keep her voice steady.

'Yeah. Nasty business. A mate of his, Bill Boyce, was found hanged from his own shower rail.'

'A staged suicide?' asked Kershaw casually, all the while wondering if Streaky could hear her heart thumping.

Streaky snorted. 'Pretty half-arsed attempt. Especially since he was worked over with a blowtorch first.'

She made a face. 'Nasty. Was he a villain?'

'No, he's clean as a whistle.' Streaky frowned. 'No clue as to motive except that he was pals with a couple of local bad boys, including your friend Steve Fisher.' His gaze fell on her knee, which she realised had been jigging up and down of its own volition.

She stilled it. 'Murder sounds a bit out of Fisher's league, though' – those pale eyes of his met hers again – 'from what I recall of his record, I mean, which isn't much.'

Streaky dug deep in his ear with his little finger, examining what he found there with an impartial gaze. 'Maybe they had a falling-out over money, or a woman. Fisher's not been seen for a few days – even missed a friend's funeral, I heard.'

'Really?'

'Yeah, another lowlife called Jared Bateman. You must have seen it on Fisher's file. The pair of them got done for handling gear from that Felixstowe lorry job – the one where the driver took a bullet in the spine?'

'Yeah, I remember now,' she said. 'So this Jared's death – is it suspicious?'

'Nah. Household electrocution. Accidental, according to the PM.' He drained his glass, pointed at hers. 'Another one of those?'

While Streaky was at the bar, Kershaw chewed guiltily on a ragged fingernail. The fact that Steve was in the frame for murder put a whole new slant on her bit of freelance detective work for Kiszka. She ought to 'fess up to the whole thing, of course, tell the Sarge what she knew. On the other hand, it wasn't like she had anything concrete yet. If, as seemed increasingly likely, Steve had murdered his mate after some job, she could get more out of Kiszka by piggybacking his hunt for Kasia. Handing him over to Streaky would only risk him clamming up – or worse, going AWOL.

The rest of the evening was spent catching up on the latest gossip from the nick. After last orders, out on the street, poised to go in their separate directions, Streaky lit a fag, before fixing his gaze on her through the upcurl of smoke. She wondered if he was going to return to the subject of Steve Fisher.

Instead he said: 'By the way, your psychologist – Paula Reeve? The one who's clueless about the Job?'

'Yeah …?'

'She was a uniform sergeant back in the day. Got a gong for bravery.'

'You're kidding?'

'Straight up. She disarmed a man with a knife trying to rob a cashier in a Tesco Express in the Lea Bridge Road.'

'Christ, I had no idea.'

'Got a punctured lung for her trouble.' Turning to go, he threw her a grin over his shoulder. 'Maybe you're not such a good detective after all.'

Twenty

Just after 9 a.m. the next morning, Oskar's Transit van peeled off from the mile-long tailback that had slowed the traffic on the North Circular to a sclerotic dribble, and ascended the relatively empty slip road onto the M11 northbound.

'Thank fuck for that,' grumbled Oskar as the diesel engine laboured its way up to 60mph. 'I still don't see why we couldn't have waited an hour, to let all the nine-to-fivers get to work.'

Janusz ignored him. After what he'd learned from Barbara the previous evening, his initial impulse had been to set out for the Forest Sanctuary Hotel there and then, but on reflection he'd decided it would be better to wait and go first thing with Oskar. A lone man checking in for the Forest Sanctuary's 'Spa Experience Package' would surely look suspicious, and if he did find any kind of lead to Kasia's whereabouts, having the van might come in handy.

'I still say they're gonna think we're a pair of *pedziow*, sharing a hotel room,' complained Oskar.

'Not with your dress sense,' said Janusz, grinning at the sight of his mate's rotund form squeezed into a royal blue jacket made of some shiny, flammable-looking fabric, paired with patent leather shoes in burgundy. 'Where the fuck did you get that outfit – a joke shop?'

'What's wrong with it?' asked Oskar, looking down at his get-up. 'You said to dress smart! I bought this for an *elegancki* wedding in Gdansk.'

'What, in 1979?' asked Janusz. 'Anyway, I told you – I'm not paying out for separate rooms just because you're insecure about your sexuality.'

Oskar gave him a considering look. 'What's got you so chirpy today, anyway? Is it the chance of seeing my naked butt in the steam room?' He did a suggestive shimmy in his seat, causing the van to swerve onto the rumble strip of the hard shoulder.

'Watch the fucking road, turniphead!' Janusz reached for his cigars. Oskar was right: he was in better spirits today. Partly because he felt he was finally a step closer to finding Kasia; but mostly because of what Barbara had confessed.

Kasia was pregnant. Saying the words to himself, he felt his mouth curve once again into a foolish smile.

It explained a lot about how she'd been acting lately, now he thought about it – the drawn look and loss of appetite, the way she'd suddenly given up smoking – as well as the preoccupied, almost secretive air he'd sensed about her. *You're some detective*, idiota, he told himself.

According to Barbara, Kasia had been planning to tell him after they moved in together. Not that she'd be worried about his reaction: the subject had come up on a mushroom-picking jaunt in Epping Forest the previous autumn. They'd been talking about his boy Bobek, and he'd let slip that he wouldn't mind having another child – the words *'with you'* left unspoken yet understood. She had shrugged, and smiled her inscrutable smile, but perhaps the exchange had sparked something in her – started her thinking about a new life, in more ways than one.

Since hearing the news, Janusz had found himself swinging from elation to despair and back again. If Steve had found out that Kasia was pregnant, it was possibly what had driven him to take such desperate measures – having realised that, this time, she was serious about leaving him. In any event, the knowledge of his lover's vulnerable state made Janusz even more desperate to find her. And the girl *detektyw*'s involvement only added to the urgency: it was surely just a matter of time before Natalia discovered the shocking mortality rate among Steve's pals, and sent the balloon up. Now more than ever, the idea of Kasia's rescue being taken over by the cops filled him with a cold fear.

The Forest Sanctuary Hotel looked a good deal less impressive when stripped of the glamorising filter of website photography and graphics, although its appeal wasn't enhanced by a backdrop of a lowering sky and the persistent drizzle which set in just as they arrived. From the tacky-looking entrance board to the static-producing carpet in reception, everything about the place looked to Janusz like it had been done on the cheap.

'Are you all right there?' asked the girl on reception.

'We're checking in for the Spa Experience Package' –

words that, until now, Janusz could never have imagined passing his lips – 'name of Beck, James and Christopher Beck.' As instructed, Oskar hung back, checking out a display stand of leaflets.

If the receptionist saw anything odd in the two middle-aged men checking in for a spa package, one with a posh yet indefinably foreign accent and wearing a threadbare military-type coat, the other dressed like an eighties game show host, she was too polite to let it show.

'Double or twin beds?'

'Twin,' chorused Janusz and Oskar.

'Sorry,' said the girl, frowning at her computer screen. 'The system's playing up today.' While she tapped away at the keyboard, Janusz dipped his head to smell a bowl of lurid peonies on the desk. *Artificial.*

'Okay. Your room is ready for you. Let's get you booked in for your treatments.' She opened the brochure on the desk in front of him and read out what was on offer.

Kurwa! This was *terra incognita* to Janusz, and yet turning down the free session included in the spa package might look suspicious. 'The, umm, aromatherapy massage with Magda?' he asked. That sounded straightforward. 'And for my brother, the one you mentioned with Agnieszka?'

'The VitaMan Special?'

'Yeah, that one.'

Their room, located in a new annexe attached to the rear of the hotel, confirmed Janusz's opinion of the place. The furniture looked fairly new but its veneer was already peeling, the cheap foam mattresses were designed to repel boarders, and air freshener couldn't quite conceal the insinuation of damp which hung about the room.

129

'What am I having done, Janek?' asked Oskar, emerging from the bathroom in a white towelling robe. 'You might have asked me first.'

'No idea, Oskar, I just picked the ones with Polish girls. If we chat them up, they might give us something useful. But don't give the girl a questionnaire, okay? Be *dyskretny*.'

'*Dyskretny, tak*,' Oskar nodded. 'So ... what am I supposed to talk about?'

'Just chit-chat. Talk to her about your blood group diet. Then you can move on to how she likes working here. And don't mention Kasia – *naturalnie*.'

'*Naturalnie*.' Oskar nodded, adopting a businesslike frown. 'But it's okay to ask for a "happy ending", right?' He hooted with laughter, slapping his naked thigh. 'Ah, Janek, you should see your face!'

Janusz eyed him anxiously. A couple of years back, Oskar had played detective on one of his cases behind his back – earning himself a brutal beating by gangsters. After that, Janusz had never let him get anywhere near an investigation again. It was only because this case involved Kasia – and a pregnant Kasia, at that – that he'd accepted Oskar's impassioned offers of help.

Ten minutes later, Janusz was lying face down on a massage table, naked but for an ancient pair of swimming shorts, the sound of panpipes coming through the speakers doing nothing to reduce his anxiety levels. Magda might be a blonde-haired slip of a girl in a white tunic, but he'd felt less vulnerable facing armed thugs.

She was certainly chatty, though. Within a few minutes he'd learned that she'd been brought up in Krakow, where she had studied for a degree in 'health and beauty'

130

– he'd had no idea such a thing existed – and that her boyfriend was English and a graphic designer.

'I went to university in Krakow, back in the eighties,' he said, trying not to flinch as she started to massage his back and shoulders with pungent-smelling rosemary oil, which she claimed would 'energise' him.

'*Naprawde?* Under Communism? My mama says it was terrible back then. What did you study?'

'Physics and chemistry. At Jagiellonski.'

'Wow, Jagiellonski! You must have been a bit of a brainbox!'

Janusz grunted, torn between a sense of gratified vanity that his alma mater still prompted respect in the younger generation, and irritation at her use of the past tense.

'I left without finishing my degree, though,' he admitted. 'There were too many distractions in those days. Demos, strikes, throwing petrol bombs at the *milicja* and ZOMO …' He stopped himself, embarrassed to hear the nostalgic note in his own voice.

'It must have been terrible,' said Magda. 'And is it true you couldn't get fashionable clothes, back then – not even branded jeans?' Her tone suggested that this aspect of life must have been at least as bad as getting tear-gassed and shot at by riot police.

Janusz decided to change the subject: reminiscing about his glory days as a *Solidarnosc* firebrand wasn't going to help him find out what Kasia had been doing here.

'I'm coming back here with my fiancée in a couple of months,' he said, 'for a pre-wedding treat.'

'Oh, congratulations!' piped Magda. 'Is that the guy with the moustache you came in with today?'

'*Kurwa! Nie!*' said Janusz, in a tone of loud protest. 'Sorry. No, my fiancée is ... *a lady.*'

'*Dobrze*. I'm open-minded.'

'Anyway, she was wondering whether you do nail extensions, you know, so that she's ready for the big day?'

'*Przepraszam pana,*' she said, apologetic. 'We don't do that here.'

'No plans to offer it alongside the spa services?'

'I don't think so,' she said.

Janusz backed off, keeping his conversation general for a few minutes before approaching the mystery from another direction.

'What's it like working here? Are they good employers?'

He felt her pause in her ministrations just for a second. 'Oh, they're okay,' she said, unconvincingly.

'It's not easy, coming to work in a foreign country,' he said. 'I remember it well.'

'I don't mind that. There's another Polish girl here and one from Lithuania.' She hesitated. 'It's just so quiet here.'

'What, out in the countryside, you mean?'

'*Nie*. I mean the business,' she went on, dropping her voice. 'The hotel is empty most of the time. I don't think they're very ... professional, you know?' Then she patted his shoulders. '*Dobrze*. Turn over for me could you, *prosze pana*?'

Perhaps regretting her indiscretion, Magda wouldn't be drawn any further on the shortcomings of the management, and Janusz was loath to press her. After finishing the massage, she dimmed the lights and left him lying there – smelling like he'd been greased and rolled in the contents of his herb rack.

By the time she came back, he'd fallen asleep.

'I checked with the hotel manager, about your girl-friend?' she said, turning up the lights. He blinked up at her, momentarily disorientated. 'He says there are definitely no plans to offer nail extensions in the spa. But he says if you ask at the front desk, we can easily arrange a booking for your girlfriend at a local beauty clinic.'

Twenty-One

Dr Nathan King sounded genuinely pleased to hear Kershaw's voice when she called his mobile.

'Hello there, stranger. How's life in the firearms unit?'

Phew. Kershaw heard nothing in his voice to indicate that he knew she'd been the shooter in the Kyle Furnell case, nor that she was on enforced sick leave – which meant no awkward questions to fend off. Nathan had been one of the main pathologists during her time in Walthamstow murder squad so their paths had crossed fairly frequently and, luckily enough given the favour she had to ask, they'd always got on well.

'Yeah, it's good – different,' she said. 'And I still get to do the odd bit of detective work, which is why I'm calling. Did you do the PM on a guy called Jared Bateman, by any chance – would have been, ooh, Monday or Tuesday?'

'Bateman ... Hang on a second and I'll check.' A minute later he came back on. 'No, I was in court the whole of Tuesday so it went to a locum.'

'I'm guessing it wasn't a Home Office PM then?'

She heard the rustle of paperwork. 'No, I'm afraid Mr Bateman only received the twenty-minute budget special,' he said.

It was something the two of them had shared a moan about more than once. All standout suspicious deaths got the full Home Office post-mortem lasting several hours which had to be conducted by an accredited pathologist like Nathan, but the more borderline cases ended up getting the economy version, at a fraction of the cost.

'To be fair, this one does look like a straightforward accidental death,' he added. 'It appears that our Mr Bateman had the misfortune to drill directly into the mains cable.'

Kershaw swallowed a laugh. Nathan was only a few years older than her, but he had that pompous way of talking she'd noticed before in pathologists – straight out of the medical lecture theatre. Maybe it was the isolated nature of the job – with only the dead for company there wasn't much human interaction to knock the corners off them.

She was wondering how to proceed without raising Nathan's suspicions, when he said, 'Look I have to run – I'm just finishing up my list. But if you have time to pop over, we can discuss the report.'

After parking up near Walthamstow Mortuary, Kershaw put in another call to Kiszka. *Voicemail again.* She'd been calling him regularly since her drink with Streaky, but he wasn't answering his phone, which – together with his failure to mention the deaths of two of Steve Fisher's close friends – had her antennae doing the conga. Of course, it was possible he was unaware of Jared Bateman and Bill Boyce popping their clogs within three days of each other, but somehow she doubted it. Remembering his unguarded mention of the Pineapple as Steve's local, she'd bet a month's rent that he'd been down there asking questions.

Inside the mortuary, the staff had clocked off leaving the post-mortem room empty. The examining tables had been hosed down, their stainless steel surfaces gleaming under the fluorescent strip lights, the raw stench of offal and bodily fluids muted by an overpowering smell of bleach. The only sound was water chuckling down count-less unseen drains and conduits. Yet no mortuary ever felt truly empty to Kershaw: she was always conscious of the silent human presence behind the doors of the lock-ers that lined one wall, the sub-zero dormitory where the mortuary's inhabitants lay, awaiting the final stage of their journey.

Seeing Nathan emerge from a side room, Kershaw sloshed across the floor in her blue wellingtons to greet him. His dark curly hair needed cutting, she noted, but he had kind eyes, and even in bloodstained turquoise scrubs she had to admit he was pretty easy on the eye.

'Good to see you, Nathan.'

There was an awkward pause: had they met elsewhere they might have exchanged a chummy kiss on the cheek but here, that felt ... *inappropriate*.

'Shall we have a quick look at our Mr Bateman?' Nathan asked, heading over to the lockers.

They stopped at a drawer bearing the scrawled name 'Bateman' in wipe-clean marker – at least it had done, until some smartarse had smudged out the middle 'e', leaving the impression that the drawer held the remains of a crime-fighting superhero. The look she and Nathan exchanged betrayed disapproval and amusement – a shared understanding that black humour was a necessary survival mechanism in a place like this.

Jared Bateman didn't look too bad, thought Kershaw – as if he were dozing and his mouth might fall open at any moment to emit a comedy snore. The unreflective pallor of his skin was the only giveaway. She'd been to so many post-mortems over the years that the sight of a dead body no longer triggered the normal, visceral, response. Whenever she'd admitted as much to her non-Job friends, they were always shocked: it was another of those yawning chasms between the world of the normal and those whose daily lives were defined by the consequences of violent death.

Nathan lifted the dead man's forearm and showed her his right hand, or what remained of it. 'There's your entry point,' he said, indicating a deep, dark red lesion that had split the palm from side to side. The fingers were desiccated mahogany-coloured claws, burned down to the first knuckle, and when he turned the hand she could see that even on the back the skin was blackened, peeled back to reveal the tracery of veins beneath. 'Because he was holding a drill, the current would have caused his muscles to contract and grip it even tighter, prolonging the exposure.'

Pulling the drawer open further, he indicated an angry-looking crater on the sole of the cadaver's foot. 'And here's where the current went to ground.'

'He wasn't wearing rubber soles, then?'

'No, unfortunately he was in his stockinged feet.'

137

'Stockinged ...?' Kershaw suppressed a grin. 'Oh, you mean he was only wearing socks. So, any signs of foul play, pre-mortem?'

'Umm,' he consulted the report. 'He sustained a broken cervical vertebra ...'

'Really?'

'I wouldn't read anything into it. Two hundred and thirty volts of alternating current can cause spasms violent enough to break limbs.' He turned one of Jared's legs this way and that. 'There are a few more burns ...'

'Could they have been inflicted before he got electrocuted?' asked Kershaw, recalling Streaky's mention of blowtorch injuries to Bill Boyce.

'Very difficult to say without a full PM. The current often arcs all over the place, trying to find the nearest route to earth.'

'No suggestion then, that the cause of death was anything other than electrocution?'

He flipped through the PM report. *'Congestion of the lungs ... petechial haemorrhages* – it's all pretty much what I'd expect to see.' Turning to the conclusion he read aloud: *'"Cause of death: cardiac and/or pulmonary arrest due to electrocution."'*

She stared down at Jared's face. 'And the drill, the wiring at his place, does it say if that all checked out?'

'Looks like it. Old-style fuse box at the property, apparently. The modern type would probably have thrown the whole circuit.'

Just then, Nathan's phone rang and he dug beneath his turquoise scrubs to retrieve it.

A moment later, his head shot up to look at her, a look of consternation clouding his face. 'Jared Bateman ...?'

Widening her eyes, she shook her head urgently.

After a bit more chat, he hung up, an uncertain half-smile on his face. 'That was DS Bacon. He was phoning to give the go-ahead for a full Home Office PM on our friend here.' Kershaw could see disappointment in his eyes. 'Um … Natalie. Why did you not want me to mention you were here?'

'I'm really sorry, Nathan. I can explain. Shall we go and have that coffee?'

Twenty-Two

'Treatment?! I call it legalised torture, more like,' complained Oskar, pausing in his demolition of a chicken and bacon club sandwich. 'I'll be lucky if my spine ever goes back to normal. I tell you, Janek, that girl would've made a good interrogator for the *milicja!*'

'Hold your muzzle, Oskar,' murmured Janusz. 'Remember what I said? About keeping a low profile?'

'There's hardly anyone here,' said Oskar, looking round the hotel brasserie.

'Even so. Keep it down.' Janusz took a sip of his coffee and scowled: described as espresso on the menu, it tasted more like boiled and reheated Nescafe.

Both men were still wearing their white towelling robes. After showering off the herbal oil slick coating his skin, Janusz had been tempted to put his everyday clothes back on. But as Oskar had pointed out, with all the other guests wearing their robes even outside the spa, he'd stick out like a duck in a hen house.

'So, did you pick up anything useful?' Janusz murmured.

Oskar folded the last mouthful of sandwich into his mouth and washed it down with a gulp of Diet Coke. 'Well,' he said, narrowing his eyes conspiratorially, 'Agnieszka doesn't like the management, I got that much out of her, just before she tried to rearrange my spine.' He rolled his shoulders cautiously.

'Go on.'

'She put me in a headlock and put her knee in my back, like this ...'

'Not that, *kretynie* – what did she say about the management?'

'Oh. Well, Agnieszka said the guy who runs the place is nice enough, but useless as tits on a boar. The place is two-thirds empty even at weekends, but he doesn't seem to care. Spends most of his time in the sauna.'

Pretty much in line with what Magda had said.

'She says he's a *maminsynek* ... how do you say that in English?'

'Mummy's boy.'

'*Tak*, he's a "mummy's boy". Mama is a widow – and loaded. She hardly ever comes here, doesn't get involved with the business. Agnieszka reckons she bought him the place like you buy a kid a train set, so he can play at being hotel manager.'

Janusz grunted. Agnieszka sounded a good deal less discreet than Magda; but perhaps Oskar's artless naivety made him a more natural confidant. 'So does anyone know how the mama got rich?'

'She's retired, but apparently she made her fortune in *zlom*,' said Oskar, rubbing finger and thumb together.

Interesting. There were millions to be made in scrap metal, that was for sure – and it wasn't a business that

141

garnered many awards for its high ethical standards. Janusz gazed out of the window over the old golf course greens. The 'landscaping' trumpeted on the website appeared to amount to a couple of overgrown beds of bamboo, an oily-looking pond, and a stretch of terrace in a lurid pink stone, its edges marked by concrete neoclassical urns that were entirely innocent of vegetation – unless you counted the weeds.

'Did you get a name?'

'The family name is Duff and the useless son is called Sebastian,' said Oskar.

'And Mama?'

Oskar screwed up his face in an effort of memory. 'Katarzyna,' he said finally.

Janusz leaned closer. 'Any suggestion these people might be villains?'

'*Nie*. Just people with more money than sense.'

Janusz sat back in his chair, feeling the motes of information float down and settle in his brain, hopefully to germinate there and produce some answers. If the hotel was just a rich kid's plaything, then why would this Sebastian bother getting Kasia out here to talk about providing nail extensions? And how might the Duff family be connected to Steve and his small-time criminal pals? He was painfully aware that this place was his sole lead. If he was barking up the wrong tree ... well, the consequences for Kasia didn't bear thinking about.

Getting to his feet, he tied the belt on his towelling robe more securely. 'I'm going for a walk,' he said.

'What am I supposed to do?' Oskar protested.

'I don't know. You could always get your balls waxed.'

Outside, the sun had burned off the clouds and the air felt surprisingly mild, which was just as well given his bare legs. He affected a meandering stroll until he'd left the terrace and passed out of view of the hotel's windows, before pausing to call up a satellite view of the grounds on his phone. The aerial image was poor resolution but it was easy to make out the red-tiled roof of the original building, and the flat asphalt of the more recent additions extending out either side. But something a couple of hundred metres behind the main hotel complex caught his eye: a rectangle of flat green, darker than the surrounding grass, with a small building alongside it, all neatly edged by trees. He blew it up as much as possible but still couldn't work out what the green lozenge might be – a badminton court, perhaps?

Only one way to find out. He struck out at an angle that would make it seem to any onlooker as though he were heading for a small artificial lake in the distance, no doubt a legacy of the original golf course. From there, the land dipped away out of sight, allowing him to cut across and back to his target unobserved.

It took him a good ten minutes via this circuitous route to reach the trees surrounding the site of the mysterious green rectangle. They were conifers, planted in neat lines, many years ago judging by their great height, apparently to screen whatever was behind. Passing through a gap between two of the tree trunks, Janusz came up against a wall of wood, two and a half metres high, made of sections of solid board with concrete footings, the kind used to cordon off building sites. Cursing, he skirted the barrier, on the lookout for a weak point. At one of the corners, he found one. A sloppy workman had failed to slot a section properly into its concrete footing, so that when pulled, it gaped at the bottom, allowing just enough room to wriggle himself through.

Inside the barrier stood an empty cement mixer and a wheelbarrow, evidence of a part-completed building project: new slabs of the same pink stone used for the hotel's main terrace had been freshly laid around the rectangle of dark green he'd seen on the satellite image. Now it was obvious what it was. Not a badminton court, but the cover for a swimming pool.

Janusz felt a stab of disappointment. He wasn't sure exactly what he'd been hoping to find behind the fence, but this wasn't it. He dropped to a squat, and lifted one edge of the tarpaulin, the dark waters beneath releasing a waft of chlorine that made his throat itch.

He turned his attention to the building he'd seen on the satellite image: a single-storey block, presumably housing a changing room for pool users. As well as the standard Yale lock on its double doors, it had a shiny-new chain and padlock wrapped around the door handles. He hefted the chain: it weighed a ton, and the padlock was a state of the art, high-security model the size of his fist, with a shackle made of what looked like 70mm-plus steel. There wasn't a bolt cutter in existence that could get through chain or lock; even a heavy-duty grinder would take a solid ten minutes' work – and make one hell of a noise.

For a swimming pool changing room in the middle of nowhere this seemed like security overkill – and it set Janusz's mind racing. He skirted the building looking for windows. There was only one. High up in the wall, a square of frosted glass. Glass over which someone had fixed, from the inside, what looked like cardboard.

144

He was just pondering whether it was big enough for him to get through when he heard a shout.

'Oi, you!'

He whipped round. Saw a guy framed in a doorway set into the fence, his body tensed, his right hand poised as if to reach inside his long leather coat.

Kurwa mac!

'Ah, hello there!' Janusz hailed him like a long-lost friend, channelling the posh diction picked up from countless black and white war movies his mama made him watch as a child to learn English. 'I was hoping I'd find somebody.'

'How the fuck did you get in here?' asked the guy, striding towards him, suspicion twisting his face. In his forties, he was lean, stacked around the shoulders, and his hard, flat London vowels matched the menace in his eyes. His greasy hair was cut longer at the back than the front – a style that Janusz recalled used to be known as a mullet.

Trying to keep his eyes away from the man's hand, still hovering at waist level, Janusz managed a lazy wave towards the door in the fence. 'It was open,' he said, taking a punt.

The guy frowned, clearly wondering whether he'd left it unlocked by mistake.

'I'm guessing I shouldn't be here?' Janusz went on, all jocular innocence. 'My apologies. I heard there was an outdoor pool and I was hoping I might put in a few lengths.' Tempted to mime a few demonstration strokes, he stopped himself – *don't overdo it*, kolego. As the guy looked him up and down, Janusz felt a sudden rush of gratitude for the absurd towelling robe that surely only a hotel guest would wear.

145

'It's not open to guests yet.'

Janusz saw the man's right hand relax down to his side – if he had a weapon, he'd evidently decided against using it. His expression had uncurled from outright menace into a disaffected scowl that appeared to be its default setting. He had a strangely concave face, sunken in the middle, as if a heavy weight had been left on it when he was a baby, his nose had suffered so many fractures it looked like a ziggurat, and he bore the dull purple scars of youthful acne on each cheek.

'You shouldn't be in here. It's … it's not safe.' Beneath his London twang, hints of another accent kept surfacing that Janusz struggled to place.

Janusz clocked a see-through supermarket carrier bag hanging from the guy's left hand, the handles bunched around a tidy-looking fist. 'That's a shame,' he said, stepping closer and lowering his voice. 'I don't suppose you could just slip the covers off, let me have a quick dip?'

Incredulity bloomed in those stony eyes. 'No chance. You need to leave.'

With a cordial shrug, Janusz made for the open door, hands in the pockets of his robe. Before stepping through the doorway, he half-turned. 'Shall I leave it open?'

The guy was standing exactly where he'd left him, his stare still fixed on the trespasser. 'No, shut it after you.'

'Right you are.'

Janusz waited until he'd reached the other side of the screen of conifers before letting out a big breath. *That was fucking close.* He'd had the misfortune of being up close and personal with too many scumbags over the years not to know that the dish-faced fucker was bad news. It wasn't just the threat of violence that shimmered off him like the heat haze off melting tarmac. There was something else. Something that Janusz had glimpsed through the clear plastic of the carrier bag that had set his mind racing.

Twenty-Three

Since Nathan King had finished eviscerating cadavers for
the day and Kershaw wasn't exactly rushed off her feet,
the coffee they'd planned had sort of morphed into a
drink in a nice old pub in Walthamstow Village.

When she confessed that her interest in the late Jared
Bateman wasn't, strictly speaking, officially sanctioned,
his response wasn't what Kershaw had expected.

'So you're actually meant to be on sickness leave?'
he asked. She dropped her gaze, gave a guilty shrug.
'Because you arrested a chap who was being boorish to a
barmaid?'

''Fraid so.'

'And now you're helping this Polish character find his
missing girlfriend, who you think is a gangster's moll.'

'Yes.'

'Good for you,' he said, raising his glass to her. 'I must
say, it all makes my life seem desperately quotidian.'

Kershaw scanned Nathan's face discreetly. Beneath the
over-long hair that brushed his shirt collar, his complex-

ion was fresh and wrinkle-free, but from the way he spoke, you'd think he'd qualify for a free bus pass. Her eyes fell on his hands: slim and long boned, the nails with perfect half-moons – more like the hands of an artist than a pathologist – and wondered what it would be like to go to bed with a man who spent much of his day up to his elbows inside dead people.

A troubled look crossed his face. 'Of course, I shall have to report your interest in Mr Bateman to DS Bacon.'

Kershaw's eyes widened.

The corner of Nathan's mouth twitched upward. 'I jest. Mum's the word. As far as I can see, you're simply trying to solve a crime.'

'Yeah, while breaking every known rule on proper procedure,' she said.

'Proper procedure can go hang,' said Nathan.

Kershaw grinned. 'Can I push my luck then and ask something else?'

'Be my guest.'

'Have you done a PM on a guy called Bill Boyce? Died a couple of days back?'

'I don't think so, but I haven't seen tomorrow's list yet. Was he a Category 1?'

'Just a bit. Someone gave him a going over with a blowtorch before he died.'

'I think I'd remember that.' He frowned. 'Are you sure he'd come to us at Walthamstow?'

'Yes. Why?'

'Because I was chatting to one of the chaps in Hackney, and he told me about a body he examined last week. I'm sure he said the guy had been burned with a blowtorch or welding gun.'

149

In a piece of unfortunate timing, a waitress was passing just as he said this. She turned to stare at him, a horrified expression on her face, before hurrying on. Nathan and Kershaw exchanged a rueful look.

'I remember thinking it was pretty unusual at the time,' he went on. 'Cause of death was two bullets in the back of the neck, execution style.'

'Really? Where was he killed?'

'Victoria Park.'

'Do you know the name?'

'Nobody does. Apparently, he had no ID of any kind on him.'

Hackney was only a stone's throw from Walthamstow, and Kershaw knew that detectives from the two murder squads talked to each other regularly. If the Vicky Park guy had been tortured in the same way as Bill Boyce then Streaky would be swift to join the dots – especially now that he was questioning the accidental nature of Jared Bateman's death.

'Have you got time for a spot of late lunch?' asked Nathan, deliberately off-hand.

Unless Kershaw's single girl radar was seriously on the blink after – what, eighteen months of celibacy? – she'd have to say that Nathan King sounded … *interested*.

She glanced at her watch. 'Shit. Sorry, Nathan, but I've got to dash. I'm meant to be seeing the shrink in ten minutes.'

'I thought you said you went yesterday?'

'I did.' She pulled a long-suffering face. 'But I'm more or less under orders to go every day while I'm off work.'

'Dinner then. If you fancy it sometime?'

That threw her for a loop. Kershaw hadn't thought seriously about starting another relationship since splitting up with Ben. She'd had offers, sure, but she'd told herself she was too busy, first with the firearms training, then with her new job … and then there'd been the shooting of Kyle Furnell and all its fallout to contend with. As she met Nathan's gaze, it dawned on her that there was another reason. The idea of getting physically intimate with a man – of someone touching, or even seeing, the knife scar beneath her ribs – that was something she wasn't sure she was ready for.

Twenty-Four

Janusz covered his glass as Oskar went to refill it with beer. 'I'm taking it easy, remember?'

'*Tak.*' Oskar waggled his eyebrows. 'I nearly forgot, *kolego*, you're on "A Mission" tonight.'

Janusz sent him a warning look.

'*Kurwa*, Janusz!' Oskar opened his arms. 'It's not like there's anyone listening.'

It was a fair point. Although it wasn't even 9 p.m., the brasserie stood empty, the last two diners, a young couple, having left a few minutes earlier. Now the only sound was the tinny sound of Britpop through overhead speakers and the distant hum and sloosh of a dishwasher.

The waitress – a Bulgarian girl called Maria – came to clear their plates. 'Everything is all right?' she asked, seeing that Janusz had left his steak and fries half eaten.

'Yes, thank you. I just wasn't that hungry.'

After she'd left, Oskar bent towards him. 'Do you really think that you might find Kasia over there, in … that pool place?' he asked in an intent whisper.

Janusz shifted in his chair. The idea that Kasia was being held prisoner in a swimming pool changing room did seem pretty outlandish now, sitting here listening to the strains of 'Wonderwall'. He shrugged. 'All I know is, the *skurwiel* who threw me out had villain written all over him.'

He didn't tell Oskar what he'd seen through the thin plastic of the carrier bag in the guy's fist. A sandwich, a bottle of water – *and a roll of duct tape*. Of course, there might be an entirely innocent explanation, but the idea that he might walk away without checking the place out? – that was out of the question.

'You stay in the room with the TV on, okay?' he told his mate. 'Then it'll look as though we both turned in for the night.'

'Why can't I come with you, Janek?' Oskar wheedled. 'I could be your lookout guy. What if the bad guy turns up again?'

Janusz eyed his mate, trying not to smile at the contrast between his serious expression and the bright blue jacket. '*Nie*, Oskar,' he said, not unkindly. 'Last time you got involved in my shit you nearly got yourself killed. I'm not risking that happening again.'

It was gone 11 p.m. by the time Janusz slipped out of the side entrance of the annexe where they were staying. He'd left Oskar working his way through the minibar, watching back episodes of *Battlestar Galactica*, thankful that his mate had given up on his campaign to play wing-man with only minimal grumbling.

He struck out into the chill moonless night, hoping that his dark windcheater jacket and black jeans would make him near invisible once he'd left the pool of light spilling from the handful of occupied rooms. In the sturdy inside pocket of his jacket he carried some basic tools that had proved useful over the years: a glasscutter with a suction pad, and a monkey wrench. The first two were intended to get him inside the changing block, the last was an insurance policy in case he should bump into Dish-face.

As the screen of conifers loomed up ahead, an unmoving wall of black against the deepest blue of the sky, something else occurred to him – might the *skurwiel* have checked the boundary fence and fixed the weak spot? If so, he didn't rate his chances of climbing over those high wooden walls. By the time he'd reached the right corner of the fence, apprehension was making his heart thump, but when he played his hands down the join, his fingers found the gap, still there. He grinned. *A good start.*

The white walls of the changing block gleamed through the darkness, but that didn't stop him stubbing his toe on the wheelbarrow he'd seen earlier. Cursing, he paused for a moment, ears cocked. Hearing nothing, he fumbled for the wheelbarrow's handles and steered it carefully over the paving slabs to a spot just below the high window he'd seen earlier. Upending it, he climbed onto its upturned base, which allowed him to reach the glass. The window was top hinged, so he clamped on the suction pad and with the diamond head of the cutter started to score a half-moon where the glass met the bottom of the frame. A single tap and the crescent of glass came free with a discreet '*pok*'. Pushing aside the flimsy cardboard inside, he groped around and flicked open the catch, sending thanks to the Virgin that it wasn't a security lock.

The process of getting himself up onto the ledge wasn't the most elegant gymnastic manoeuvre, but by using the struts of the wheelbarrow to boost himself up, he made it with nothing worse than a few scrapes to his ribs and shins.

Lowering himself down into the profound darkness, his questing foot touched something solid. Pulling out his phone, he flicked it into torch mode – and found that he was standing on a sink, facing two dank-smelling shower cubicles, everything monochrome in the bluish light of the torch. The only sound was the *tink ... tink* of a dripping tap. His beam illuminated a balled towel on the floor. He crouched to touch it. *Still damp.* Feeling his heart start to pummel his chest wall, he pushed open the shower room door – and felt his breath slow and solidify in his lungs.

Not three metres away, bullseyed in the blue circle of light, lay a sleeping figure swathed in bedclothes.

'*Kasia*,' the word came out of him, harsh as an old man's dying croak, or the cry of a raven. Falling to his knees, he reached for her. His fists closed on ... fabric. A bunched-up sleeping bag. *Empty.* A pillow. Nothing else. His vision darkened as a curtain of black despair engulfed him. He fell back on his haunches, breathing hard. His heart was booming so hard he felt it might burst through his chest like a piston thrown by a defective engine. *Don't die here, you stupid old fucker*, said a voice in his head.

Janusz took a giant breath, held it ... and after a long moment, managed to master himself. Unzipping the sleeping bag, he pressed its lining to his nostrils. Was it his imagination, or could he discern, beneath the character-less smell of human sweat, the faintest trace of Kasia's scent?

The sleeping bag lay on a cheap blue mattress. It was badly stained, which gave him a nasty moment, but on closer examination the blotches appeared neither recent nor sinister. He could find no clue around the makeshift bed to its recent occupant, and a search of the lockers that lined the wall behind yielded nothing. Pausing to straighten and stretch out a threatened cramp in his side, Janusz cocked his head. He had heard something from the direction of the shower room. He waited. There it was again. The faint but clear sound of *snuffling*.

Killing the torchbeam, he got to his feet and padded softly in the direction of the sound. Listening at the half-open window he'd used to break in only confirmed his fears. It was the sort of noise a dog would make, investigating an alien scent. *A big dog.*

Kurwa mac! Where the fuck had it come from? Janusz got along fine with most of the mutts he came across, but the flutter in his gut told him that the thing snuffling around beneath the window wouldn't be greeting him with a big doggy grin and a wagging tail. The thing was likely to start up barking at any moment, and the idea of being cornered in this *straszne* place by a vicious guard dog – and perhaps its master, too – didn't appeal.

Tiptoeing back through the changing room, Janusz located the double doors to the outside and gave them a hefty push. The big chain and padlock securing the handles on the other side gave a deep, satisfying rattle. Pressing his ear to the door, he waited. Ten or twenty seconds passed. He was about to try again when he heard the faint scratch-scratch of claws crossing paving and then the sound of sniffing at the crack between the doors. Bending down, Janusz pressed his open palm against the spot where he reckoned the thing's snout would be. Sure enough, the snuffling intensified, accompanied now by an alarmingly deep-throated growl. Having piqued its interest, Janusz took hold of the door handles and shook them as hard as he could, rattling the chain so violently it would put Marley's ghost to shame.

That triggered a paroxysm of baying and snarling, quickly followed by a series of door-shaking thuds, which Janusz realised was the beast flinging itself at the obstacle standing between it and its quarry. Backing away, Janusz headed for the shower room, and clambered up onto the sink, grateful for his adrenaline-charged agility. He manoeuvred himself carefully onto the window ledge – and paused. From the front of the block he could still hear the mutt's hysterical snarling and intermittent thumps as it continued trying to demolish the locked door. *Dogged*, he thought, suddenly understanding the English word.

Knowing that he'd only have seconds once the beast cottoned on, Janusz decided against jumping down, gambling that silence would buy him more time. Turning face-on to the ledge and gripping the bottom of the window frame, he began to lower himself, his feet blindly seeking any toehold in the wall's surface. As his shoulders and arms took the weight, he felt his muscles starting to scream. He pictured the individual fibres snapping, like overstretched piano wires. Jaw clenched in a rictus of pain, he was close to letting go when his right boot touched something. The life-saving strut of the upturned wheelbarrow.

No sooner had Janusz reached the ground, than he realised that the barking had stopped. A split-second later, a black ball of muscle on legs came tearing around the corner. It was the biggest pit bull he'd ever seen, shoulders as broad as it was tall, and he was confused to see the bottom half of its face glowing white through the gloom, till he realised its jaws were lathered with foamed spittle. Hearing himself mutter something, Janusz realised he was reciting the 'Hail Mary'.

The only upside was that taking the corner so fast caused the dog to veer off-course, and as it tried to correct its trajectory, claws scrabbling on the paving, Janusz took his chance. Grabbing the handles of the wheelbarrow, he yanked it up in front of him like a shield, just as the thing launched itself at his face. There was a dull clang as its skull rang against the steel edge and it bounced off to one side. It rolled onto the grass but within seconds was back on its feet, shaking that great head.

The beast stalked him, dodging left and right in his hunt for an opening, while Janusz pivoted his wheelbarrow-shield this way and that, ducking to protect his throat and face and trying to keep his arms safely tucked in. The dog leapt again, and he danced backwards, the meaty snap of its jaws so close to his hand that he could feel the hot damp breath on his knuckles. Janusz cast around for something to use as a weapon, his breathing ragged from the exertion. There was nothing. It came to him with absolute clarity that the loser of the standoff would be the one who tired first – and eyeing the dog's pitiless stare he had a pretty good idea who that would be.

Then, above the bass rumble of the dog's hate-filled growl, Janusz heard an unexpected and piercing sound. An inanely chirpy, five-note whistle. A mobile ringtone.

What the fuck …?

The dog turned to look over its muscled shoulder towards the source of the noise. A second later, the piercing sound came again. Its flat, murderous eyes returned to Janusz, who stayed stock-still, remembering that a fighting dog's attack impulse was triggered by movement. Again the whistled ditty sounded. The beast's gaze flickered and then, with a jerk, it spun round and headed in the direction of this intriguing sound, its trot horribly purposeful. As he watched its rear quarters recede into the darkness, Janusz let out a breath.

Then, setting the wheelbarrow down as if it were a porcelain vase, he sprinted for the fence, setting a new personal best. Pulling open the loose section he clambered through, before risking a final look backward through the gap.

He could just make out the dog, silhouetted against the boundary fence on the opposite side. It was trotting along the fenceline, following the chirruping ringtone, like one of the children in the fairy story, mesmerised by the Pied Piper's refrain.

Twenty-Five

The morning after his encounter with the *psychol* dog, Janusz was packed and dressed before Oskar had even emerged from the bathroom. 'Get your stuff together,' he told him. 'I'm going to go track down this Sebastian Duff, see what he has to say about the mystery guest they've had staying in the changing block.'

'Are you sure you don't need me to come along?' Oskar winked. 'In case you come across any wild animals that need taming?'

'*Dobrze, dobrze*, Oskar! We already heard plenty about your dog whispering exploits.'

'I'm only saying, you wouldn't be sitting here now if I hadn't distracted that thing.'

Janusz sighed. Since last night, he'd heard the story retold from every possible angle half a dozen times. How Oskar had experienced a 'funny feeling' after Janusz left and decided to follow him, to 'watch his back'. On hearing the frenzied barking and snarling he'd realised what was going on beyond the fence and, at a loss for what to do, had hit on the idea of trying to distract the dog by playing his phone's bird-whistle ringtone.

'And I must have told you twenty times how grateful I am, *kolego*,' said Janusz. 'So shut the fuck up now.'

Oskar shrugged modestly. 'Are you going to call the girl *detektyw*? Get the cops to raid the place?'

Janusz ran a big hand roughly over his face. He'd barely slept last night, amid his mind's ceaseless churning, going over and over what he'd discovered. *The guard dog, the bedding, the padlocked door* – everything about it screamed prison cell. And the thing his mind kept circling back to compulsively: *what if he'd taken on the hard-faced skurwiel and broken in earlier? Would he have found Kasia in that sleeping bag?* He gave his head a violent shake in a bid to dispel the thought. If experience had taught him anything, it was that to indulge in 'what-ifs' was to disappear down a never-ending rabbit hole of self-recrimination and pointless regret.

'What's the point?' he said, in answer to Oskar's question. 'They'll only find what I found. And these Duff fuckers are already on the alert. No point making it worse.'

'Good thinking,' said Oskar, before picking up the treatment brochure. 'While you're talking to the manager, I might get the reflexology foot massage. It says here that it's particularly beneficial for people who've been through a stressful situation.'

'There's no time for that,' growled Janusz. 'You need to get the bags into the van and wait in the car park. We might need to make a swift exit.'

He made his way to the spa, where by a stroke of luck he found Magda, the therapist who'd given him his massage, on reception duty.

161

'*Dzien dobry*, darling,' he said, laying on the charm. 'I have an appointment to see Sebastian Duff.'

She consulted her computer screen. 'Umm. He went into one of the tanning booths but he should be coming out any second. You say he's expecting you?'

'Yes, he said to meet him there, actually. He's going to give me the full tour.'

'*Naprawde?*' Magda widened her false-lash-fringed eyes. 'Are you thinking of having your wedding reception here?'

'Perhaps,' said Janusz, adopting the bashful expression he considered appropriate to a would-be groom.

'*Fantastycznie!*' She clapped the tips of her fingers together. 'It will be our first wedding! *Dobrze*. You just head down this corridor here and keep going. The booths are at the very end – he's in number 1.'

After she'd buzzed him through a security door, Janusz strode down the corridor feeling a familiar thrill. A kinetic crackle coursing through his body that always marked the imminence of justified violence.

He slipped in through the door marked '1' as quietly as possible. He needn't have worried: inside the cubicle, music was playing at top volume, and through the clear blue glass of the upright tanning booth he could see a fair-haired guy in his thirties. Pale-skinned and naked but for protective goggles and an indecently attenuated pair of briefs, he was jiggling in time to the beat.

Janusz squinted at the control panel next to the booth, before turning off the speakers and the cooler fan. The man carried on shimmying for a second or two before peering out through the glass – his goggles steamed up from the heat.

162

Janusz put his head closer to the booth door. 'Sebastian Duff?'

'What's it to you?' The guy squinted up at him through the glass. 'You're not supposed to be in here.' His voice rang with the timeless entitlement conferred by money, although wealth hadn't been able entirely to erase his Cockney roots. 'I'm calling security.'

He tried to open the door of the booth but Janusz had already set the sole of one boot firmly against its bottom edge, heel braced against the floor. 'We need to chat,' he said.

The guy shrank back, his hands shooting to cover his groin in an unconscious gesture of vulnerability. 'I can't talk to you if you won't let me out,' he blustered, but a worm of panic had entered his voice.

'We can talk like this,' said Janusz amicably.

'I've got to come out now. I've already been in longer than I'm supposed to.'

Janusz made a show of examining him. 'You still look pretty pasty to me,' he offered. Then, keeping his boot wedged against the door, he turned back to the control panel. 'Let's give you another ... what, ten minutes?' He punched in some numbers, choosing the highest UV setting available. 'And I've whacked it up to 250 watts.'

'That's the maximum!' he gasped.

'Sometimes we must suffer for our beauty.'

'But I'll get burned!'

'Well, let's do a deal. If you're extra helpful, I'll let you out while you're still medium rare.'

'How am I supposed to help when I don't even know what it is you want?'

Janusz detected an undertone of pleading in his voice. *Excellent.*

163

'Who was it you had locked up in the changing block of the outdoor pool?'

'Locked up?' The guy sounded scared. 'I've no idea. I haven't been over there in ages, not since the builders arrived.'

Janusz gave him a hard look, but it wasn't easy to work out through the misted glass and the goggles whether he was telling the truth. 'Try again.'

'I'm telling you, I don't know anything!'

When Janusz fell silent, the guy pressed his face to the door. 'What are you doing?'

'Lighting a cigar. I reckon we could be here a while.'

'I'm roasting in here!' – his voice rose to a desperate moan.

Janusz responded by blowing smoke at the glass.

'Look! I don't get involved in the … family activities. All I do is manage the place.' He slapped the glass in frustration. 'I'm just a fucking hotelier!'

Janusz shook his head, his expression more disappointed than angry.

Sebastian flattened both palms on the glass, dropping his voice. 'Okay, okay, all I know is that there's *something* going on. But I don't know nothing about the changing block – except it's totally out of bounds all of a sudden.'

'Says who?'

'My older brother. *Joey.*' He made no attempt to hide the dislike in his voice.

'Tall skinny guy? Wears a leather coat?' A nod. 'What's he doing here?'

'No idea. I don't have nothing to do with him – it's the first time he's even been here. My mum won't let me get involved in anything except the hotel.'

The woman Oskar had mentioned – who'd supposedly made her pile in scrap metal.

'What else is there to get involved in, other than the hotel?'

'I haven't a clue! She says she "didn't spend all that cash giving me an education just to see me end up inside".'

Janusz studied him for a long moment, decided he was telling the truth. 'So where does your brother usually hang out then?'

'I don't know! I haven't seen him since Christmas. Then a few days ago, he turns up out of the blue and throws out the builders working on the pool.' Resentment bubbled to the surface of his voice. 'Nobody tells me anything!'

Duff barged the door with his shoulder a couple of times, but the only impression he made was a smudge in the thickening condensation. 'I'm burning up in here,' he cried, his eyes desperate behind the goggles. 'This is GBH!'

Ignoring him, Janusz pulled out the photo of Kasia and Steve – the one he'd found at the flat. He took his time flattening it against the glass. 'Have you seen this woman? Kasia Fisher? Runs a nail bar in Stratford?'

The guy squinted through the glass before shaking his head. 'No never.'

'What about the guy, Steve Fisher?'

'I've never seen either of them before! On my life!' It came out as a wail.

Janusz gave the guy a considering look before pocketing the photo. Then he leaned close to the glass. 'If I were you,' he said confidingly, 'I'd have a good long think about retiring from the family business. You could always go run a nice B&B on the coast somewhere.'

He lifted his boot off the door and Sebastian Duff collapsed across the threshold, the heat coming off him in waves, his sweat-sheened skin already flushing red from his UV overdose.

Janusz made a wincing noise. 'You need to get some aloe vera on that,' he said, before turning to leave.

Twenty-Six

Dozing in bed on Saturday morning, Kershaw received an unexpected alarm call.

'So here's a funny thing ...' said the caller, without preamble.

Streaky.

'Sarge?' Kershaw sat bolt upright. As a wake-up aid, a guilty conscience beat a triple espresso hands-down.

'First off, I find you've been digging around on the PNC for info on Steve Fisher, a close associate of two local gents who recently shuffled off this mortal coil – and who has mysteriously gone AWOL.'

'Well, like I said ...'

'Stow it. Now my team tells me that this Steve Fisher is married to a certain Polish lady who also seems to have gone walkabout. She's called Kasia. Ring any bells?'

Fuck.

'As you may recall, among my many talents I am blessed with what some have been kind enough to call a photographic memory.'

It was true, Kershaw reflected glumly. Streaky could always recall the most insignificant details of a case long after the rest of the team had forgotten even the name of the defendant.

'It took me a while but I finally managed to retrieve it from the old memory banks.' He paused. 'Your Polish chum Janusz Kiszka had a girlfriend called Kasia who lived in Stratford, I recall. And this Kasia, unless I am mistaken, was married to a Cockney called ... wait for it ... *Steve*. Am I right or am I right?'

'You're right, Sarge, but I don't see ...'

'Spare me, Kershaw.' Streaky dropped the bantering tone. 'I spoke to Toby Greenacre. I know he signed you off sick after you pulled some comedy arrest stunt while nine sheets to the wind. So even running a PNC search puts you in breach of about a dozen regulations.'

Bollocks.

'I don't know what the fuck you're playing at,' he went on, 'but if you don't fill me in I'll have you up before Divisional Standards before you can say knife.'

Hearing him breathing heavily down the phone, Kershaw could visualise his face turning pillar-box red. Deciding there was no alternative, she told him everything, only missing out her cousin Jason's search of the Alicante flight manifest and her unofficial visit to the mortuary: there was no way she was dropping anyone else in the shit.

'And that's all of it?' asked Streaky, when she'd finished her upsum.

'Yes, Sarge.'

'So Kiszka hasn't officially reported his girlfriend missing?'

'No, Sarge. You know what he's like about the cops.'

'But you think she's an accessory, passive or otherwise, to whatever criminal caper Fisher and his Cockney muckers have pulled off?'

'Seems likely, don't you think? She's been with him for twenty-odd years – she can't have just not noticed he's a villain.'

Streaky made a non-committal noise. 'Right,' he said. 'Here's what's going to happen. You're going to carry on helping Mr Kiszka as though nothing's happened, see if he turns up anything useful about Fisher's whereabouts.'

'You want me to be a CI?' Kershaw couldn't keep the dismay out of her voice.

'Well I wouldn't call it a Criminal Informant exactly, since I don't intend to pay for your services, but a grass of sorts, yes – and operating strictly in a civilian capacity. Why, did you have any objections?'

'I guess not.' *What else could she say?* 'So what do you reckon to all this, Sarge?'

There was a pause before he replied. 'I think your theory's got legs. Steve and his pals do some job, then fall out while divvying up the proceeds. And since it's Steve who's done a bunk, I make him our prime suspect for the murder of Bill Boyce, and very possibly of his chum Jared Bateman who managed to connect himself to the ring main despite being a qualified electrician.'

She fell silent for a moment, digesting the information. 'I was thinking, Sarge. I know Steve was only the fence for the gear from the Felixstowe lorry job – but is it possible that he might have got in deeper with the gang who did it?'

'Funnily enough, I was speaking to my old mucker in SOCU about that only this morning,' said Streaky, going on to relay what his contact in the Organised Crime Unit had told him: not only was the Felixstowe job still unsolved, nearly a year on, but there had been two further armed robberies targeting lorries with high-value cargoes. 'The exact same MO as Felixstowe, apparently. Almost certainly the same villains.'

'But no leads?'

'Not a dicky bird – they're tearing their hair out over there.'

'So could Steve be working for the gang now?' she persisted.

Streaky thought about it. 'I can't see it,' he said finally. 'This lot are professionals. They spend weeks recceing the job, they're forensics-aware, they torch their getaway motors ... It's all a long way out of Fisher's league. If they're Chelsea, he's Leyton Orient.'

'So we've got nothing to go on?'

'I wouldn't say that.' She heard him sucking his teeth. 'I'm only telling you this in case it might help you winkle something out of Kiszka. A stolen car was reported abandoned last weekend.'

'And?'

'And it's got Steve Fisher's prints all over it.'

'You're kidding! Where was it found?'

'The outskirts of dear old Sarfend.'

Within the hour, Kershaw was standing outside Kiszka's swanky mansion house block in Highbury, leaning on his buzzer. When she got no reply, she tried the flat numbers above and below his, finally getting hold of one of his neighbours, a grumpy old git called Ron. Kiszka had knocked the previous morning, he told her, to say he was going away and asking him to feed the cat. He'd said he hoped to be back the next day.

Returning to her car, she settled in for a wait. It wasn't too long before a battered Transit van pulled up outside, discharging Kiszka onto the pavement before tearing off in a plume of oil smoke. She reached him before he even got his key out.

'Hi there!'

Kiszka whipped round, looking paranoid.

'You don't look very pleased to see me,' she said. All she got in reply was one of his caveman grunts, but he did at least invite her up.

As he opened the door to the flat, his ginger tomcat greeted them with an aria of hungry miaows.

'Shhh, Copetka.' Kiszka bent to stroke him before straightening to follow his urgent trot into the kitchen.

Kershaw clocked the difficulty he had getting himself upright again – and noted the hint of a limp in his gait. *What had he been up to?*

After feeding the cat, he folded his big frame into a chair opposite her at the kitchen table. She was shocked by how he looked, close-up. The skin under his eyes was purple-dark, the symmetry suggesting lack of sleep rather than a beating, and his face was markedly thinner, making his features even craggier than usual.

'I'm forgetting my manners,' he said, setting his hands on the table to lever himself up again. 'Coffee?'

'Hey, you look done in. I'll make it.' Seeing her determination, he raised a hand in surrender, before slumping against his seat back.

'I don't suppose you've got any food?' she went on. 'I haven't had breakfast.' In truth, she wasn't especially hungry but Kiszka looked like he was in serious need of a feed.

He told her there were eggs and cheese in the fridge and she started to whip up an omelette big enough for two. She was suddenly reminded of cooking her dad breakfast when she'd been nine or ten – it had been their Saturday morning ritual.

'So any news on where Kasia and Steve might have got to?' she asked.

Janusz scratched his jaw, the stubble reminding him he hadn't shaved that morning. There was plenty he wanted to ask the girl *detektyw*, but he'd have to tread carefully. By now the cops would surely be all over the murder of Bill and probably Jared's death, too. Recalling his discovery of Bill's body, he sent up a silent prayer that he hadn't left any fingerprints at the flat.

'Nothing as yet,' he told her. 'You?'

The fat in the frying pan sizzled a greeting to the beaten egg, the smell making Janusz realise how hungry he was.

'Not really. Just a few bits and pieces,' she said. 'So, Ron was telling me, you weren't here last night?' From the state of him, it was obvious he'd been up to something.

He suppressed a scowl. He'd let Ron know he was away for the night just in case someone came calling with information about Kasia, but he hadn't anticipated the girl *detektyw* turning up. 'I was out of town.'

'Really? You weren't anywhere near Southend, I suppose?'

'Southend-on-Sea? No – why?'

After sliding the two halves of the omelette onto plates, Kershaw put the larger portion in front of him. He sawed some hunks off a wheat and rye loaf and offered the board to her before taking a mouthful of omelette. 'This isn't half-bad – for an English person.'

His grin up at her was a bit more like the old Kiszka. 'We think that Steve might have been there recently,' she said, pouring coffee from the stovetop pot. No harm in mentioning it – she didn't think for one minute he'd still be there now. She'd lay serious money that Steve had picked Kasia up from Epping tube station for the short drive to the Essex coast – and they weren't going there to sample the whelks. Southend had a tiny airport that had recently added a bunch of European routes: the missing couple were probably already sunning themselves in Faro or Tenerife.

Janusz had picked up her lapse into 'we' – which confirmed what he'd half-expected. Natalia wasn't simply helping him out in the search for Kasia any more: she was working the case for the cops. He'd better stay on his toes.

'You do know Southend?' she persisted.

'The beach with the view of the power station, right?' Janusz had been dragged out there once by a girlfriend who'd lived in Stepney. Brought up on summer holidays amid the white dunes and chilly jade waters of the Baltic, he'd been appalled by Southend's muddy beach with its grim vista of a giant smoke-spewing chimney, its noisy 'amusement' arcades.

Kershaw felt miffed at his dismissive tone: East Londoners were proud of 'Sarfend' – their nearest seaside resort, which boasted the longest pier in the world. Day trips there had been a fixture of her childhood summers, and long after her mum died, she and her dad made a pilgrimage every August bank holiday, rain or shine, to fish off the pier.

Janusz set his knife and fork on his empty plate at 'twenty to five' as he'd been taught; even after getting on for three decades here, he still couldn't bring himself to line them up soldier-style, like the English. 'What makes you think Steve was in Southend, anyway?'

'Prints on an abandoned car.'

'Nicked?'

'Yep.'

He grunted. As far as he was concerned, the strongest lead he had to Kasia's whereabouts was still a certain Essex spa hotel. He topped up their cups with coffee before levelling his gaze on hers. 'I'll tell you where I've been and what I've found out if you'll get me some information.'

Kershaw took her time finishing her final mouthful before replying. 'Okay ...'

'Do you swear it?'

'Yes, all right, I swear it.' No detective would ever make such a promise – but then hadn't Streaky made it crystal clear that she was 'strictly a civilian'? Well, that cut both ways.

'I've come across an Essex family who I think tie in with the Steve business somehow.' He tossed a few of his suspicions about the Duffs into her lap, the fortune the mother made in scrap metal, his visit to the hotel in Epping, omitting a few minor details like his microwaving of the younger Duff that morning.

174

'So why do you think they're involved?'

'I can't say.' He saw no point in sharing his hunch about Kasia being held prisoner in the changing block.

'You'll have to give me more than that or I can't help you.'

'Look. All I can tell you is that there's a connection to Steve. And if this Duff family are just innocent hoteliers, I'm Pope Francis.'

'Where does that leave your idea that Steve abducted Kasia? Are you saying the Duffs were doing him a favour when they took her?'

'Maybe,' he shrugged. 'Perhaps it was a reward for some job he did for them? I don't know yet. But trust me, I'll make it my business to find out.'

Hearing his tone darken she looked up at him. 'Okay. I can make some calls, check them out. Until I do, don't go doing anything stupid.'

He pulled a wolfish grin. 'You can't make an omelette without breaking eggs.'

Kershaw gazed at him: with his fierce eyes and drawn face, unshaven jaws sprinkled with grey, he looked like a pirate returned from an all-night raid. *An undeniably attractive pirate.*

'Who was it said that, anyway?' she asked.

'Joseph Stalin, supposedly.'

His face split in a giant yawn, which he covered with one hand. 'I don't wish to be discourteous,' he said, 'but I'm afraid I really need to get some sleep.'

After she'd gone, Janusz made another pot of coffee, double strength, in a bid to keep himself awake. Copetka jumped up onto his lap and he sat stroking his ginger fur, mulling over what Natalia had told him and trying to work out how it might fit into the tantalising jumble of facts he'd amassed in the last couple of days.

Kasia

A jolt to the spine catapulted Kasia out of her perpetual fog –
and into the back of a vehicle. A ridged steel floor, the reek of
diesel … a van. She registered the familiar bite of plastic into her
wrists, her taped mouth, and a blindfold – tied so tight it
squashed her eyeballs.

Then she remembered the baby. Obudz sie! she told herself
– Wake up! – deliberately knocking her head against the floor.

So few of these lucid moments, no time to think. Had the
drugs harmed her little one? How long now since she was taken?
Five days? Six? It seemed as if she'd been sliding in and out of
the muffled darkness for weeks. The man only roused her to eat,
or to push her into the toilet. Never spoke a word. She'd seen
him – once, early on, when the blindfold had slipped off – but
he'd been wearing a balaclava. His eyes were as stony and pitiless as a cemetery angel. She knew then, that if and when he
chose to, he would kill her without hesitation or remorse.

Where was Janusz? She'd been so sure he'd have come for
her by now. Then she remembered her dream. She'd been
underwater again, but this time she could see Janusz just a few

metres away. He was waving to her, his lips moving, but she couldn't hear him. The sight of him, so solid and dependable, filled her with a heady rush of hope and love, but when she'd swum towards him, her hand struck something. She realised that she was in some sort of tank and he was on the other side of the glass, unable to reach her.

She still had faith. He would still come for her. She started to pray.

Then she felt it. Nie! A dragging sensation in the pit of her belly. The baby! It expelled every other thought. She knew what would come next. Bleeding.

Hold on, maluszku, she murmured. Hold on, little one.

Twenty-Seven

After the girl *detektyw* left, Janusz drifted into a fitful sleep on the living room sofa. When he finally opened his eyes, it took him a few long seconds to register the profound navy blue of a spring dusk through his bay window. Rousing himself, he had the niggling feeling that while he'd been asleep, he'd learned something important. Something that, now that he was awake, dangled frustratingly just out of reach.

He decided to make some *pierogi*: it might persuade his brain to offer up its subconscious machinations. Pouring boiling water onto some dried mushrooms he left them to soak, before finely chopping a red onion together with fresh parsley and thyme for the filling. Letting his mind drift, he found himself thinking about Southend, where Natalia had said the cops had found a car Steve had dumped. It struck him as an odd place to go into hiding, unless it was all just a decoy and he'd actually circled back to the Forest Sanctuary Hotel. He certainly couldn't see Steve tempting Kasia out to Southend: hadn't she once said something about how depressing she found the Essex coast?

Setting down the knife, Janusz went to his greatcoat and, delving into the pockets with parsley-specked hands, found what he was after. The faded photo he'd found in Steve and Kasia's flat a few days earlier. It captured them in younger days, standing in a field, holding ice-cream cones, except now that he looked properly, wasn't that thin, greenish line on the horizon that almost merged into the sky's uniform grey, the sea? And on the extreme left of the picture, just visible, something he hadn't noticed before. Something that looked like a van, but with its roof angled at the rear.

It all came rushing back. A couple of years back, he and Kasia had been lying in bed, daydreaming about going on holiday together one day. She'd said that her last proper holiday had been years ago when Steve had taken her to stay in a *karawana* belonging to his parents on the Essex coast. Thinking it over now, he was ninety-nine per cent certain she'd said it was in Southend.

It was too much of a coincidence. Was Steve using the caravan as a hideaway? Might he have had Kasia moved there, after the changing block became unsafe?

Janusz kissed the young Kasia's freckled face. '*Brawo, kochanie,*' he murmured, before picking up his coat and heading out of the door.

It was nearly 9 p.m. by the time Janusz got off the train at Southend along with a crowd of late-returning City workers. He drew his coat tighter – he'd forgotten how much colder it was out in the sticks compared to London.

Reaching the line of cabs waiting at the taxi rank he stuck his head in the window of the first. 'I'm looking for a caravan park. But I've forgotten the name.'

The elderly Asian driver thought for a moment. 'There's two,' he said. 'The Ivydene or the Sea View?'

'The Sea View,' said Janusz, picturing the photo – with a private smile at the helpful literalness of the name.

Ten minutes later, he was climbing out of the cab onto a cinder drive. He squinted at the board advertising the comforts of the Sea View – judging by the faded yellow of a big smiling sun, the place hadn't had a makeover since Kasia visited. A sudden gust from the sea whipped his coat open – it was even colder out here, and pitch black once you stepped away from the streetlights. He crunched off down the path, using the torch function on his phone to light the way.

A hundred metres on, past an empty car park, he came upon a wooden chalet, a light visible through the curtained window and the word 'Office' on its door. When he knocked, the curtain was whipped back to reveal the face of an elderly woman peering out at him. For a fanciful moment, he felt as if he had just found Baba Yaga, the child-eating witch with the iron teeth from the folktales, who had filled his childhood nightmares.

'Good evening,' he said when she opened the door a few centimetres. 'I'm looking for the Fishers' caravan?'

She squinted at him, her gaze openly curious. Janusz guessed she probably didn't get many raffish-looking foreign blokes turning up at her caravan park on a cold March night. After a long pause, apparently expecting him to elaborate, which he declined to do, she eventually handed him a map showing the park layout.

'Number 17,' she said.

Janusz thanked her and, as he turned to go, asked, 'Oh, is he in, do you know?'

She gave him an evil look. 'No idea.' And slammed the cabin door shut. Janusz could hear her sliding the bolts across, top and bottom, making a production of it for his benefit. He imagined her heading back to her cauldron to chuck in another lizard.

The rows of darkened caravans slumbered under the sickly light cast by the solar-powered lamps along the path; they stood on breeze blocks or steel struts, their touring days long past, each plot precisely marked out with its own picket fence. Stowed underneath them were the discarded flotsam and jetsam of last year's summer holidays: a deflated lilo here, a windbreak there – its once-jaunty stripes looking tattered and mournful.

As he passed the end of the third block of caravans, Janusz spotted something down the path that branched off to his left. A window-shaped glow that punched a sepia-coloured hole in the darkness. He consulted the map: the light came from plot 17.

Janusz abandoned the noisy cinder path for its soft turf edge, and headed for the rectangle of light. Here, at the park's seaward edge, a salty breeze lifted his hair and he could hear in the distance the faint yet insistent sound of the surf shushing the beach.

Finding a wooden lean-to at the edge of number 17's plot, he ducked behind it and peered around the edge. What he saw made the breath congeal in his throat: somebody had pasted newspaper in the caravan's windows. He cocked his head. Was that a voice he could hear inside, beneath the wind whickering in the trees?

He strained his ears towards the murmur. Yes! A *woman's* voice.

Then two things happened at once. The woman laughed, and he realised that the sound was coming from a radio, just as a shadow loomed onto the grass in front of him. Long and thin, it put him in mind of a praying mantis.

Instinct took over. He ducked right. *Thwack!* A blow struck him between neck and shoulder. He staggered into the wall of the lean-to so hard it drove splinters of wood into his palms. Hearing the breathing of a man behind him, he turned and dropped to a crouch in a single movement. Made a grab for the denim-clad legs coming towards him. The impact knocked the breath out of his lungs but he hung on and the pair of them wrestled to and fro, his attacker raining blows on him with what looked, and felt, like a length of two-by-four timber. But Janusz was holding him too close to allow a good swing, and the weapon just bounced off his back. Loosening his grip around the man's legs for an instant, he felt his centre of gravity shift a fraction. Dropping his hands to the man's ankles, he gave a mighty wrench. The guy crashed backwards with a grunt, before kicking out wildly. Just avoiding a boot in the face, Janusz scrambled to his feet. But the other guy was younger and nimbler, and by the time Janusz was upright, he was already disappearing into the darkness beyond the caravan, heading in the direction of the sea. From his size and shape – skinny, below average height – it was clear to Janusz that the guy who'd jumped him was Steve Fisher.

He took off after him at a sprint, casting a sideways glance at the paper-covered windows of the caravan. Told himself that even if Kasia were inside, he first had to neutralise the threat.

Once he got going, his long stride meant he covered ground fast, and soon had Steve's outline in his sights, backlit by the rising moon. Janusz grinned to himself, having just made a happy discovery: *Steve Fisher ran like a girl*. On the downside, he clearly knew the lie of the land – wheeling right as he approached what looked like an impassable hedge, he disappeared through it without breaking step.

Janusz knew he could be waiting the other side to ambush him but couldn't risk losing ground by slowing down. Following Steve's route, he charged through the gap in the hedge head down, branches raking his scalp. Emerged into the colder air of the beach, the black North Sea so close now that the smell of salt and ozone made his nostrils prickle. Steve was still there ahead of him, closer now, but Janusz could feel his progress slowed by the soft-going sand. Within a few minutes, the punishing surface was making his thigh muscles scream, but he kept his gaze glued to Steve's back. Getting closer with every stride, the dim roar of the sea growing ever nearer, he saw Steve cast a frantic look over his shoulder before throwing a desperate jink to the right – exactly like an impala Janusz had once seen in a wildlife film, trying to evade a leopard. Then, as the sand gave way to a band of shingle, Steve stumbled. He scrambled back to his feet, but it was clear his heart wasn't in it. Putting on a final spurt, Janusz jumped on his back with a roar and manhandled him down onto the beach.

Steve offered no resistance, and they lay there, in an awkward embrace, the surf growling over the shingle in their ears, until Janusz had recovered his breath. Pulling at Steve's shoulder, he flipped him onto his back so he could see his face.

'Is she … is she in the caravan?' he got out finally.

'Who?' Steve's eyes were wild with fear.

'Kasia!' Janusz snarled, giving him a shove.

'No!'

'So where the fuck is she?'

'I …, I th …, I th …' Steve was stuttering like a stuck record.

Janusz whacked the back of his head onto the shingle to jog the needle. It did the trick.

'I thought she was with you!'

Twenty-Eight

Janusz frogmarched Steve up the steps to the caravan – pushing him ahead through the door in case he'd been lying about being alone. Inside, he made him shuffle along to the farthest point of the semicircular banquette around the dining table so he couldn't easily do a runner. After that, it took him all of twenty seconds to scope the place – there was just one bedroom, the bed empty but for a coverless duvet the colour of weak tea, and a tiny shower and toilet cubicle next door – before returning to the kitchen-cum-living area.

Steve had recovered a good deal of the surly insouciance that Janusz remembered from their only encounter, when, assuming the guise of Kasia's visiting cousin, he'd had to demonstrate the unpleasant consequences that would follow if he ever lifted a finger to her again. Three years on, Steve looked much the same, the only alteration to his rat-like features a modish, jaw-skimming beard that made Janusz's fists itch.

'How long have you been here?' Janusz asked, wrinkling his nose: the place reeked of Chinese takeaway and stale male sweat, a fan heater rattling at their feet contributing the smell of burned dust to the mix.

'Why should I tell you anything?' – his voice rose to an angry mosquito whine – 'I know all about you and Kasia. I never did buy all that bullshit about you being her cousin.'

Janusz lifted a shoulder. 'What do you expect, if you use your wife as a punchbag?'

'It only happened once!' burst out Steve. Janusz raised an eyebrow. 'Maybe twice. Anyway, I don't have to fucking explain myself to you.'

Janusz's arm shot out to grab the neck of his T-shirt, and yanked him half-upright out of his seat. 'Yes. You. Do.' Each word underlined with a sharp tug. 'Now, answer me, toerag. Where is Kasia?'

'I told you! I thought she was with you.'

'If you don't tell me what the fuck's been going on and why you're holed up here ...' Janusz gave his collar a vicious twist, forcing a gargling noise from Steve's throat. Seeing him nod in surrender, he released the T-shirt, before wiping his hand on his coat.

Steve massaged his throat, and when he spoke again his voice was hoarse. 'Kasia told me she was leaving, but I got her to agree to stay for my birthday. I'd bought us surprise flights for ... a mini-break.' He gave a defiant shrug. 'I thought if we went away, it'd give me one last shot at getting her to stay.'

Aside from the tickets being one-way, it was a version of events that Janusz judged to be more or less truthful. 'Then what?'

'My plans changed. I had a ... falling-out with someone and decided to get out of town for a bit.'

A falling-out. A funny way to describe the murder of two close associates, thought Janusz. 'Really. What was that all about then?'

'Oh, just one of those things down the pub, after we'd had a skinful. You know, handbags' – for all Steve's attempts at a dismissive tone, the effort of inventing on the hoof was written all over his face.

'Right. And when you left, you took Kasia with you?'

'No! I haven't seen her since Sunday morning. We had a bit of a dust-up, when I told her about the flights. Her last words to me were that she'd be moving out on Monday "come hell or high water".' His voice was shot through with self-pity.

Studying his face, Janusz decided he was telling the truth – about Kasia, at least. He felt a complicated sensation in his chest: relief that she hadn't changed her mind at the last minute – something he realised he'd still half-feared – and deep anguish that somebody had prevented her from doing so. But if not Steve, then who? And with what possible motive?

Steve worried at a bit of peeling veneer on the table-edge with his thumbnail. 'So when did *you* see her last?' he asked.

Lighting a cigar, Janusz ignored the question. 'Let's go back to this "falling-out" you say you had. Was it the guys who did the robbery with you?'

Watching Steve's face light up like a pinball machine, Janusz had to stifle a grin: he'd be the dream opponent in a high-stakes poker game.

'What robbery?'

'Don't fuck me around, Fisher. I spoke to your mate Bill.'

It was almost comical the way his eyebrows shot up. 'Bill Boyce?'

'Yeah. He was worried about you. He wanted to get a message to you. Or a warning.'

'A warning?' Steve wasn't sounding quite so dismissive now.

'But you haven't been answering your phone.'

A look of self-congratulation flitted across Steve's face. 'Before I left town, I stuck it in a post box, addressed to a friend of mine in Glasgow.'

'Glasgow? Why?'

'It's an anti-surveillance tactic I read about. If someone tries to trace you via your mobile signal, it throws them right off track.'

Of course, thought Janusz: *going 'off-grid', the caravan hideaway – it would all gel perfectly with Steve's fantasy world.*

'There must have been a lot at stake for you to dump your phone.'

Silence.

'Listen to me,' Janusz went on. 'I know that you and your mates pulled off some kind of criminal job.'

'I haven't got the foggiest what you're on about.'

'You stitched them up afterwards, didn't you? Did them out of their share of the booty, whatever it was.'

'No comment,' said Steve, his face relaxing into a complacent sneer.

So maybe that wasn't it, thought Janusz. He leaned across the tabletop. 'You're not talking to the fucking cops now, Fisher. All I care about is finding Kasia. But if you don't tell me what the fuck's been going on I'll happily haul your skinny arse out of here and hand you in to the nearest nick.'

189

'What have the filth got to do with it?'

Janusz stared at him. 'Well for starters, they're keen to find out who plugged Jared Bateman into the mains and strung Bill Boyce up from his own shower rail.'

Steve's response took him aback. Paling to the colour of fresh putty, he stood and tried to scramble out of his seat. Janusz had to grab him by his skinny shoulders but despite the difference in bulk and strength, it took some effort to restrain him. He seemed in the grip of a visceral panic, like a nervous animal in a thunderstorm. It took thirty seconds for Janusz to wrestle him back down on the banquette.

Eyeing the slick of sweat on Steve's upper lip, Janusz felt his own heart thumping. Unless he'd suddenly acquired virtuoso acting skills, this was clearly the first Steve Fisher had heard about the grisly demise of his two friends.

After giving him the basic facts about Bill and Jared's deaths, Janusz sought Steve's gaze. 'Someone has taken Kasia,' he told him. 'And if I'm going to get her back safe then you have to tell me everything.'

Steve put his head in his hands. After a moment, he nodded at Janusz's cigar tin. 'Can I have one of those? I'm out of fags.'

The nicotine hit seemed to calm him down, and the story came spooling out.

'There's this guy, Simeon – he's been coming down the pub on and off for years. I only ever knew him to nod to, but Christmas before last we started getting friendly.' Janusz remembered Simeon: he was the chunky guy with the high-pitched voice Bill had introduced him to down the Pineapple that day, the one who'd eyed him so charily. 'He starts giving me and Jared the odd bit of work. Nothing massive – sourcing a fast car to use on a job – that kind of thing. Fucking good money, though.'

'So it was him who got you and Jared involved in that lorry hold-up? A load of iPads, wasn't it?'

Steve squinted at him, plainly trying to work out how he seemed to know so much. 'We wasn't involved in the actual job – but yeah, he gave us some of the merchandise to shift, afterwards.'

'And you got caught red-handed by the cops flogging them in a pub,' said Janusz. 'How did that go down with your new chum?'

'We kept our mouths shut about where they came from, which is more than a lot of people would do,' said Steve self-righteously.

Janusz felt a surge of bile towards the twisted morality of the criminal class, which considered covering up for a bunch of thugs who'd shot and paralysed an innocent man the honourable course of action.

'So your … discretion earned you brownie points.'

'Yeah, it did,' said Steve, oblivious to Janusz's distaste. 'After that, he knew me and Jared were solid, you know?'

'What about Bill? Was he one of your crew?'

'Nah, Bill's straight as a die. He's just someone we hang out with down the pub.'

Picturing Bill's mournful expression, Janusz sent him up a silent apology. Like Kasia, he'd simply been an innocent bystander who'd paid the price of being close to Steve. 'So tell me about the job this Simeon gave you.'

'He said he wanted a crew who could be trusted, to knock over a place in Stratford, above a launderette.'

'A launderette? Why in the name of God would anyone want to rob a launderette?'

Steve took a pull on his cigar, clearly enjoying his role as gangster with the inside track – his former terror forgotten for the moment. 'The launderette was neither here nor there. But there was some geezer living in the flat upstairs who Simeon said kept a load of cash on the premises.'

'Why didn't he use a bank?'

'Search me,' Steve pulled down the corners of his mouth. 'Some people like to keep their money close.'

Which suggested two options, thought Janusz: *an old timer who, perhaps with good sense, didn't trust banks – or someone with something to hide.* 'So Simeon gifted this information to you and Jared? Presumably for a cut of the take?'

'Nope. He didn't want a penny!' Steve grinned, revealing a missing tooth in his upper jaw. 'He called it a "golden hello" – a way of testing us out for a proper job.' He paused for effect. 'And he gave us both a piece.'

Janusz stared at him, incredulous. The idea of a criminal gang handing out intelligence and guns without any expectation of a return just didn't add up. If there really had been easy money on offer, then why would they tip the wink to a lowlife punk like Steve?

'So, you and Jared broke in and stole this guy's money?'

'Yeah. It was a pushover. Some foreign girl let us in, and told us the cash was hidden in the freezer.'

'Did you have to persuade her?' growled Janusz.

'No! As God is my witness.' As Steve set a skinny hand over his heart, Janusz got an unpleasant jolt to see the letters K.A.S.I.A. tattooed in flowery script across his knuckles.

192

'So you got the cash – but why the sudden exit from London? What happened?'

Steve squirmed in his seat, looking anxious. 'Me and Jared dumped the guns in the canal, but after that we didn't contact each other for a few days. We was meant to meet up on Sunday to split the cash. So I leave the flat and head back to where I parked the Merc ...'

'You've got a Merc?'

'Nah. The one I nicked to pull the job?' – his upward inflection indicated this was a statement of the obvious.

'You kept the getaway car?'

'It was a Kompressor convertible,' protested Steve – as if this could justify his stupidity in keeping hold of a stolen car used in an armed robbery. 'And I didn't park it near the flat, did I? Anyway, just as I'm going down the road where I left it, I spot a bloke standing there, giving it the once over.'

'What did he look like?'

'Stocky geezer' – Steve sank his head into his shoulders to demonstrate – 'Around my height. Had a crew cut, red in the face. Ex-army type, you know?'

Janusz frowned: the description sounded a lot like the guy who'd chased him round N1 a few days ago. *Who was he? One of Joey Duff's henchmen?*

Steve closed one eye. 'I had his number, right off.'

'Is that right.'

'Yeah, plain clothes copper. Probably Flying Squad.'

'Really. So that's why you did a runner? Because you thought the cops were onto you?'

'Yeah.' Janusz watched as realisation crept across Steve's face, like time lapse footage of the sun rising through thick fog. 'He wasn't Sweeney, was he?' he said after a moment. 'Do you think it was him who killed Jared and Bill – and took Kasia?'

From Steve's tormented gaze, it was clear to Janusz that the torch he carried for his wife was a long way from extinguished. He felt no sympathy: if it weren't for this worthless *skurwiel*, right now, Kasia would be lying next to him, safe at home in bed – instead of out there somewhere, in mortal danger.

He tapped cigar ash into an empty beer can. 'Whoever he is, I don't think he's the one pulling the strings. And your friend Simeon doesn't strike me as someone at the top of the food chain either. So who does *he* work for?'

'No idea,' said Steve, just a fraction too fast.

Janusz stared at him through the blue fug that had filled the caravan, letting the silence grow for ten or twenty seconds. Steve examined the end of his cigar intently, before reaching for the lighter lying on the table between them.

Janusz's hand shot out to catch his wrist in an iron grip. 'Listen to me, you worthless piece of shit. The guy who ordered the raid on that flat is going round torturing and killing your mates. He's taken Kasia, and if I don't find where she is, he'll probably do the same to her.'

He watched Steve's expression work for a moment or two, before folding in surrender. 'All right,' he said. 'I'll tell you what I know – though I can't see how it's gonna help.'

He told Janusz about the day the previous April when Simeon had sought him out down the Pineapple. After the pair had gone outside for a fag, he'd asked if Steve would be interested in shifting a couple of hundred brand-new iPads.

'I bit his hand off,' said Steve. 'Even if I cut Jared in on it, I stood to make an easy couple of grand.' They agreed a time for Steve to collect the phones from a lock-up garage in Leyton, but in his anxiety not to be late for the appointment, he turned up half an hour early.

'I was all set to wait in the car, but then I see the garage door's open. So I go over, but when I get closer I hear two voices. Simeon's, and someone else I didn't recognise. He's doing most of the talking and he sounds properly pissed off.'

'Pissed off? Why?'

'He's telling Simeon that he hates "stupid fuckers like that who play the hero".' Steve cocked an eyebrow, seeing if Janusz had got it.

He'd got it all right: *the lorry driver who'd refused to open up his wagon to the armed gang.*

'The last thing I hear before I got my arse out of there, is him saying he lost his rag and gave the guy both barrels. Then he laughs and says, "I wonder how long FreightFast keeps paying the stupid twat's salary."'

Janusz's fists clenched reflexively beneath the table.

'Mind you,' said Steve, 'I never breathed a word of this to the cops. I'm no grass.'

'Yeah, you already said. So the way he was talking, the other guy – did he sound like he was the boss?'

Steve nodded.

'So what did you do? You wouldn't want them to know you'd overheard them.'

'Too fucking right I didn't. I legged it back to the car. I was about to take off, when a geezer comes out of the lock-up and gets into a four-wheel drive.'

'Did he see you?'

'Nah. Thank Christ. I've got tinted windows – best four hundred and fifty quid I ever spent.' He chuckled.

'Did you get a proper look at him?'

'Yeah. Big long streak of piss in a leather coat. Never seen him before.' He shrugged. 'I told you it wouldn't be any use.'

'Let me guess,' said Janusz. 'He had a face like a fat lady sat on it, acne scars here' – he used his fingers to draw stripes down each cheek – 'and a nose that goes in about three different directions, right?'

The way Steve gazed at Janusz – slack-jawed with amazement – brought to mind an old Polish expression: *'like a dog that's been shown a card trick'*.

'Does the name Joey Duff mean anything to you?' Janusz asked.

'Well … not really,' said Steve. 'The Duff Family used to be a big East End firm, back in the day. Joey was Frankie Duff's boy, from memory. But I haven't heard anything about them for … ooh, I dunno – ten, fifteen years?' He widened his eyes. 'Are you saying that geezer was Joey Duff?'

Janusz didn't answer. Steve had confirmed his hunch that Joey Duff was up to his neck in this business, and yet he felt no closer to understanding the chain of events that could have led to him having two men murdered and Kasia abducted. Why would Joey Duff order the raid on the flat over the launderette, only to then come after those he'd tasked with the job?

'You're absolutely sure that Simeon didn't demand a cut of the money you and Jared stole from the flat?'

'As God is my witness, he said we could keep it all.'

196

'Show me what you took.'

Going into the caravan's living area, Steve dropped to a crouch and pulled up the edge of the carpet. Reaching into a cavity beneath the floor he retrieved a bulging plastic carrier bag.

Janusz emptied the bag's contents onto the table. The sexy-dirty smell of used banknotes rose from the pile: some of it in neat single denomination wads secured with elastic bands, some in apparently random amounts in creased envelopes of varying sizes. There was a leather pouch, too, holding a dozen heavy gold coins which Janusz recognised as sovereigns.

He rifled through the envelopes, which had different names and postcodes printed on the outside.

'Do you know any of these people? Marcus E11 ... Amit E15 ... Dragomir E15 ...?' There were various initials written alongside each name, too. 'What about these letters? LB, M, ML, BH, CL ...?'

A shake of the head. 'It's all Greek to me, mate.'

Janusz sat silent, frowning. The cash reeked of some kind of criminal enterprise – but what exactly? Did the initials stand for the names of working girls? If so, what about that single 'M'? Or were they some kind of code for different drugs? Giving up on the puzzle, he embarked on a rough and ready tally of the cash. Finding it to be almost entirely made up of twenties and tens, he soon realised it wasn't as much as he'd been expecting.

'Where's the rest of it?' he growled.

Steve looked surprised. 'That's all there is.'

'But there's only ...'

'Just over fifteen grand,' said Steve, with a modest grin.

'*Fifteen grand?*' Janusz stared at him. 'You're kidding, right? So once it was split, you and Jared were going to make seven and a half grand each from an *armed robbery*?'

His grin dissolving, Steve folded his arms. 'That's six months' rent on a bar in Alicante.'

Just as Janusz had suspected, the real reason behind the one-way flights to Spain had been to start a new life abroad – him and Kasia. *The guy really was a fantasist.*

Janusz picked up a handful of notes. 'So this is definitely all you took from the flat?' Catching Steve's eyes cut to the left, Janusz lost it, backhanding him across the face.

Steve raised both hands. 'Okay, okay!' Reaching behind him, he started to feel along the hem of the curtain, looking for something. 'It's no big thing. Just a souvenir really.' Something chrome-shiny winked as it fell from his hand, rattling onto the tabletop between them.

A bullet. But oversized, Janusz realised – even for the largest calibre gun. Picking it up, he found that the top twisted off to reveal a data stick.

'Where did you find it?'

'It was in the bag with the rest of the stash.'

'What's on it?'

He shrugged. 'No idea. I haven't got a computer here.'

Janusz rolled the bullet in his hand. 'This guy you robbed? What do you know about him?'

Steve shrugged. 'Fuck all. I don't even know his name. Just some guy who kept a lot of cash at home.'

'And the girl – you said she was foreign. What kind of foreign?'

'Search me,' he shrugged.

'Think, for fuck's sake!'

'One of your lot, maybe? Wait – Jared asked her name, trying to keep her calm.' He screwed his face up. 'Lara. That was it.'

Lara. The short form of Larissa, which would make her most likely Russian or Ukrainian. Janusz started to return the cash to the carrier bag, stacking it neatly.

'Take the money,' said Steve. 'Maybe it'll help you get Kasia back.'

Janusz grunted. Picking a free sheet newspaper off the floor, he folded it into the top of the bag to hide the contents. 'You stay here. You contact no one. Whoever killed Jared and Bill – they'll still be looking for you. If I need you, I'll call the old lady in the office.'

Steve shifted in his seat, his expression becoming mournful. 'I'd give anything to turn the clock back, you know – to make Kasia safe again.'

'Well, let me know how you get on with that,' said Janusz, getting to his feet.

'I know you probably won't believe me – but Kasia and me, we were all right for a long time,' Steve was apparently in confiding mood now that Janusz was leaving. 'Up till the moment we lost the baby.' Their eyes met, and this time it was Janusz who looked away first. 'You didn't know about that, then?' Steve sounded defiant but it was plain from the way he spoke, mouth twisted to one side, that he felt the loss still. 'Yeah, we had a little girl, stillborn. Almost full term, she was – eight years ago this year. After that, Kasia just couldn't fall pregnant again.'

Until now, thought Janusz. *Until now.*

Twenty-Nine

First thing the following morning, Janusz got a call from the girl *detektyw* saying she had some information that might interest him, but refused to say more till they met in person. Now he sat waiting for her in a greasy spoon in Walthamstow, sipping a lemon tea.

In a bid to still his impatient speculation as to what she'd discovered, Janusz went over what Steve had told him for about the hundredth time, attempting to fit it alongside what he already knew. He was reminded of an Impressionist painting he'd seen in a gallery one time. Standing up close to the canvas, all you could make out were the formless daubs and dashes of paint; it was only when you stood back that the countless individual brush-strokes resolved themselves into a picture – bathers and sightseers around a sunlit lake. Right now, Janusz felt as though he were standing way too close – that the bigger picture was still eluding him.

Steve and Jared's raid on the flat above the launderette was at the heart of this business, of that much he was sure. And the envelopes full of cash were clearly the proceeds of some kind of racket. Of course, gangsters raiding each other's stash was nothing new, but he was struggling to understand why Joey Duff would hire a pair of jokers like Steve and Jared to do the job – and ask for nothing in return?

Through the window, he saw the slender little figure of Natalia coming into view, beetling along the pavement under an umbrella. She paused in the doorway to give it a shake before joining him.

'Sorry I'm late. It's caning it down out there.'

'So I see.'

He eyed her with an amused glance: her fair hair looked damp and messy, her cheeks pink. He was suddenly reminded of the trip they'd taken to Poland, where he'd acted as her interpreter, and especially the night when, in the heat of a blistering row, he'd come perilously close to kissing her. He and Kasia had been going through a rough patch at the time so it was fortunate that Natalia had been more or less engaged to some other cop: people's entire futures turned on such split-second decisions, he mused.

'I've been doing some digging on your Duffs,' she told him with a triumphant grin, after taking a gulp of the Diet Coke he'd bought her.

'Tell me.' Janusz's voice was urgent, the daydream forgotten in his desperation for anything that might take him a step closer to finding Kasia.

'It turns out that Frankie Duff was a bit of a legend in the sixties and seventies. The Duff Family was the biggest criminal gang east of Hackney. They had a string of pubs and clubs, but that was all just a front for the real business

– which was mainly drugs and prostitution. Anyway, in the nineties, the family firm decided to diversify – and guess what their new venture was?'

'Armed robbery.'

'Got it in one.' She shot him a quizzical look.

'Educated guess,' he shrugged.

'Okay. Anyway, in 1999, SOCU got some intel and Flying Squad ambushed a gang in the middle of a raid on a warehouse. The leader was Frankie's son, Joseph – more commonly known as Joey – Duff.'

'He went down, I take it?'

'Yep. Twelve-year sentence. After he'd been inside a year, his dad died of a stroke and he got let out to attend. It was one of those East End gangland funerals.'

Janusz recalled seeing one such affair on TV news a few years back – the horse-drawn carriages, the ageing bottle-blonde 'celebrity' mourners, and lavish wreaths spelling out 'D-A-D'. He'd been appalled and fascinated by the crowds it drew: back in Poland, only religious figures or heroes of the Solidarity movement got funerals like that.

'I assume he's been out for a while now?'

'Yep. He got early release after six years, and as soon as his probation was finished, he buggered off to Australia.'

'What happened to the family firm?'

'With Frankie Duff dead and the son gone, that was the end of them. Or that was the story that was put about, anyway.' She took a leisurely sip of her Coke, her eyes on his, mischievous.

'Come on, Natalia.'

She felt herself blush: simultaneously pleased yet embarrassed by him using the Polish version of her name.

202

'All right. Passport records show that Joey Duff flew back into Heathrow on the 16th of January last year. Three months later, an armed gang held up a lorry – the one I told you about at Felixstowe? And we think the same gang pulled two other similar jobs.'

'I don't get it,' said Janusz. 'Are you telling me that your lot *didn't know* Joey Duff was back in the UK? Didn't anybody put two and two together?'

'It's like my old Sarge always says: the public have a touching faith in our powers.' She pulled a wry face. 'Fact is, after his probation order ended, Duff became pretty much like you and me. Unless he announces he's joined Al-Qaeda or something, he can come and go through passport control ten times a year, and we'd be none the wiser.'

Janusz ran his finger around an old mug ring on the tabletop. 'But now you know he's back, I suppose you'll be wanting to speak to him about these lorry robberies.' He kept his tone casual, but in truth, the thought of the cops chasing after Joey Duff and putting Kasia in worse danger filled him with dread.

'There's not much point till we get some evidence,' said Kershaw. 'Even if we knew where he was.' She'd suggested the exact same thing to Streaky, after he'd told her the Duff family history, only to earn herself one of his dismissive snorts. *Never confuse coincidence and evidence*, he'd told her.

Janusz looked out of the fogged and rain-streaked window at people scurrying by, hunched under umbrellas. 'Have you got a photo of him?'

She tapped the screen of her phone and handed it to him. 'His arrest mug shot.'

Back in the nineties, Joey Duff still had the mullet, but gelled into spikes on top, a style which Janusz remembered being popular among footballers and celebrity chefs at the time. But there was no mistaking the stony gaze, that twisted nose: the mug shot put it beyond doubt that Joey Duff and the hard-faced guy from the Forest Sanctuary Hotel were one and the same. Janusz heard again his strange, bastardised accent – Cockney intermingled with a twang picked up from somewhere or other ... Australia, as it turned out.

'Well?' Her blue-grey gaze on Janusz's face was unblinking.

'Ugly bastard, isn't he?'

'Do you recognise him?'

'No,' he lied, handing back the phone. 'What's the story with the mother?'

'After her husband died, Katherine Duff sold the scrap business she'd inherited from her father and retired. She bought herself a big pile in the country and a golf club in Epping, which she had converted into the Forest Sanctuary Hotel. It's all above board – on the face of it, anyway. The business is in the name of Sebastian Duff, the younger son.'

Recalling his tanning booth encounter with Duff Junior, Janusz felt a twinge of conscience. 'Yeah. I came across him at the hotel,' he said. 'For what it's worth, I don't think he's involved in the dirty side of the business. There's certainly no love lost between him and his brother.'

'Interesting,' she said, filing away the information. Then she saw a smile spreading across his face, lifting his habitual scowl. 'What is it?'

Janusz was recalling his stay at the hotel, and the moment when Oskar had told him the name of the owner. He'd called her Katarzyna – the Polish version of the English name Katherine, as Natalia had just confirmed.

'You said that the Duffs used to own pubs and clubs, right?'

'Yeah ...'

Narrowing his eyes, Janusz pictured the woman who'd been serving behind the bar of the Pineapple the first time he went there. The woman who Bill had called 'Kath'. He remembered she'd struck him as surprisingly well turned out for the landlady of such a cruddy pub, with her expensive clothes, jewellery, and winter tan – she and her younger son apparently shared a weakness for sun beds. And now he thought about it, hadn't her ears pricked up when he'd asked after Steve Fisher?

'I think if you check, you'll find that Katherine Duff still owns the Pineapple.'

'No shit!'

'Bill said something about her being out of practice changing a beer barrel,' he said, thinking aloud.

The girl's face snapped shut quicker than a sprung trap. 'You met Bill Boyce?!'

'Uh, yes. Ages ago.' Janusz cursed himself. 'Didn't I say?'

'No. You didn't. In fact, you gave me the definite impression that you'd never set foot in the Pineapple.'

She suddenly sounded like *milicja*. Opening his big hands on the table, Janusz sent her his most innocent look. 'I go to a lot of pubs, darling, I can't be expected to remember them all. Anyway, the conversation we had, it was just bar chit-chat.'

'You know he's been murdered, right?' she asked, her gaze skewering him.

'Yes, so I heard,' he said, making a split-second decision that she'd never believe a claim of ignorance. 'Looks like being friends with Steve Fisher can seriously damage your health.'

'You're right there,' she said.

Seeing her drop her gaze, Janusz drew an inward sigh of relief – *he'd got away with it.*

Kershaw drained her glass. She didn't buy his story for a minute – but what was the point in picking a fight?

'Anyway, where does it get us?' she went on. 'If you're right, I mean, and Katherine Duff really does own Steve's local?'

'She's a retired millionaire – her idea of a busy day is probably getting her nails done *and* her legs waxed. Why would she put herself behind the bar of a pub unless she was desperate for something?'

'Like what?'

He ran a considering hand along his jaw. 'To eavesdrop on the gossip. Find out if anyone knows where Steve has got to.'

'Which would suggest she's up to her ears in her son's dirty business.'

Janusz shrugged, non-committal. He was aware of walking a tightrope: handing Natalia just enough to earn reciprocal intelligence about Joey Duff, but not so much that it risked the situation slipping out of his control.

'I'll text the Sarge,' said Kershaw, reaching for her phone. 'See if we can find out who owns the Pineapple.'

As she tapped out a text, Janusz's brain was racing. It felt to him as if parts of the picture were finally starting to coalesce, shapes emerging from the formless mass. From the clamour of his thoughts a sudden conviction emerged: whatever his motives when he ordered the raid on the flat above the launderette, *Joey Duff had bitten off more than he could chew.*

One thing was as clear as the sun: the idea that all this angst and bloodshed could stem from the theft of a paltry fifteen grand was implausible, if not laughable. His thoughts turned to the bullet-shaped data stick sitting in his coat pocket. The minute he'd got back from Southend he'd tried opening the thing on his laptop, but it was password-locked. Had Steve lied to him? Had the data stick been the real target of the robbery all along? Something else occurred to him. The break-in at the nail bar had happened right after Steve went missing. Was it an attempt by Duff to recover the stick, thinking Steve might have hidden it there?

Janusz turned the bullet shape over in his pocket, toying with the idea of handing it over to Natalia – the cops had whole departments dedicated to unlocking data – before dismissing the idea. He couldn't bring himself to hand over his only clue, his single hope of bringing Kasia home unhurt. If only his degree had been in computing rather than physics.

Suddenly, he leapt to his feet, jogging the table and startling Kershaw, who caught her empty Coke glass as it threatened to topple. 'What the f ...?'

'Sorry, darling. I just remembered, there's someone I have to see.'

Before she could protest or press him further, he was gone, leaving the bell above the door jangling in his wake.

Thirty

'I brought my laptop,' Stefan told Janusz, as the younger man set down two pints of Tyskie. Stefan had suggested the George, a sprawling Victorian gin palace opposite Wanstead tube for their rendezvous, due to the privacy offered by its ornate high-sided booths. 'Do you have the article?' The old boy evidently relished the cloak and dagger nature of their rendezvous: his voice was tense with suppressed excitement, blackbird eyes hooded yet alert.

Stefan had been unable – or unwilling – to say over the phone whether he'd be able to access the contents of the locked data stick, and Janusz had been loath to return to St Francis's, where he would only be reminded of the unfinished business of Wojtek Raczynski's fraudulently inflated annuity. He still felt duty bound to report the matter to Haven Insurance at some point, but told himself that asking Stefan for advice on a separate matter didn't, strictly speaking, breach the terms of his contract. Anyway, in the strange state of limbo that he'd inhabited since Kasia had gone missing, he'd learned not to look too far ahead. One step at a time: that was the only way of coping with the sickening sensation of vertigo that engulfed him whenever he thought about where she was, or what might be happening to her.

After firing up his laptop, Stefan inserted the data stick. 'Any clues at all to the password? Such as the owner's name, birth date, so forth?'

'Not really. Only that it might be in Russian.' Janusz eyed the laptop – a large and expensive-looking black number.

'It's my single extravagance,' said Stefan, with that unnerving knack he seemed to have of reading unspoken thoughts. He tapped the keyboard. 'I just downloaded the latest "brute force" software. And luckily for you, it accepts a Cyrillic character set.'

'So, are you saying it can crack a password, just like that?' Janusz tried not to sound sceptical.

'Well, that depends entirely on the complexity, of course. If it's eight or nine characters and a simple words and numbers combination, then probably, yes. It runs a billion guesses ... *per second.*' Stefan chuckled at the look on Janusz's face.

Recalling that his own favoured password was Kasia's name and birthday, Janusz wondered guiltily how long it would take to crack. 'What if it's more complex?'

'Then I might need some help from one of my young *wunderkinds*. Some of them have access to some serious hardware.'

Janusz squinted at the screen, which was filled with scrolling lines of flickering text. 'Is there any password that isn't breakable?'

'Probably not,' Stefan chuckled at Janusz's shocked look. 'But rest assured, there are very few people with the requisite skills and a computer large enough to do the job.'

Having arranged to talk again when Stefan had any news, Janusz left him to it. At the door to the street, he threw a backward glance at the booth where the old man sat. Hunched over the laptop, his face illuminated by the screen, he looked like a medieval alchemist in an old master painting, transmuting base metal into gold.

Before leaving the caravan park the previous night, Janusz had extracted from Steve the address of the flat that he and his mate Jared had robbed. Half an hour after leaving Stefan, he had located the Bubbles Launderette on the outskirts of Stratford. The place stood in a straggle of dismal-looking shops – an Asian newsagent, a Polski *sklep* and a Paddy Power, alongside a couple of empty units that had been boarded up long ago. He found the flat's front door down a side turning, but after ringing and knocking he got no answer. Flipping open the letter-box, he peered through – and saw a pile of junk mail overflowing the mat.

Back at the parade of shops, as twilight fell, the launderette was empty but for a man watching his clothes tumble dry, so Janusz decided to try his luck at the Polish shop next door. Seeing that the lady behind the counter was a soberly dressed sort in her late fifties, he rapidly reconsidered the direct enquiry he'd been planning, which he knew someone of her generation might view with distrust.

'*Dzien dobry, pani.*' He gave her a respectful nod, before turning his attention to a glass-fronted cabinet filled with cakes. 'Ah! It's my lucky day,' he said, as though to himself.

She sent him a look of polite enquiry.

'I'm flat hunting in the area,' he explained. 'But I never expected to find my favourite cake on sale.'

'*Naprawde?* Which one is that?' A complacent smile hovered around her lips now.

'The *makowiec*, of course.' It was true – since he was a boy he'd always loved the yeasty yellow cake, rolled and stuffed with rich poppyseed paste – and this one really did look a cut above the usual mass-produced stuff. He sent her a playful look. 'Is it homemade, though, *pani?*'

'*Naturalnie!*' she said, bridling. 'Here, try a little.'

After handing him a small slice on a napkin, she pretended to busy herself tidying behind the counter, all the time keeping half an eye on his reaction.

'Mmm. *Smaczny*,' pronounced Janusz, shaking his head. 'You know, that's as good as my mama used to make.' He ordered half a kilo and, as she was cutting it, added, 'I'll definitely have to move into the neighbourhood now.'

'It's not too bad – for a cheap area,' she said, turning down the corners of her mouth. 'Westfield is only a few minutes on the bus.'

'I heard there's a flat above the launderette that might be coming up for rent?'

Unspooling some cling film from a catering-sized roll with an expert flourish, she set the rectangle of *makowiec* on top using a cake slice. 'That would be where the Russian couple used to live.'

'Oh yes? Did you know them?'

'The girl, a little – she had a sweet tooth, like you. A nice girl, Larissa, very quiet. As for the man, Vasily, I only ever saw him when he ran out of cigarettes' – her lips turned down again, more decisively this time. 'He was a rude man, and flashy with it, you know the type. Drives a Porsche but lives above a launderette!'

Janusz pulled a mystified face. 'That is strange. Did the girl say what line of work he was in?'

'"Accounting", she said.' A single lift of her eyebrow intimated that, as a description of his activities, it might prove less than comprehensive. '*Dobrze*,' she said, moving to the till. 'That'll be £4.50, *prosze pana*.'

He proffered a note. 'And you're sure they've left now? It's just that I was hoping to view it, but the agent hasn't called me back.'

'Oh yes. Larissa came to say goodbye – terribly upset to be leaving, the poor thing – she said there was a visa problem and they needed to go back home.' Handing him his change, she went on in a confidential whisper, 'I'll tell you something strange, though. That was over a week ago, but yesterday, I happened to see his Porsche, still parked back there in the car park.'

A minute later, Janusz was standing in the block's underground car park, admiring the hard-earned proceeds of accountancy – a new model 911 Cabriolet in custard yellow. Pulling out his phone to snap its registration plate he was just tapping in his pass code when he paused, something suddenly occurring to him.

He dialled Stefan's number.

'Stefan? ... Have you got anywhere with that password yet?'

212

Janusz headed back towards the street, still talking. Had he not been so focused on his conversation, he might have noticed that he wasn't alone. Parked two rows away from the Porsche, partly hidden behind a concrete stanchion, stood a black estate car.

The red-faced man in the driving seat sat utterly still: the only thing that moved were his eyes as they followed the big man in the greatcoat out of the car park.

Thirty-One

'Like I told your Sergeant, I wanted to bring you along because your chum Kiszka's got his big mitts all over this business, okay?'

DS 'Streaky' Bacon was driving his former protégée Natalie Kershaw through Essex countryside, on their way to interview Katherine Duff, widow of East End gangster Frankie and mother to convicted armed robber Joseph.

'Yes, Sarge,' said Kershaw, leaning forward to adjust the control on the passenger air vent – for like, the twentieth time. It would be the first interview she'd attended since leaving murder squad over a year ago and while she wasn't getting the raw rollercoaster buzz that accompanied an armed op, she was surprised by how excited, how *energised*, she was feeling.

'It's just an informal chat – we're not interviewing her under caution or anything. So, you keep that gob of yours shut unless I give you the nod.'

'Sarge.' She reached out to twist the air control knob again.

'And leave that chuffing thing alone, will you?' Streaky sent her a look of amused exasperation. 'You're sending my blood pressure up.'

Council records had confirmed Kiszka's hunch – the Widow Duff *was* still the official licensee of the Pineapple – thus establishing a link, however tenuous, between the Duffs and Steve Fisher and, more importantly, with his murdered associates. Unfortunately, interviews with the pub's regulars hadn't proved especially productive – or, as Streaky had put it to Kershaw, less diplomatically, *'The fucking Cockneys are sticking together like shit to a blanket.'*

Meanwhile, the pressure had just cranked up another notch. Nathan King's full post-mortem on Jared Bateman had revealed subcutaneous bruising suggesting his wrists had been bound at the moment of his 'accidental' electrocution. Although his burns weren't as extensive as those found on Bill Boyce – probably because he'd died of a heart attack before the torture properly got going – the two cases were now being treated as a double murder investigation. Except now, the prime suspect was no longer Steve Fisher, but Joseph Francis Duff. And without a single lead as to his likely whereabouts, Streaky had decided it was time to put the screws on his mother.

He turned the car onto a driveway, between two tall redbrick pillars surmounted by statues of lions – their grandeur somewhat undermined by being made of newly cast cement.

'Do you think the Duff family firm really had shut up shop, till Joey came back from Australia?' asked Kershaw.

'I'm not so sure,' said Streaky. 'I'm starting to think that maybe Kath Duff kept things going on the QT all these years. She's no shrinking violet, that's for sure. One of the retired guys was telling me she got spotted once, luring a rival gangster into a car outside a pub in the Mile End – thirty years ago, this was. A few weeks later, his remains were found stuffed in a suitcase, floating in the River Lea.' Streaky sprayed breath freshener into his mouth. 'She was never charged, of course.'

'How come?'

'The witness had a nasty attack of sudden onset amnesia, no doubt connected with the injuries he sustained while falling down the stairs.'

'He was nobbled.'

'No shit, Ms Marple.'

Kershaw grinned: although he was being sarky, it felt good hearing him use her old nickname.

'But you think it was Joey who took the firm back into the armed robbery game.'

'The timing certainly fits with his return from Oz.'

She narrowed her eyes. 'So we reckon Duff hires Steve and his mates to do some job, but when he comes to collect his share, he finds Steve's done a runner.'

'Leaving Steve's mates up to their necks in the proverbial. What does the torture of Boyce and Bateman say to you?'

'That Joey was desperate to find out where Steve was hiding with the loot.'

Streaky grunted his agreement. 'It must run in the family. Frankie wasn't averse to a bit of torture, back in the day. His favoured method was electric shocks to the privates using an old army field telephone, if memory serves.'

Kershaw stared out at the greenery speeding past for a moment. 'Sarge? You think Janusz Kiszka was right all along, don't you – about Kasia being abducted?'

Streaky nodded. 'Yes, but not by her husband – by Joey Duff.'

She pictured Kiszka's face when she'd more or less told him that his girlfriend was a gangster's moll who'd done a runner with her criminal boyfriend. As usual, his expression hadn't given much away, but there had been the hint of something behind his hooded eyes that she couldn't remember seeing there before: vulnerability. The memory made her wince. *Nice one, Natalie.*

Leaving the car in an otherwise empty parking area to one side of the house, they crunched across the gravel towards the front of the building, Streaky brushing debris off the shoulders of his brown pinstripe suit.

'Do you think she'll give us anything, Sarge?' she murmured.

'Probably not,' he admitted, breezily. 'But sometimes it's worth turning the gas up under villains, just to see them dance.'

Kershaw would be the first to admit she knew sweet FA about architecture – but she knew crap taste when she saw it. She was taking in the Duff residence's Disney-style turrets and Provençal window shutters, when she caught a movement at one of the windows, the fleeting impression of a man, fair-haired – Sebastian Duff. At the massive oak front door, Streaky rang the bell. Before the deep chimes had faded away, the door opened to reveal not some flunky, but the lady of the house herself.

Katherine Duff wore a canary yellow silk suit with serious shoulder pads over a black blouse, gold hoops in her ears to match her strappy gold sandals – and an expression that could curdle cream.

'DS Bacon and PC Kershaw, ma'am,' said Streaky. 'I think you're expecting us?'

'Take your shoes off,' she snapped, before turning to walk away. The hallway was carpeted two inches deep in cream wool, gilt mirrors either side throwing back a gallery of reflections, reproducing the three of them over and over till they became too tiny for Kershaw to make out.

'What's all this about then?' demanded Katherine Duff, settling into a throne-like armchair covered in striped chintz. She ignored Kershaw, focusing solely on Streaky. 'I thought your lot had finally given up harassing me after my Frankie died, God rest his Soul.' She touched a fist bristling with gold beneath her nose as if to staunch tears.

'Actually, it's your son we're interested in, Mrs Duff.'

Her face contracted with hostility. 'My Sebastian? That boy's as straight as a die – he's got a City and Guilds in hospitality management.' Her voice was low, roughened by decades of smoking – a nicotine habit she hadn't quite kicked, judging by the long black and silver vape pen on the arm of her chair.

'I meant your eldest son. Joey.'

'Joseph is in Australia,' she said, studying a coral-painted fingernail. 'He went there three years ago. He works in the motor trade, in Queensland. I haven't seen him since.'

Yeah, right, thought Kershaw: her reply was so off pat she might as well have been reading from an autocue. Letting her gaze drift around the room, she noticed a large oil painting in an elaborate gilt frame above the marble fireplace. A boy of about fourteen, dark-haired, gazed out of the picture, hands set on his hips. The painter had given him unnaturally blue eyes, and a hundred-yard stare that, together with the heroic pose, predicted a date with destiny. At his feet sat a much younger boy, white-blonde, perhaps four or five years old, who was depicted gazing up at his older brother adoringly. *Joseph and Sebastian Duff.*

Streaky was scratching his neck, acting dumb. 'Three years, you say? Did you and him have a falling-out then?'

'No.'

'So you'd say you get on with him?'

'We talk on Skype all the time. We're a very close family.' Her eyes looked like bits of tarmac, black and glittering.

'I'm sure you are,' said Streaky, all sincerity. 'Which is why I'm finding it hard to understand why your first-born would come back to London and not look up his dear old mum.'

'I don't know what you mean.'

Way too fast, thought Kershaw. She knew all right.

Streaky opened his notebook. 'According to passport control records, Joseph Duff re-entered the country via Heathrow Airport on the 16th of January last year.'

'Rubbish. They've made a mistake.' She was fiddling with the vape pen now, no doubt gagging for a puff.

'No mistake, Mrs Duff.' An edge had entered Streaky's voice. 'I'm afraid we need to speak to your son as a matter of the utmost urgency. It's in relation to a double murder investigation.'

'Murder? Don't be ridiculous.'

'I'm afraid so. You must have heard about Bill Boyce and Jared Bateman?'

'Never heard of them.' She directed a bored stare past Streaky.

'Really? Two of your best regulars down the Pineapple?'

Her eyes flickered over his face. 'I'm never down there any more – I'm enjoying my retirement,' she pulled an icy little smile.

'That's funny,' said Streaky, consulting his notebook again, 'I've got an eyewitness who puts you behind the bar the day after Jared Bateman got himself electrocuted. A death which we now believe involved foul play.'

She opened her mouth – lipsticked coral to match the nail polish – about to say something, before stopping herself.

'So I have to ask you again for any information you have regarding your son's whereabouts.'

'I told you, I haven't seen him in years.' Kershaw watched as Katherine Duff writhed self-righteously in her chair – *working herself up into one*, as her nan would have described it. 'I've got nothing to hide – which is why I agreed to you coming here in good faith. But now I'm asking you to leave.'

Streaky gave a single, sorrowful shake of his head. 'You're aware, I'm sure, Mrs Duff, of the Proceeds of Crime Act?'

'Oh, I'm aware of it, all right. It's a legalised extortion racket where your lot takes money off hard-working people without an ounce of proof.'

'Oh yes,' smiled Streaky. 'It slipped my mind. The courts awarded against you after Joey went down, didn't they? Took just over four hundred grand off you, which

220

the judge deemed to be the illegal proceeds of organised crime.'

'A fucking disgrace is what I call it.' Kershaw watched, fascinated, as Katherine Duff ranted on, flecks of spit collecting in the corners of her mouth. 'We earned every penny of that money above board in our pubs and clubs but your lot never stop persecuting me and my family.'

Streaky gave her a beatific smile. 'Sadly, the court didn't share your view, Mrs Duff. In any event, since I am sure your current finances are all perfectly legitimate, I'm sure you wouldn't object if the Fraud Squad decided to mount another inquiry into your financial affairs?'

She glared at him, speechless for once.

Acting on a sudden impulse, Kershaw leaned over to Streaky, and said under her breath, 'Sorry Sarge, I forgot I've got to make an urgent call. I'll just pop out to the car. Excuse me, ma'am.'

He opened a file on his lap. 'Now, I've got a little list of your son's former contacts and girlfriends, and old addresses ...'

Streaky hadn't missed a beat, but she could tell he was wondering what the hell she was up to – this wasn't in the script. As for the Widow Duff, she had a death stare locked on Streaky and didn't even glance up as Kershaw left the room.

Returning to the entrance hall, she opened the front door but, instead of stepping outside, she counted *one, two, three* to herself – before shutting it noisily.

Padding over the thick carpet to the bottom of the wide staircase, she put her foot on the first step – and froze. The last time she'd done something like this, she'd ended up with six inches of steel in her gut. This is totally different, she told herself: how much harm could come to her with the Sarge right next door? Dry-mouthed, and missing the pressure of a Glock holstered on her hip, she forced herself to climb the stairs.

On the first floor landing, she started trying the door handles of rooms at the front of the house. She found bedrooms, expensively wallpapered, windows hung with elaborate swags of pastel satin – all of them empty and smelling of air freshener.

Until she opened the third door.

'What do you think you're doing?' A man's voice, tetchy-sounding, came from behind the cream silk drapes of a large four-poster bed.

'Christ, I'm really sorry. I was just looking for the loo.'

He pulled a drape aside to check out the intruder, revealing a raspberry-red face under pale blonde hair. 'It's at the end of the corridor. Anyway, there are two bathrooms downstairs.'

'Of course, silly of me,' she said. Then, with a sympathetic expression, 'That looks painful. Dodgy sun bed ...?'

'You could say that,' he said, falling back on the pillows. The irony in his voice suggested some hidden meaning that Kershaw couldn't interpret. 'They're rubbish, some of them, aren't they? I had the same thing happen once.'

'Really? How long did it last?'

'The pain goes after a day or so, but you'll be peeling for ages, I'm afraid.' She drifted a bit closer to the bed, taking in the blisters on the guy's shoulders. 'And you're really fair skinned, like me. I have to use factor 50 all over on holiday.'

'Me too – *and* wear a hat.' He pulled himself up to a sitting position with a wince. 'Are you here to see my mother?'

Obviously bored shitless and glad of the company.

'Yes. I'm a cop.' She braced herself for a hostile response.

Instead, he rolled his eyes. 'What a surprise.'

'Why do you say that?'

He gave a little hoot of laughter. 'When I was a kid, the police called more often than the Jehovah's Witnesses. I lost count how many times I had my bedroom turned upside down. Till I got sent to boarding school, that is.'

She pulled a sympathetic face – the bitterness in his voice clearly wasn't directed at her. 'That sucks. Especially when it's got nothing to do with you.' She noticed that even the skin on his earlobes was starting to peel.

'And now it's kicking off all over again, isn't it?' He shifted tentatively against the pillow.

'Well … I can't really say. I'm just a junior cop.'

'It's *my brother*, isn't it?' Sebastian Duff said the words like someone else might say 'rattlesnake'.

Kershaw gave an embarrassed little shrug, as if she'd like to say more but couldn't. He patted the bed, inviting her to sit, and she parked herself on the edge. 'Between you and me?' she said confidingly. 'Yes. We know he's back in the country and we need to talk to him.'

'Good luck with that. He's good at disappearing. Leaving other people to deal with the fallout.' He put his fingers to the blisters on his lips, his touch as tender as a lover's.

'I got the impression that Joey and your mum, they're … close?' It was a shot in the dark, based on Sebastian's resentful tone – and the nauseating portrayal of the first-born Duff in the oil painting downstairs.

'"*Like peas in a pod*".' He said it in a mocking, singsong tone, as if quoting someone, presumably his mother. 'For years, we got on fine without him – now it's all "Joey says this" and "Joey thinks that".'

Kershaw decided to take a risk. 'I don't suppose you've got any idea where we might find him?'

Instead of replying, Sebastian suddenly tipped his head, his eyes focusing somewhere over her shoulder. Bemused, she sent him a questioning frown, but then she heard it, too. The *thunk* of one of the doors off the hallway closing, followed a second or two later by a soft click as the next one was opened. *The sound of someone checking out the bedrooms* – just as she'd done a few minutes ago.

Their eyes met and he mouthed '*Go!*' – jabbing his finger towards a nearby door. Needing no further encouragement, she made it there in three soundless strides, grateful for the thick carpet. Found herself in a wetroom, lined in a pinkish veined stone.

Her heart was beating so fast it felt like it was spinning in her chest: *what if Joey Duff was in the house, after all?* She wrapped her arms around her ribs. Last time she'd been cornered like this, she'd been just seconds away from getting stabbed.

Stop. Think. She scanned the place – *no window*. Made a monumental effort to steady her breathing, reminded herself that the Sarge was downstairs – if she hollered good and loud, he'd hear her. No sooner had she formed this comforting thought than she heard a noise. *The distant but distinctive clunk of a car door closing.* Streaky's car door. The interview with Katherine Duff must have ended.

Fuck!

Then came the sound of Sebastian's bedroom door opening.

'Don't you ever knock?' – his voice was petulant.

'Sorry, sweetheart. Have you seen a girl up here?' The fag-raddled tones of Katherine Duff.

'Don't be ridiculous. What girl?'

'The police have been here, harassing us again. You sure you haven't heard nothing?'

'Yes, Mother – I'm quite sure' – the word 'mother' iced with teenage venom. 'Why don't you look in the study? Isn't that where all the deep dark secrets are hidden?'

In the agonising silence that followed, Kershaw stared down at the bathroom doorknob, bracing herself to see it turn. Instead, the silence was split by a cascade of chimes: *the front door bell.*

'Fucking hell!' Katherine Duff's voice. 'I bet it's that fat ginger cop again ...' Kershaw heard the volley of abuse receding as she left the room.

Seconds later, Sebastian opened the wetroom door, wearing a robe.

'You'd better get going,' he murmured. 'Turn right in the hall and take the back stairs. There's a door at the bottom that'll bring you out in the parking area.'

'Thanks,' she said, sending him a smile of genuine gratitude. She could hear Streaky from the front door step, talking loudly – keeping Old Ma Duff busy.

Sebastian's cheeks grew even redder. 'That's okay.' He thrust a folded pink Post-it note in her hand. 'My brother's new number,' he said. 'I overheard them on the

225

phone a couple of days ago. When she read it back to him I wrote it down.'

'Why?'

He smiled wearily. 'If you'd grown up in my family, you'd know that information is power. Look, I hope you find him. And do me a favour?'

She cocked her head.

'Make sure they throw away the key this time.'

Thirty seconds later, she was back at the car, wondering if her heartbeat would ever return to normal. When Streaky came back he climbed into the driver's seat whistling. It was only once they were off the Duff premises and back onto the main road that he turned to her.

'So where the fuck did you get to?'

She admitted what she'd done, bracing herself for a proper bollocking. Instead, there was a moment's silence, before the car filled with a strange wheezing sound. It was the sound of Streaky cracking up.

Thirty-Two

While Kershaw and Streaky were driving back from Essex, Janusz was on the phone to Stefan, pressing him on whether he'd been able to crack the password-locked USB stick.

'I ran a series of combinations of the name and possible birth years that you suggested,' said Stefan.

'And?'

'You were right. It only took me a couple of dozen attempts. It's Larissa1989.'

Just like Janusz, it seemed the Russian who lived above the launderette had used an obvious, and woefully inadequate, password: his girlfriend's name and birth year.

'That's great news!' said Janusz.

'I wouldn't break open the Bollinger just yet. The files are encrypted, too.'

'*Kurwa!* Can you unlock them?'

'Decrypt them. Well, for a disagreeable moment, I thought they might be PGP-encoded but it's actually just a standard Windows package.'

'So, can you do it?'

'*Promises are like babies: easy to make, hard to deliver,*' he quoted. 'Give me a little more time, I'll do my best.'

After Janusz hung up, it struck him that he hadn't spoken to his boy Bobek since Kasia had gone missing. He wouldn't win any prizes for world's greatest father but a few years ago he'd taken a private vow to call him once a week, without fail. What had begun as a small gesture to make up for the long periods of absence from the boy's life had become something he'd grown to look forward to – even now that Bobek had entered his troublesome mid-teens. Just thinking of the boy, Janusz felt his mood lift. The Easter holidays were only a few weeks away: he could come over to stay for a week or so. Kasia would surely be back by then and Bobek liked her, might even have a little crush on her, Janusz suspected.

Back at the apartment, after feeding Copetka and putting the kettle on, he called the boy's mobile.

'*Czesc*, Tato.' The boy sounded a long way away.

'You don't sound very pleased to hear from me,' said Janusz.

'Sorry.'

Janusz still hadn't got used to the deep voice – its timbre almost that of a man's – his little boy had recently acquired. 'So, what have you been up to?'

'Nothing.' He spoke in a bored monotone and Janusz could visualise his awkward shrug as if he were only an arm's-length away. He reminded himself how he'd felt at that age: the feeling that your skin didn't quite fit, the constant anxiety that perhaps it never would.

'I was thinking, it would be great to see you at Easter.'

'Are you coming to Poland, then?'

'*Nie*. I meant you coming to London, for a bit of a holiday, if your mama will let you out of her sight?'

Silence.

'Well? Did you swallow your tongue?'

'I arranged to see my friends at Easter' – a whiny note entering his voice.

'You see your friends all the time,' said Janusz, trying to keep his voice light and reasonable, 'and I haven't seen you since Christmas.' The boy's monosyllabic responses only made his desire to see him, to give him a hug, all the more powerful. 'We could go to the London Aquarium again – you loved it there last time.'

There was a painful silence. *Idiota*, he chided himself, *the boy will have grown out of penguins, for Christ's sake.*

Bobek sighed theatrically. 'Anyway, they're bound to give us tons of homework.'

Janusz felt a flare of irritation. 'Bring it with you – Uncle Oskar and I could help you with it, like we did last summer.'

'No way!' The boy's tone suddenly sounded amused. 'I lost marks on my biology project because of Uncle Oskar!'

'*Naprawde?* How come?'

'You know I had to do that diagram of a frog?'

'Yes ...?'

'After I handed it in, I found out he'd written "Kermit" on it – without even telling me!'

They laughed together over 1,600 kilometres of cable.

'Well, listen, *kolego*, you're a big boy now and I understand you wanting to hang out with your friends. How about I come over there for a weekend in May, instead?' The weather would be picking up by then and Janusz knew a homely inn on a nearby lake where he and Kasia could stay. It would be a good time to tell Bobek the news – that soon he'd be getting a little brother or sister.

'*Mega!* You can come and watch me play football.'

The boy launched into a convoluted story about a recent critical match, and the goal he'd definitely have scored if he hadn't been fouled by a *kutas* called Slawek. Janusz smiled to hear him prattling on, suddenly as unselfconscious as a six-year-old, the surly teenager gone.

'*Dobrze*, Bobek. Tell your mama I'll call her so we can work out a good weekend to come over.'

'*Spoko*. Ummm. Dad?'

'What is it?'

'I wanted to tell you, nobody calls me Bobek any more.'

'Why not?'

'Everyone calls me Piotr now, even Mama. It's my real name after all.'

'Why the change?'

'Bobek's a baby's name.'

Afterwards, Janusz sat for a long moment with the phone in his hand, feeling as though someone had reached up under his ribs and given his heart a sharp tug. He and Marta had nicknamed their son Bobek – little berry – when he was just a few months old – a round and cheerful baby whose favourite mode of locomotion was scuttling around on his bottom.

His mind drifted to last summer, when he'd taken Bobek – *Piotr* – go-karting in Romford. The boy had turned out to be a bit of a speed freak, and Janusz had struggled to keep up with him, sweating in the cramped kart, leaning into the corners. He felt that way again now

230

– as if he were straining every sinew just to keep him in view.

A tentative tap at the flat door interrupted his reverie. It was probably his next-door neighbour, moaning about the mattress he'd left by the bins. Janusz opened the door, his expression arranged into a semblance of neighbourly cordiality – only to be met by a fist full in the face. He staggered backwards, his vision darkening, with no idea who'd hit him. *Kurwa mac!*

He threw a wild right hook, only to receive a vicious crack on the wrist. Reeled back against the wall, blinking rapidly. When his vision cleared, he found himself facing a stranger holding a metal baseball bat. Opening his bomber jacket, the guy let him see the well-worn grip of a pistol holstered against his ribs. After this brief and wordless exchange he used the baseball bat like a cattle prod to direct Janusz into the kitchen, where he nodded him into a chair.

'About our friend Steve Fisher,' said the man, as if they were picking up a long-running conversation. Taking in the reddened face – as pocked and pitted as a firing squad wall – Janusz suddenly recognised him: it was the guy who'd chased him, after tailing him on the tube. Sadly, it appeared his fracas with the mail van had left him with no lasting injury. 'I know you've been looking for him. So where the fuck is he?' His accent was one that had always made Janusz think of sloe berries bubbling on a low gas. *Russian.*

Fighting a gust of nausea, Janusz said nothing. Leaning across the table, the Russian gently rapped the surface between them with the baseball bat, a gesture as eloquent as it was economical. Janusz realised what he should have guessed from the first encounter – this guy was a professional, and it had only been a matter of time before he turned up on his doorstep.

'I'd love to help you out,' growled Janusz. His upper lip throbbed, already thickening, and he could taste the salty tang of blood. 'But I've been looking for the guy for a week now and no one has a clue where he is. It's like he evaporated.' *No point lying about his search – too many people knew he'd been sniffing around.*

'What do you want with him?'

'I'm a private detective,' said Janusz. 'I've been hired by a client to find him, someone he owes a pile of money to.'

Crack! The guy whacked the bat on the table before shoving it in his chest. 'Wrong answer, Polak. The dogs in the street know you're fucking Fisher's wife, so quit jerking me around.'

Janusz needed a moment to think. 'Okay, okay. But I need a smoke.'

The guy cursed in Russian, but threw him a pack of cigarettes. 'You can light me one while you're at it.'

After lighting their cigs, Janusz said, 'Look. I couldn't give a flying fuck about Fisher. But he kidnapped my girlfriend because she was about to leave him. My only interest in finding him is to get her back.'

'That's all?'

'That's all.'

The Russian squinted sceptically at Janusz, but after a moment his face relaxed into an expression of mocking amusement. 'You're going to a shitload of trouble just for a piece of pussy, aren't you?' Janusz didn't rise to the bait. 'So, loverboy, have you got any idea where he would take her?'

Janusz guessed that his best hope of surviving this exchange would be to hold out some hope of success. 'Nothing concrete, but I've put the word out with a bunch of contacts, people who might know where he'd go. He can't hide for ever.'

'Like the people he hangs around with in that shitty pub in Stratford?' He locked his eyes onto Janusz's face.

'I talked to a few of them, at the beginning, but I'm pretty sure they don't know where he is either.'

The Russian gave a little nod to himself – as if Janusz had confirmed his own analysis of the situation. 'So who are these contacts of yours?'

'You know, guys he's worked with in the past, mostly on the building sites.'

'Family?'

'Nope. His parents are long dead, and he's got no brothers and sisters.'

'Does the name *Duff* mean anything to you?'

'Duff? No, that's a new one on me.'

'What about Simeon?'

'I've heard of him, but I can't trace him. I think he's done a runner, too.'

Leaning across the table, the Russian gently tapped the side of Janusz's face with the baseball bat. 'You wouldn't be fucking with me, would you, Polak?'

Tap, tap, it went, cold and insolent against his cheekbone. The only thing that stopped Janusz from grabbing it and shoving it down the *skurwysyn*'s throat was the thought of Kasia.

Hearing a clattering from the window behind him, the Russian whipped round. It was Copetka, who'd just come

233

in through the cat-flap onto the kitchen worktop. He stood to reach for the cat, who lashed out, claws raking the back of the stranger's hand. *Mother of God!* Janusz rose from his seat – *if the* skurwiel *hurt his cat* ...

Instead, the Russian turned to him, a delighted smile on his face. 'Holy fuck! He's got some balls.' He tried again to stroke the ginger fur but Copetka sank his stomach to the worktop, his spine as sinuous as a snake's, before bolting out through the cat-flap. Watching him streak down the fire escape stairs, the Russian chuckled. 'That's a nice animal. I've got a Siberian Forest Cat at home. Great little hunter – he brings back rabbits, squirrels, pretty much every day.'

He pulled up his sleeve to examine the bloody scratch, revealing his forearm for a second or two – long enough for Janusz to glimpse an indigo-coloured tattoo on the inside of his wrist. Two characters – '*IV*'.

Sitting down again, the Russian gave Janusz a long considering look. 'I could persuade you to tell me who these "contacts" of yours are ... but then I'll only have to go find them, get them to talk. So, I'm thinking, why make extra work for myself? I hear you're pretty good at finding missing persons.' He leaned forward. 'Listen, loverboy. Steve Fisher has stolen something that I need to recover. You've got forty-eight hours to locate him and deliver him, and what he took, back to me. Alive. Understood?'

'How can I do that, if I don't know what he stole?'

The Russian put his tongue in his cheek, thinking it over. 'A USB stick. Looks like a bullet. Don't even think about opening it. I hear the cops are looking for Fisher, too, so you need to get a move on.'

234

Janusz took his time grinding his cigarette butt out in the ashtray. 'My usual charge for a missing person job is five hundred a day. Sterling.'

'I see you've acquired an English sense of humour,' said the Russian, with a cold smile. 'So let me explain the deal. You deliver Fisher – and you and your girlfriend get to walk off together into the sunset.'

'On your word as a gentleman?' Janusz made no attempt to hide his sarcasm.

'Listen, Polak. From where I'm sitting, you don't have a lot of choice in the matter.' He pulled out his phone and scooted it across the table. 'Put your number in there. And I'll send you mine.'

'All right,' said Janusz.

'You know, we have a common interest here. You find Fisher and that USB stick he stole, and I guarantee he'll never bother you or your girlfriend again.'

'And if I can't? Find him?'

The Russian smirked at him. 'Do you want me to paint you a picture?'

He stood up, stowing the baseball bat inside his jacket. 'The Americans have a name for this kind of arrangement, don't they ...' he mused. '*Da*, I remember. It's called an "incentive program".'

235

Thirty-Three

Predictably enough, Katherine Duff had failed to produce any useful information as to where her elder son might be hiding out, and since Streaky's threat of a Fraud Squad investigation was no more than a bluff, that left Joey Duff's mobile phone number as the only live lead.

The Sarge had agreed to drop Kershaw home on the way back to Walthamstow nick, where he'd start the process of requesting access to the phone company's call data. His expression was wistful as he drew up outside her flat. 'I was hoping for fish and chips at the Moon,' he said, 'not a pasty at my desk and a bloody great form to fill in.'

Kershaw opened the passenger door, wishing that she was the one pulling a late one, instead of going home to a cold and empty flat. 'You'll let me know, won't you Sarge, as soon as we have anything?'

'Yeah, I'll call you,' he said. 'And get in touch with Kiszka – see what he has to say about the latest from your new boyfriend.'

'Sorry?'

'Nathan King.' He lifted his eyebrows meaningfully. 'The Doctor Kildare of Walthamstow Mortuary.'

'Who's Doctor Kildare?' Kershaw shot back, sidestepping the wind-up. Streaky's jibe was probably just a lucky guess: the pub where she and Nathan had had drinks wasn't one of the boozers on the Walthamstow nick drinking circuit.

Once she was inside, she put in a call to Kiszka. He answered on the second ring, sounding grumpier than ever.

'Any news?' she asked.

'Nothing,' he said. 'What about you?'

'Same here. Everything okay? Your voice sounds a bit weird.' He was speaking in a mumble, like he'd just had a tooth filled.

'I'm fine.'

'This is probably unrelated, but we just got the results of a PM ...'

'A what?'

'Sorry, a post-mortem – on a body, found in Victoria Park. It had similar injuries to those found on Steve's associates.'

'Oh, yes?'

'The guy had no ID on him, so they sent casts of his teeth off to some specialist.'

'What did he say?'

'*She* said that the work was probably Russian. Apparently, the way dentists do things there hasn't changed much since Communism.'

He made a non-committal sound.

'So, did you ever hear of Steve hanging out with any Russians?'

'Russians?' he laughed. 'No, Steve never struck me as the cosmopolitan type.'

Kershaw felt her interest waver: she found it hard to see where a murdered Russian might fit into any scenario involving Duff and Fisher. Russian organised crime had certainly been on the rise in the capital for several years, but the Duff Family didn't strike her as the type to hire foreigners.

'Okay. It was just a thought. And you're sure nothing else has happened that I should know about?'

'No. It's all quiet here.'

Kershaw chewed at a nail. She knew what she ought to do – *had* to do if she was going to keep him on board – but she'd always found saying sorry, the kind of apology that meant something anyway, agonisingly hard.

'Listen, Janusz. I wanted to say I'm sorry for any impression I gave that I … had doubts about Kasia being taken against her will.'

His silence said: *not good enough*.

'I mean it. I was wrong and you were right – we're all working on the assumption now that she was abducted.' His only response was a grunt – but having got used to his Neanderthal communication methods, she took it as an acknowledgement of the apology. 'I know you didn't want a full-on police search for her, but, obviously, the case is much bigger than one missing person now.' She paused. 'Any chance you could email me a recent photo?'

'… Okay.'

'And promise me something? That you'll let me know if you get any clue about where she is? … Janusz?'

'I'm afraid I have to go, there's somebody at the door.'

There was definitely something funny about the way he was talking, she was sure of it, but before she could quiz him further, the line went dead.

Later that evening, Janusz Kiszka would pop back into Kershaw's thoughts – and not in a helpful way.

She and Nathan King had been out to dinner in town – a trendy American-style place where the waiters dressed like Midwestern farm workers at a hoedown and the starters and mains came in a haphazard order, which was apparently the new normal. The pair of them had enjoyed taking the mick out of the restaurant's *Little House on the Prairie* pretensions and she'd discovered more of Nathan's droll sense of humour beneath the geeky intelligence. All in all, it had been a good night – a solid 8 out of 10.

Afterwards, Nathan wanted to find a bar, but she had baled – if there were any developments on the Joey Duff case, she didn't want to be hungover – so the night had ended with one of those awkward partings at the bottom of an escalator under the tube lights' knowing glare. After a moment's hesitation, Nathan went in for the kiss on the lips – and it was a good one – not too keen, while leaving no doubts about the nature of his interest.

But anyone who'd noticed the compact blonde girl riding the escalator down to the Central line platform a moment later might have described her expression as troubled. Kershaw had spent the day fretting about the moment when Nathan King might kiss her – worried that it might trigger unwelcome images of his day job. In fact, the thought that had flashed into her mind as they'd kissed had been something different – and totally unexpected.

What would it be like to kiss Janusz Kiszka?

Thirty-Four

The lady behind the counter at the Polish café was too polite to comment on Janusz's swollen and scabbed lip as she took his order – a scruple not shared by Oskar when he arrived a few minutes later.

'What happened to your face, sisterfucker?'

Janusz shushed him with a gesture – the waitress was just setting down his bowl of *zurek*.

'*Mniam, mniam!*' Oskar wafted the steam towards him. 'Could I have the soup, too, *prosze pani*? It smells delicious.' After she'd gone, he examined Janusz's face. 'So was the guy who hit you a midget?'

'Yeah. He was about your height.'

'He had a good punch on him,' said Oskar, his tone admiring, before loading a hunk of bread with pork dripping and crispy fried onions from the pot on the table.

Back in their national service days, when he'd weighed in at a good twenty kilos lighter, Oskar had been a pretty useful flyweight boxer, winning a bunch of medals in military competitions. His boxing career had come to an abrupt halt, however, after he'd accepted a challenge to fight Sergeant Golombek.

Since Golombek was a swivel-eyed *kommie* with a reputation for bullying the weaker lads, Janusz had advised his mate to throw the match. Instead, Oskar took the guy apart. The fight made Oskar the hero of the compound, but it also earned him months of latrine-cleaning duty and – even after Golombek's transfer – he was never entered for any more competition matches. When Janusz saw him after the fight, and asked why he'd done it, Oskar had shrugged and said, 'He took the piss out of Andrej's stammer.'

Oskar washed down his mouthful of bread and *szmalec* with a draught of beer. 'So who thumped you?'

'Somebody who wants to find Steve.'

'Well, if you can't find him, then what chance has Shortarse got?' said Oskar with an air of complacent confidence.

'I wouldn't be so sure about that, *kolego*. He has some persuasive methods.'

Janusz hadn't breathed a word to Oskar – or anyone else – about Steve's caravan hideout. It was a piece of information evidently worth a great deal to his pursuers, although Janusz still had no idea why Joey Duff – and now some Russian *psychol* – were so desperate to find him. The only thing he was sure of: that the stolen data stick held the key to the mystery.

'You've got some Russian mates, haven't you?' he asked Oskar.

Oskar nodded, tucking into his soup.

'Have you ever heard of a tattoo that spells out "IV"?'

'What, in Cyrillic?'

Learning Russian had been compulsory under Communism and, by the end of their schooldays, Oskar and Janusz had been force-fed the basics of the language. Only now did it strike Janusz that the letters 'I' and 'V' didn't exist in the Cyrillic alphabet.

'No. In Latin script. Here.' He tapped the inside of his wrist.

Oskar shook his head. 'I'll ask Arkady.' Pausing in his demolition of the soup, he dug out his mobile and punched out a text. 'Done.'

'*Dzieki, kolego.*'

Oskar studied his friend, his expression grown doleful. 'How are you bearing up, Janek? You know, with … the Kasia thing.'

Janusz stared at the table. 'It's funny,' he shrugged, 'I don't have a clue where she is and yet, I'm starting to feel like I'm getting close to finding her.'

'And you still think she's …' Oskar didn't finish the thought.

'Alive? Yes, I'm sure of it.'

'I can't imagine how I would cope, if Gosia went missing, or – God forbid! – one of the girls.'

Both men crossed themselves.

'Listen, Oskar. I don't want you coming round my place for a while.'

'Don't tell me – you've shacked up with a couple of rent boys.'

'Very funny. I'm serious – it's too dangerous, now this Russian *skurwiel* knows where I live.'

'Sounds to me like you could do with some backup. You never were much of a boxer.' Oskar put up his chubby fists, feinted a few jabs.

242

'I'm not screwing around, Oskar.' Janusz paused, weighing up the risk of revealing his suspicions. 'If I tell you something, you've got to swear you'll keep it to yourself, *dobrze*?'

Oskar nodded, adopting his serious face.

'This Russian, I'm pretty sure he murdered two of Steve's mates,' he said, in a murmur. 'But not before using a blowtorch on them.' He recalled how the guy had nodded, when Janusz had said nobody knew where Steve was holed up.

The Russian had nodded because in his experience, when people knew something, he always got it out of them.

Before Oskar could respond, his phone chirruped its irritating ditty. 'It's Arkady,' he said.

Janusz watched as he scrolled through a text message. 'Well?'

Oskar's eyebrows shot up. 'It's not "IV",' he said, staring at Janusz. 'It's the number four.'

'*Naprawde?* Why would he have the number four tattooed on his wrist?'

'It's his blood group: the Russians use numbers instead of letters.'

'I don't get it?' Janusz frowned at his mate, uncomprehending. 'Does it mean he has some kind of medical condition?'

Oskar met Janusz's gaze, his expression troubled. '*Nie, kolego.* It means he is Spetsnaz.'

Thirty-Five

'*Voyska spetsialnogo naznacheniya ...*' Stefan pronounced the phrase like a roll of thunder. 'Russian elite special forces.' He cocked his head at Janusz, eyes bright with intrigue. 'Why the interest in those bastards, all of a sudden?'

Three miles east of the Polish café, at the St Francis of Assisi Residential Home, the late afternoon sun was shining through the bare branches of the apple trees. Janusz and Stefan had taken their mugs of tea outside into the orchard so that Janusz could smoke.

'It's just some article I read recently,' he said, lighting his cigar. 'Are they part of the FSB?'

'No. Spetsnaz always came under GRU – military intelligence. They're a driving force behind Putin's nasty little games in Ukraine.'

'They've got a pretty tough reputation, right?'

'Oh, yes – they make a positive fetish of their barbarism. The training includes bare knuckle fighting, getting dragged behind trucks, breaking roof tiles over each other's heads ...' Stefan rolled his eyes. 'Adolescent nonsense.'

Janusz was reminded of an anecdote he'd once heard about Spetsnaz training. A unit had been ordered to swim across a freezing cold river at dawn carrying full kit, prompting an observer to ask their commander: *What if they drown?* His reply: *If they drown, they're no good for Spetsnaz.'*

'For all the talk of honour, they're just a bunch of murderous criminals,' Stefan went on. 'They tortured and killed thousands of civilians in Chechnya, women and schoolchildren included.'

Janusz wasn't surprised to learn that his assailant boasted such a CV. 'What about the data stick?' he asked. 'You said you'd managed to break into the files?'

'I have.' Stefan sounded pleased with himself, but made no move to open the black laptop lying on the seat between them.

'So are you going to tell me what's in them?'

Stefan's expression was as genial as ever but the look he sent Janusz was as piercing as a raptor's. 'We do still have the awkward matter of Wojtek's annuity to resolve,' he said. 'It seems to me that these are circumstances in which both of us could benefit from a little *quid pro quo.'*

'In other words, you're not going to tell me what's on there unless I agree to hush up Wojtek's fraudulent medical records.'

Stefan inclined his head a fraction.

Janusz drew on his cigar. He'd expected the demand, of course, but that didn't make the dilemma it presented any more attractive. If he reported Stefan's fraud to Haven Insurance it would almost certainly trigger an investigation of all annuitants at St Francis, and the resulting court cases and scandal could close the place. The thought of any of the residents having to move – many of them to places where the management would have less regard for the dignity and self-determination of their residents – was more than he could bear.

And yet … He had always lived by the principle that his word was his bond. Tomek was a friend who had given him a break by hiring him to do a job in good faith – and the idea of abusing that trust … Well, it made him feel profoundly uneasy.

'What's to stop me getting someone else to unlock the files?' he asked.

'Be my guest,' said Stefan with a magnanimous gesture. 'Although, personally speaking, I would think twice before sharing such … *sensitive* information with any Tom, Dick, or Harry.'

They surveyed each other for a long moment. Janusz was the first to break the look. 'Okay,' he sighed at last. 'Here's what I'm prepared to do.'

Five minutes later, after a free and candid exchange, Stefan fired up his laptop, positioning it at an angle that allowed Janusz to view the screen.

There were five files on the stick: the first three were bank statements, two of the accounts with UK high street banks, and one with a private bank based in Mayfair that Janusz had never heard of. Even a cursory glance revealed that a tidal wave of money passed through these accounts every month.

They were all in the name of a company calling itself Brunswick Entertainment Group, and when Janusz read the address at the top of the statements, supposedly the head office of this apparently highly profitable outfit, he felt a jolt of recognition. *It was the address of the flat above the launderette in Stratford.*

'See how the cash gets paid into the private bank account first,' said Stefan, pointing out some of the transactions. 'And always in amounts of just under ten thousand pounds, the maximum single deposit that can be made without the bank needing to report it to the authorities. Once in the system, it's "clean money" that can legitimately be transferred to the bigger banks.' He maximised another file. 'Finally, it all ends up here.' The balance shown on the final statement was a seven-figure sum, its masthead naming a bank based in Nicosia, Cyprus.

'But the EU, the banks ... everyone's supposed to be all over money laundering these days.'

'Quite so.' Stefan sent him a look over his reading glasses. 'But where there's a will, and a friendly bank manager, there's always a way.'

'So who does the money belong to?'

'It's hard to say. There are substantial transfers to solicitors, some of them London-based, which would appear to be property transactions. But money is never paid to any individual's bank account.' He shot him a look. 'Or should I say, *almost* never.' Janusz felt his heart rate step up. Stefan scrolled through one of the statements. 'Here we are.'

Janusz craned to read the tiny print. 'Two hundred grand in euros, paid into what looks like a Russian bank account.' He shrugged. 'But no account name – just a string of numbers.'

Stefan raised a finger in the manner of a conjuror about to produce a turtledove from an unexpected orifice.

247

'Ah, but here's the interesting bit.' He clicked on the icon for the final file, which turned out to be an email. Addressed to one Vasily Vetrov, it consisted of a single line.

'My Russian's pretty rusty,' Janusz confessed, squinting at the unfamiliar script.

Stefan lifted his chin in order to read it through the bottom of his lenses. 'It says: "*Transfer €200k to the Moscow account. Urgently.*" Signed "*SB*".' He looked at Janusz to make sure he'd got it. 'That sum arrived in the Moscow account ...' after scrolling through another statement, he pointed out a deposit, 'the very same day.'

Janusz checked out the address the email had been sent from. '*SBelyakov@MinskTel.com,*' he read out.

'Anyone you know?' asked Stefan.

'No,' said Janusz, shrugging.

'This email is the single slip-up, the one thing that links this highly interesting flow of cash from the UK with the person I assume to be the final beneficiary in Russia.' Stefan took off his reading glasses to polish the lenses. 'If I were you, I'd be asking why anyone would risk keeping such dangerous information on a data stick.'

Janusz grunted – he was thinking precisely the same thing. 'Listen, Stefan,' he said. 'If your heart's set on dying peacefully in your sleep one day, I'd advise you to erase those documents from your computer and forget you ever saw them.'

Stefan unplugged the data stick, chuckling. 'It's a bit late for me to start fretting about my mortality. As my father used to say: "I'm old, my book is already closed."' Handing Janusz the oversized bullet, he caught his hand in both bony paws. His touch was warm and papery, oddly comforting. 'You, on the other hand, would be wise to proceed with extreme caution. You're a young man, with half your life still to live.'

Halfway across the garden he glanced back at Stefan, who was standing now, feeding the birds from a plastic bag. Raising his stick in a valedictory gesture, the old boy called out: 'Don't forget our agreement!'

Back outside, Janusz crossed the road to George Green and put some distance between him and the main road before calling his mate Tomek at Haven Insurance.

'*Czesc*, Tomek … You know the final paperwork I was going to send in on Wojtek Raczynski? Well, I've just had some news from the rest home where he stays. I'm afraid the old boy has "kicked the calendar" …' He gazed up into the budding branches of the ancient oaks. '*Dobrze*. Yes, it was quite sudden. Haven will be formally notified, of course, but I thought I'd let you know so you can terminate his annuity payments straight away … It's a pleasure. And Tomek? I'm sorry, but I'm afraid my other commitments forbid me from taking on any more work in the foreseeable future … It's a great shame, yes. It's been good working with you, too.'

As he cast a final look across the road at the home's Gothic facade, Janusz thought of the lives within, picturing the faces of the old people he'd come across during his visits to the place. Sometimes, he reflected, doing the not-quite-honourable thing was the only honourable thing to do.

Thirty-Six

That night, Kershaw was already in her pyjamas and standing over the kettle in her kitchen, when her mobile sounded.

'What are you doing?'

Streaky. Calling from a car.

'Uh, making a cup of cocoa, Sarge.'

'What, at ten past ten?' He sucked his teeth disapprovingly. 'Young people today. Well, you'd better down it in one, Ms Marple, 'cos I'm on my way to pick you up. And Kershaw?'

'Sarge?'

'When you answer the door, make sure you're decent. I've got a weak heart.'

Before she even had a chance to ask what it was all about, he'd rung off.

Kershaw had only just pulled on her boots when she heard the throaty growl of a car engine outside. Downstairs she discovered Streaky in the passenger seat of a BMW pursuit vehicle with a uniformed driver: wherever they were going, he wanted to get them there fast. But since he spent the next few minutes giving the driver directions, all she could do was speculate, fidgeting with frustration, in the back seat. The M11 was mentioned, which could mean they were heading back to Katherine Duff's mansion in Ongar – or maybe to the Forest Sanctuary Hotel in Epping?

It was only once they were accelerating up the ramp to the motorway that Streaky finally deigned to fill her in.

'So there I was, sitting in the Moon having a quiet pint, trying to decide whether to go for an Indian or a Turkish' – this thrown over his shoulder from the front passenger seat – 'when I get an email. It's the mobile phone company sending me the call records for "Gerald Doherty" – or as we know and love him, Joseph Francis Duff.'

Streaky delved a hand into his coat pocket, but instead of the phone records Kershaw was expecting, he produced two packets of peanuts, before lobbing one backwards in her general direction.

'You mean they've got a location for him?'

'Looks like it.' He broke off to remind the driver, Aaron, to take the first exit, for Loughton, before continuing. 'It seems our pal Joey did spend time at his mum's hotel last week, after all. And they speak on the phone every day. Must have slipped the old girl's mind.'

'Is that where we're going?'

Streaky shook his head. 'Two days ago, in the early hours, he was on the move again.'

'Sounds like something spooked him,' said Kershaw, recalling Kiszka's admission that he'd checked out the Forest Sanctuary Hotel a couple of days back.

'Apparently.'

251

'So, where is he now?' Kershaw raised her voice over the engine's growl as they dropped into a lower gear, descending the exit ramp.

'Well, the bad news is, shortly after leaving the hotel, he turned his phone off. Must be getting paranoid.' Streaky threw a handful of peanuts into his mouth, taking his time to dispatch the mouthful.

'And the good news?' she prompted – struggling to keep the exasperation out of her voice.

'This morning, just after 0900 hours he turns it on again, to call his dear old mum. Only for a couple of minutes, but long enough for his phone to start talking to nearby mobile masts. Lucky for us, there were enough masts within range to triangulate his calls. It's not perfect, but it should get us to within a hundred metres of his location.'

'Are you going to tell me where the fuck we're going, or what?' Kershaw caught Aaron's shocked gaze in the rear view mirror.

Streaky, though, just gave her an innocent look 'Oh, didn't I say? He's in Epping Forest.'

An unusually quiet night at Walthamstow nick had allowed the Sarge to borrow a fast car and trained driver, which meant they reached the forest's eastern fringe, where Joey Duff had used his mobile that morning, in just thirteen minutes. The plan was to try to discover Duff's hiding place and, if he was still there, to call in backup before going in. 'Quicker than getting the Essex boys to check it out,' he told her with a significant look. 'Even if they made it a priority, which I doubt, the last thing I need is a bunch of uniforms trampling all over a potential scene.'

As they plunged into the forest, the probing beam of the car headlights seemed to carve a tunnel out of the bare branches overhead, the dense undergrowth either side. 'We're looking for an abandoned electricity substation,' Streaky told Aaron, consulting his phone. 'There should be an unpaved road on the right in about half a mile.' He turned to Kershaw. 'It's the only possible hideaway around here so far as I can see – unless he's sleeping in a tent.'

'Do you think he's still got Kasia – out here in the middle of nowhere?'

'No idea,' he sighed. 'But it's all we've got to go on.'

A minute or two later, they spotted the overgrown entrance to a dirt road leading into the forest; fifty metres further on, Aaron pulled onto the verge and killed the engine. There was a moment in which all Kershaw could hear was the tick of cooling metal, before Streaky opened his door. As she went to follow suit, he turned to her – clearly about to tell her to stay put – but on seeing the look in her eyes, he just gave a nod.

They walked back along the verge, the woods to their left an impenetrable black, the only illumination the moonlight reflecting off the asphalt surface of the road. The going was soft and uneven and Kershaw was glad she'd chosen to wear her sturdiest boots. When they reached the dirt road, Streaky signalled her to stop.

'This is as far as you go.' This time, his expression brooked no objection. 'Got your Airwaves on?' Double-checking her radio, she nodded. 'Okay. I'll go ahead, have a little butcher's. If you hear anything untoward, no schoolgirl heroics, okay? You toddle on back to the car and tell Aaron to radio for backup.'

It only took a minute or two for the darkness to swallow up Streaky's outline. Until that moment she'd felt only a surging, restless excitement, but now there came a backwash of anxiety. It wasn't so much for the Sarge – she couldn't really think of him as anything other than indestructible – but for Kasia, who might be just metres away, *right now* – her life hanging in the balance, in the hands of the ruthless criminal holding her.

Straining to hear any sound from the velvet-dark depths of the forest, all she could make out was a faint wind susurrating through the trees, punctuated by the occasional distant cry of some nocturnal animal. 'Come on,' she muttered to herself, desperate to follow Streaky, find out what was going on. What stopped her wasn't the fear of what might await her in the darkness, but the knowledge that by staying put, she'd be in a better position to raise the alarm.

When her radio issued a burst of static, she jumped like she'd got an electric shock.

'Kershaw. All clear here.' She could tell from Streaky's voice that he'd found something. *Kasia?*

She jogged down the dirt road, heart bumping, zigzagging around potholes. Reaching the end of the road, she saw the outline of the disused substation. It was a sinister sight: so heavily overgrown with ivy that it looked like it had been struck by some ancient vegetal tsunami. On the six-foot-high chain link fence surrounding it were hung faded signs with red lightning bolts, and fresher ones that warned 'DO NOT ENTER! UNSTABLE AND HAZARDOUS STRUCTURE.'

Through the undergrowth, she glimpsed Streaky in the building's doorway, waving her towards a point in the fence. Groping along it, a whole section gave under her hand: someone had cut out a makeshift door – and very recently, judging by the bright glint of the wire's cut ends. Stepping through it, she followed a rough path trodden through the ramparts of buddleia and stinging nettles.

At the door, she found Streaky on his Airwaves talking to Essex Police control room.

'Kasia?' she mouthed.

He shook his head.

Shit. Kershaw exhaled, realising that she'd been holding her breath for the last minute or so.

'What about Duff?'

'Gone to a better place,' said the Sarge out of the side of his mouth.

'What the ...?' Kershaw was gobsmacked – Joey Duff was *dead*?

But the Sarge was talking again, asking for roadblocks on routes out of the forest. Too impatient to wait, she went past him into the substation interior.

Inside, a cluster of dim shapes leapt to life under the light from her phone screen – the station's defunct electrical apparatus, furred with decades of dust, which took up most of the interior. The place smelled of ... *dead electricity* – if there was such a thing. On the floor she made out footsteps in the dust, leading towards an inky black rectangle – a doorway.

At the threshold, she paused, feeling the hairs on her arms prickle upright – before forcing herself to go on. Her phone screen dimmed, choosing that moment to conserve power, and she blundered into something hard. Cursing, she tapped the phone back to life, illuminating a metal filing cabinet. She could hear a faint sound. *Dap ... dap ... dap* a couple of seconds apart. *The sound of dripping.*

She directed the faint blue light of her phone towards the source of the sound. Out of the blackness sprung the outline of a hanged man. Her hand shot to her mouth. Breathing fast, she stepped closer. Recognised the greasy-looking mullet and flattened features of Joey Duff, darkened with blood. He was hanging from a high barred window, wrists bound in front of him with plastic ties.

Dap ... dap. Playing the light downward, she saw a single drip fall from the toe of his trainer onto the tiled floor below: remembered from her pathology module at uni that hanging victims often soiled themselves.

It was a relief to hear Streaky approaching, holding a pocket torch.

'Let's get him down,' he said.

Streaky manhandled the filing cabinet over from the opposite wall, before fishing inside his coat and handing her a pair of latex gloves.

'Showtime,' he grinned, meshing his hands to give her a leg-up.

Using the penknife he handed up to her, Kershaw started to saw at the thick leather belt Duff was hanging from, trying to concentrate on getting the job done as fast as possible. It wasn't easy, with the still-warm body pressed intimately against her, the ammonia waft of urine in her nostrils, trying to ignore the purple face bobbing just inches from hers. And the width and thickness of the belt made the job even more difficult. When she'd got halfway through the leather, she paused, her raised arms starting to ache. Streaky, who was holding the bottom half of the body steady, shifted his position, causing the ligature around Duff's throat to slacken its grip a fraction. A sound like a sigh escaped Duff's lips. Kershaw ignored it. Having heard cadavers moan before, she knew it was just the last bit of air leaving the lungs, passing over the vocal cords.

It took her another ten seconds of sawing to reach the last few fibres, the body shifting and twisting as the Sarge took more of the weight from below. Finally, as the last strand of leather gave way, the belt flew loose. Something made her glance sideways at Joey Duff's face. His eyelids flickered, then snapped open – and he fixed her with a bloodshot stare.

Christ on a bike!

After that, everything went into fast-forward: Duff started to hyperventilate with a harsh rasping sound, Streaky shouting, 'I've got him, I've got him!' After a moment of horrified paralysis, Kershaw jumped down to help.

Once Duff was on the deck and in the recovery position he lapsed back into unconsciousness, but his breathing – although hoarse – remained regular.

'Just as well,' Streaky told Kershaw as they stared down at him. 'If he carks it, it won't be me giving him the chuffing kiss of life, I can tell you.'

Fifteen minutes later, an ambulance was ferrying Joey Duff away down the dirt road, its blue lights flickering against the trees.

'He got the same treatment as Bill Boyce, didn't he?' asked Kershaw.

When the paramedics had torn open Duff's shirt to affix sensors to his chest, they had exposed angry-looking welts extending from his abdomen down beyond the waistband of his jeans. 'Yep,' said the Sarge. 'The torture, the mocked-up hanging – it looks like the same MO. Except this time, the killer screwed up.'

They'd pieced together the puzzle of Joey Duff's lucky escape. After torturing Duff, presumably in a bid to extract information, the killer had tied his wrists and strung him up. But he must have been in a hurry, because when he'd left, Duff was still alive – just. A single nail they found protruding from the wall behind him may have provided a minute but critical heel hold which, together with the inefficient ligature made by the chunky leather belt, had bought Duff a few extra precious minutes of air.

'Takes a lot to kill a man,' mused Streaky. 'Especially a scumbag like Duff.'

'He couldn't have been up there long though, could he, Sarge?' She looked up at him. 'Do you think we just missed the boat?'

Streaky's grimace said it all. They both knew what that meant: if they'd arrived earlier, Kasia might be safe by now.

Beyond the substation's perimeter fence they found a freshly crushed patch of undergrowth, suggesting a struggle – Kershaw hoped it was Kasia, putting up a fight against whoever took her – but beyond that, nothing. There were no obvious tyre tracks on the dirt road, and the only other way out would involve navigating a route through the forest's tracks and paths, which would be quite a feat – even by daylight and without a hostage.

Kershaw was still getting her head round the abrupt change of direction the case had taken. *If it hadn't been Joey Duff who had murdered Steve's mates, then who? And where the hell was Kasia?*

'D'you think Fisher could be behind it all, Sarge?'

'No chuffing idea. Right now we can't even prove positively that Kasia was here.' Streaky handed her a pouch containing a protective suit. 'Forensics won't get here for hours. Why should they have all the fun, anyway?'

Kershaw grinned: for all his old lag banter, Streaky was a grafter and he wasn't about to delay the hunt for Kasia Fisher just so they could get a few hours' sleep. They started to search the substation interior using torches and the light from a high-wattage lamp that the Sarge had hung from the ceiling.

It took them over an hour to sweep the building, by which time their once-white suits were streaked and mottled with dust. Streaky straightened and, digging both hands into the small of his back, stretched out his spine.

Kershaw wiped sweat from her forehead with the back of her sleeve. 'She's got to have been here, Sarge.'

'If I'm going to persuade the office wallahs to fund a national manhunt, I probably need something a bit more solid than woman's intuition.'

'We've got this,' Kershaw picked up the evidence bag holding the empty water bottle she'd found. 'Her DNA might be on it.'

'Maybe,' he sighed. 'It all takes time though, and I'm not sure Kasia has a lot more of that commodity.'

Kershaw returned to the corner where the decades-deep dust showed signs of being slept on – the spot where they suspected Kasia had spent the last two days and nights – and tried to think herself into Kasia's headspace. Seven days a prisoner, terrified, probably drugged – but surely not the whole time. She must have been conscious now and again in order to eat and drink – might even have witnessed Duff's murder, just a few metres away. Treading carefully in her plastic shoe covers, Kershaw played the torchbeam over the wall, in the faint hope of finding something, perhaps a word or message scrawled there. *Come on, Kasia,* she urged, silently. *You're a smart girl. Surely you'd have left something for us?*

Nothing.

She dropped to a crouch, focusing on the foot of the wall. The walls, painted an institutional green, ended in a narrow strip of skirting board. The filler between wall and wood had shrunk over the years, leaving a narrow, meandering crack. Kershaw trained the beam of her torch on this gap, moving along it centimetre by centimetre.

By the time she shuffled the length of the sleeping area, her thigh muscles were screaming. And then she saw it.

'Sarge. I think I've got something.'

Thirty-Seven

If Kershaw had been expecting any gratitude from Kiszka for the progress they'd made in the search for his girl-friend, she was in for a disappointment.

Sure, it wasn't ideal, dragging him into Walthamstow nick to break the news, but Streaky was right: it was high time that Janusz Kiszka spilled his guts. He needed to share everything he knew with them, let the profession-als take over the search for Kasia – and the best place to bring that home to him was an interview room.

That morning, she'd put her uniform back on for the first time since being signed off sick. The Sarge had cleared it with Toby Greenacre, explaining that he needed her officially back on duty to question a contact in a murder case. After pulling on the regulation socks and boots, the dark blue trousers, she zipped up the jerkin, and stood staring in the mirror for a long moment. She'd been out of uniform less than a week and yet she was finding the sensation strangely unnerving – like a snake might feel, slipping back inside its discarded skin.

Now she was sitting in interview room 3, with Janusz Kiszka glowering across the table at her and the Sarge.

'Am I to be questioned under caution?' he asked Streaky.

'No ...'

'Well, that makes a refreshing change,' he growled.

It was obvious to Kershaw that someone had recently split Kiszka's upper lip, and badly, leaving the area around it black as a plum – which would explain the way he'd been mumbling on the phone the day before.

'We wanted to update you officially on our search for your girlfriend, Kasia Fisher,' said Streaky, before giving him an edited version of last night's activities.

'Let me see if I understand you correctly,' said Kiszka, when the Sarge had finished. On the surface, his voice was silky smooth, but Kershaw could sense the riptide of rage beneath. 'You trace this Joseph Duff's phone signal, but by the time you turn up, you find him half-dead – and my girlfriend gone.' He made a derisive noise. 'While you lot were knocking on the front door, whoever it was who took her was probably walking out the back.'

'I think that highly unlikely,' said Streaky. 'We put roadblocks up locally: if he'd still been anywhere in the vicinity we'd have caught him.'

Kiszka emitted a percussive gust of air, a response that Kershaw translated as *police bullshit*.

'Anyway. I have to say you don't seem very surprised to hear that we think it was Joseph Duff – and not Steve Fisher – who abducted Kasia and who's been holding her captive all this time,' said the Sarge. 'What do you know about him?'

'I already told *your colleague* everything I know,' he shot Kershaw a cold look. 'He's some villain who Fisher got himself mixed up with.'

'How did you come by this information?'

'Pub gossip.'

'Nothing more than that?'

'No.'

'It seems to me that you know an awful lot more about this business than you're letting on,' said Streaky. 'For a start, what motive Joey Duff might have for kidnapping Kasia in the first place.'

Kiszka shrugged. 'I wish I knew.'

'And who might be holding her now.'

'No idea.'

Leaning forward, Streaky spoke in a confiding murmur. 'Do you think it might be the same person who punched your lights out?'

Kershaw noticed Kiszka's top lip lift a fraction: evidence of the Herculean effort he was making to control his temper.

A subtle change in Streaky's body language indicated that she should have a crack. 'Look, Janusz,' she said, 'I understand how you must feel. It was frustrating for us, as well, getting there too late for Kasia. But you've got to admit, at least we were able to find out where she was – because we've got the resources to do that.' *And you haven't*, her eyes said.

He met her gaze, but all she could see there was an accusation of betrayal. 'I can't tell you anything.'

'Can't – or won't?'

'Do you even have any proof that she was there, at this mystery location?'

In her peripheral vision, she saw Streaky blink. Opening a box file on the table in front of her, she pulled out a plastic evidence bag. Clearly picking up on the tentative way she pushed it across the table, Kiszka's eyes flickered up to meet hers.

'Do you recognise this?' she asked.

He hesitated a moment before drawing the bag towards him, bending his head to squint at the black fragment inside. He looked blank, until it clicked. His head shot up. 'It's ... one of Kasia's fingernails!' Taking a ragged breath he stared up at the ceiling for a long moment. When he spoke again his voice was hoarse. 'You don't think ...'

'No, no. It's not her actual nail,' said Kershaw, soothingly. 'It's acrylic – an extension. She did wear black varnish, then?'

'Always.'

'We think perhaps she broke it off herself. To leave some sign that she'd been there.'

Kiszka was clutching the bag in one big fist, staring down at the nail fragment, a muscle in his jaw working. Kershaw knew she ought to be pleased to have thrown him off guard; in fact, seeing him like this churned her up in an unexpected way.

Would anyone ever love her that deeply? she asked herself.

'So you see, Janusz,' said Streaky, breaking the silence, 'we think Kasia left it there for the police to find – to give us something to go on. If you'll give us your full cooperation, tell us everything you know about what's been going on, I'm confident that working together, we can find her and bring her home safely.'

Janusz looked up, his gaze travelling from Streaky to Kershaw, as if he'd forgotten they were there. For a second, she thought he might actually play ball.

Instead, visibly composing himself, he produced his most charming smile. 'I hope you'll forgive me, but unless you are going to arrest me, I'm afraid I need to go now.'

Within seconds of leaving the interview room, Janusz had his mobile – which had been switched to silent for the interview – in his hand. A missed call and a waiting text. No surprise who they were from: the number was the one belonging to the red-faced *skurwiel* with the Spetsnaz tattoo. The text said simply *'Call me.'*

He flew down the two flights of stairs to the exit, a cocktail of relief, hope and gut-loosening fear racing through his veins.

Once outside, he leaned against a wall, willing his breathing back to normal, before making the call.

'This is Kiszka.'

'Have you tracked down our mutual friend, the *rogonosets*, yet?'

Janusz frowned – he knew the word was an insult, but he was having trouble recalling what it meant.

'Didn't we teach you people Russian in school? The guy whose wife you are fucking!'

'I know where he is, yes.'

'You do?' The guy gave a grunt of begrudging acknowledgement. 'What about the mislaid item – the one I'm keen to have returned?'

'I've got it locked away somewhere safe.'

Janusz heard the guy lighting a cigarette, followed by an unhurried inward breath as he drew smoke into his lungs – and had to bite down hard on his lip to stop himself asking about Kasia. *Come on*, skurwiel, *spit it out*, he urged silently.

'Describe it to me.' The voice was sceptical.

'A carrier bag full of cash, about fifteen thousand sterling, and a data stick shaped like a bullet, just like you said.'

On the other end of the line came the sound of the guy exhaling smoke. 'Okay. Here's what's going to happen. I'm going to tell you a safe place where you will leave the items, and when you get home to your flat, your favourite lady friend will be waiting for you. Maybe she'll already be in bed, with her legs open.' His chuckle turned into a cough as the smoke caught in his throat.

'No.'

A moment of disbelieving silence before the mocking tone turned to ice. 'What the fuck do you mean, *no*?'

'You don't get what you want until I see her. We do a swap – the stick for the girl.'

A tiny, considering pause. 'Why not. Somewhere nice and quiet.'

'No. Somewhere nice and public.'

The Russian exploded. 'You don't get to decide how this fucking goes, cocksucker!'

'The deal's off then.' As he said the words, Janusz could feel his heart bouncing around behind his ribs like a rubber ball – but he knew he couldn't give in. Agreeing to do the swap in the middle of nowhere would be tantamount to suicide. Whoever was the final recipient of the dirty money sluicing through the labyrinthine pipework of international bank accounts recorded on the data stick, he would clearly go to any lengths to keep the information under wraps. Which meant that even after the Russian got what he'd been sent to recover, he might still be under orders to eliminate Janusz and Kasia.

The guy swore to himself in Russian. 'Why don't we do it in Trafalgar Square?' he sneered. 'We can feed the pigeons afterwards.'

'I'll choose the place.'

'What makes you think I'd let you do that, Polak?'

'Because I know London and you don't.'

Janusz said nothing. He could hear the guy rethinking his calculations.

'Okay. Text me the place and *I'll* decide if it's okay. We do it tomorrow at dawn.'

'Okay.'

'And the "inconvenient husband" – where can I find him?'

'I'll tell you after I see the girl – he's not going anywhere.'

'He'd better not be.' The guy laughed suddenly. 'I'll be doing you a favour: no need to waste money on a pricy divorce.'

'Works for me.'

'I'll bet it does. And Polak – I don't need to tell you what happens if I sniff cop anywhere tomorrow?'

'I hate the fucking cops.' Janusz's words rang with unfeigned hostility.

'Good.' The hint of a sigh came down the line. 'Let's get this over and done with.' There was a weary note in his voice, as if he were sick and tired of the whole business. Janusz was struck by a bizarre notion: maybe the ex-Spetsnaz hard man was homesick, pining for his Siberian Forest Cat.

Thirty-Eight

Joey Duff's room in the private wing of St Margaret's Hospital in Epping wasn't hard to spot, thought Kershaw: it was the only one with an armed cop standing outside, albeit at a discreet distance. Duff had only just regained consciousness since being admitted the previous night but his doctors had agreed, after a bit of persuasion, that their patient could manage a brief chat with police about what had happened at the electricity substation.

'He's using the name Gerald Doherty,' Streaky told Kershaw in a murmur as they neared his room.

'So he has no idea that we know his identity?'

'Well, he's going to be wondering why the cops turned up at his hidey-hole in Epping Forest. But if he refuses to speak to us it only looks more suspicious. He's just got to tough it out and hope we don't know who he is and what he's been up to.'

Gerald, aka Joey, greeted his visitors civilly enough: if he remembered either of them from the previous night, he was making a good show of hiding it, thought Kershaw.

'Right then, Mr ...' Streaky allowed a blank look to come over his face.

'Doherty.' Kershaw noticed that the whites of Duff's eyes were a uniform red – the result of the dozens of tiny haemorrhages sustained during his strangulation. *Petechiae* – that was what pathologists called them, she remembered. His recent brush with death had also left a band of livid bruising around his throat, curving up behind his right ear.

'Ah yes. Sorry, Mr Doherty. We just wanted to get a handle on what happened to you in, er ...' Streaky shuffled paperwork on his lap, doing a solid impression of an old lag dragged out of a warm office to do a tick box job. '... Epping Forest.'

'It's obvious, isn't it, officer?' His voice came in a sibilant rasp, presumably, thought Kershaw, a result of the damage to his throat.

'Obvious?'

'I wanted to end it all.'

'I'm sorry to hear that.' Streaky didn't actually stifle a yawn but he might as well have done. 'Why was that then?'

Duff trotted out a hard luck story involving getting dumped by his girlfriend and money troubles, all of which had led to him becoming homeless, and finally, to deciding to top himself.

'So, this substation you were found in,' Streaky went on. 'You say you'd been sleeping rough there?'

'That's right.' His smile was insincere beneath his stony stare. 'I was wondering, officer – who was it called the police?'

'I wouldn't know,' said Streaky, shrugging. 'I know there's a big traveller problem in Epping – the forest

269

authorities are always on the lookout for trespassers.' He went back to his notes. 'So, was there anyone else kipping down in the substation?'

Duff's gaze flickered between the two of them but evidently found nothing in their glazed expressions to alarm him. 'Not that I know of. 'Course, there might have been someone else using it before I got there.'

'Fair point.'

'Where did you say you were from, officer?'

Meaning which police station, thought Kershaw. If Streaky told him Walthamstow rather than Epping, he'd be bound to suss this was more than just a routine enquiry by Essex Police.

'I'm from the West Country, originally,' said Streaky, deliberately misunderstanding the question. He turned to frown at Kershaw. 'Have you got that report?'

'I think it's in your file, Sarge.'

'No, it isn't … Oh, yes, here it is.' He glanced at Duff. 'The medical report says that you'd suffered recent burns to your abdomen?'

'I was into self-harming.'

'And the plastic ties around your wrists?'

'Yeah, I put them on myself.' Putting his wrists together and raising them to his lips, Duff mimed the act of pulling the ties tight with his teeth. 'In case I changed my mind once I was up there.'

It was almost impressive, thought Kershaw. In the short time Duff had been awake, he'd already constructed a near-plausible explanation for the way they'd found him.

He massaged his throat. 'I'm not being funny, officer, but is there much more of this? I'm getting tired.'

'Just a couple more questions and we'll be out of your hair.' Streaky lifted one buttock from his chair and fumbled with his trousers, apparently extracting his underpants from the crack of his backside. 'Just so I'm clear, you fixed the belt up first? And then got up there and got your head through the noose.' Duff nodded. 'Do you recall how you got yourself up there?'

Duff's gaze wavered.

'Was it on the filing cabinet mentioned here in the report from the scene?'

'Yeah, that's it, I climbed up on the cabinet.'

Streaky lifted a gingery eyebrow. 'That was quite a feat.'

'Yeah, well, when you're desperate.' Duff hadn't noticed a subtle shift in his questioner's manner.

'You are pretty tall, though,' Streaky conceded.

'Six foot one. Why?'

Streaky looked down at the map of the crime scene. 'Not eight foot one?'

'Come again?'

'PC Kershaw here measured the distance between the noose and the cabinet.'

Duff stared at her, as if he'd only really noticed the blonde girl for the first time.

'What was the distance again?' Streaky asked her.

'Two and a half metres, Sarge.'

'It can't have been.' The face in the hospital bed darkened.

'I'm afraid it was, Mr Duff.'

He was about to say something but then he clocked the use of his name, and his mouth snapped shut again.

'It's a cock and bull story, isn't it, Mr Duff?' said Streaky pleasantly.

'No comment.'

'I think somebody whacked you over the head and then strung you up with your own belt. You ought to be thanking me and Kershaw here – the docs said you only had minutes to live once you were up there. We got there in the nick of time, I'd say.'

'No comment.'

Streaky dropped the light-hearted tone. 'We have very good reason to believe that you had company in that substation. Female company – of the non-consenting variety.'

Folding his arms, Duff drilled him with a stare.

'A lady who wore black nail varnish,' Streaky continued. 'Forensics are running DNA tests as we speak.'

'I want my brief.'

'I'll bet you do.' Streaky turned to Kershaw. 'Do the honours, PC Kershaw.'

'Joseph Duff, I am arresting you for the suspected abduction of Kasia Fisher, on or about March the tenth. You do not have to say anything. However, it may harm your defence if you do not mention when questioned something which you later rely on in court ...'

Thirty-Nine

Kershaw followed Streaky down the hospital corridor, having to perform the occasional skip-step to keep up with him.

'I want a second armed guard on that room – I don't trust that bastard not to pull something,' said Streaky. 'And chase up the lab for the results on the water bottle and the nail, will you? We need a match to Kasia's DNA if we're going to charge him in the next twenty-four hours.' He slowed down to let her catch up. 'On second thoughts, I'd better get Ackroyd to do it.' Seeing her crestfallen look, he said, 'There's already whingeing in the ranks.' He adopted a whiny, little girl's voice. '"*Why is she going out on a shout when she's not even a detective, Sarge?*"'

Kershaw bit her lip. 'What about Kiszka, Sarge?'

'What about him?'

She pictured again the way he'd raced out of the interview – like there was somewhere he needed to be. 'He knows *something* about what's going on – I'm sure of it. He might even know who took Kasia.'

'You could be right,' he said, 'but we can't prove it.'

They'd reached the hospital car park now, Streaky's car greeting him with a chirrup.

'Why don't I go and talk to him, on his home turf?' she persisted. 'Try to persuade him that if he has any idea where she is, he could use some firepower on his side.'

'I'm not convinced that he shares your touching faith in the armed wing of our glorious organisation,' said Streaky, opening his car door. 'On the other hand, if you were to speak to him, entirely in an unofficial capacity, of course, I suppose he might let something slip.' He sucked his teeth. 'He does fancy the pants off you, after all.'

And with that parting shot, he climbed into the driving seat leaving Kershaw standing there, a raspberry-red tide climbing her cheeks, wondering if what he'd said was true.

Forty minutes later, she arrived outside Kiszka's apartment block. Deciding that ringing his bell would only risk getting a knockback, she hung around outside until she saw a delivery guy arrive. When he was buzzed in, she tucked behind him with a smile and a routine thank you as if she lived there.

Remembering Kiszka's hostility during the interview, she braced herself for a torrent of abuse when he opened his door. Instead, he stood aside, inviting her in with a laconic gesture. In the living room, he stood with his back to her, looking out of the bay window. It was the first time, she noticed, with a little pang of sadness, that he hadn't invited her to sit or offered her coffee.

'Look, Janusz, I can understand I'm not exactly flavour of the month with you at the moment.' She left a pause, which he didn't use to contradict her. 'But you need to hear me out. You've got to realise that once people started dropping dead all over East London, it was inevitable that the police were going to get involved. I couldn't stop that happening – even if I wanted to.'

She stared at that broad back. There was something in the slope of his shoulders that felt different today. When he turned to face her, she squinted at him, trying to make out his expression, backlit by the fading light.

'It's not your fault, darling,' he said. 'You have a job to do. I know it's not personal.'

That 'darling' triggered a flare of irritation, but it was the last bit that really stung. She pushed down the feeling. 'I'm going completely off the record here,' she said. 'But I wanted to be the one to tell you that we've arrested Joey Duff for abducting Kasia. There's a good chance we've got enough to charge him.'

'Congratulations. I'm sure that would be a great comfort to Kasia, if she were in a position to hear of it.'

'Janusz, you surely know we're focused on the same outcome as you here. All we want is to find Kasia.'

'It's not quite "all", though, is it?' he said, tipping his head to one side. 'You want to see the "bad guy" incarcerated.'

'And you don't?'

He lifted a big hand, let it fall. 'In TV cop shows, sure. In real life? It's not always possible.'

The setting sun sank behind a cloud, allowing Kershaw to see his face properly. She was shocked to see how he looked – the wrinkles at the corners of his eyes etched deeper by a look of profound melancholy.

'What's wrong?' She felt an impulse to go over and give him a hug, but stopped herself. Something made her say, 'You're not planning to ... kill someone, are you?'

Later that evening, Janusz would reflect that the girl *detektyw* had hit the nail on the head – even if she had no clue about his intended victim. For the moment, though, he just shook his head.

'Janusz, I can see that something's up. There must be something I can do to help.'

'You need to go now.'

She didn't move for a moment. 'Okay. But I want you to know you can call me anytime, even if it's the middle of the night.'

It was a relief for Janusz finally to close the door behind the girl *detektyw* and return to his own thoughts. Ever since the call with the Spetsnaz *skurwiel*, he'd been wrestling with a dilemma that was making his insides churn.

What to do about Steve?

The Russian had made it clear that he was expecting Janusz to deliver Steve's current location as part of the deal to ensure Kasia's safe return – and there could be little doubt of the fate he had planned for the small-time hoodlum who'd caused such a shit-storm of trouble.

Of course, after he'd got Kasia back, Janusz could warn Steve, tell him that his only hope of survival was to leave the caravan and go on the run. But whichever way he played out this scenario, it was just too risky. If the Russian so much as suspected a double-cross – or caught up with Steve and got him to talk – then Janusz and Kasia would be next in line for his vengeance.

Janusz had told himself a hundred times that this whole mess was of Steve's making, that it was he who had put Kasia's life in danger in the first place. Yet none of it made him feel any better about being the emissary of another man's death. Because no matter how many times he played it out in his head, the answer came back the same.

Save Kasia. Sacrifice Steve.

After putting in a call to the caravan office, he left a message with the old woman who ran the place, and waited. Ten minutes later, the phone rang.

'It's me,' said Steve.

'I wanted to let you know that there have been some developments.'

'Have you found Kasia?' Steve's voice dropped to a murmur – the old biddy was probably hovering, trying to listen in. 'Is she okay?'

'I'm working on it,' said Janusz. 'I should have news tomorrow.' He hesitated. 'It's important that you stay in the caravan all day, okay?'

As Steve started to burble his thanks, Janusz hung up.

Forty

At 5.45 a.m. the following day, Janusz was in the back of a cab, turning off Poplar Street towards the Blackwall roundabout. One hand was wrapped around the carrier bag of dirty money retrieved from beneath his floorboards, while the other delved inside his greatcoat for perhaps the twentieth time, clasping the bullet-shaped data stick like a talisman. Through the windscreen, the sky had lightened to a dishcloth grey and looked like it planned to stay that way for the rest of the day.

Coming up with a rendezvous location that would be sufficiently busy at six in the morning to head off any rough stuff by the Spetsnaz *skurwiel* was enough of a challenge, but it also had to be a place where nobody would pay them too much attention. That ruled out any tourist hotspot at a stroke: the last thing he needed was a bunch of Japanese sightseers taking snaps of him and the Russian with their iPhones.

In the rear view mirror, hung with what Janusz took to be a Koranic inscription, the cab driver – a young Asian guy – shot him an uncertain look.

'You sure you want the fish market, yeah, bro?'

'Yep.'

'You buying some fish, innit?'

'No, I'm … meeting somebody.' Janusz had managed to head off any chit-chat during the journey but now they were nearing their destination, the guy's curiosity was clearly getting the better of him.

'They do amazing king prawns – my mum buys them in five-kilo bags.'

'I'll bear it in mind.'

The cantilevered roof of Billingsgate Market, an unlovely wedge of corrugated iron painted beige, came into view ahead.

'You got a friend who works here, that's it, yeah?'

'That's right. You're going to park up and wait for me, okay?'

'Yeah. Extra twenty for the wait, you said, righ'?'

'Yes. And turn the car around, would you, so we're ready to leave? We'll be in a hurry.'

As Janusz climbed out of the cab he was assailed by the ozone scent of fresh fish – a smell that pitched him back to his childhood, playing on the harbourside at Gdansk. Before he'd reached the entrance to the market, a horn sounded behind him. It was the cab driver.

'What is it?' he asked.

'Have you got a quid for the car park, bro?'

Having been open since 4 a.m., the market should be entering its final act, but the aisles were still heaving with customers and the competing shouts of traders ricocheted off the iron roof. Janusz shuddered: he had an intense aversion to crowds. As he shouldered his way down the thronged central aisle, he was jostled by an elderly

Chinese lady haggling noisily over a big ugly fish with whiskers. Then a red-faced Cockney boomed in his ear, 'Get your clams, two bags for a fiver!' making his blood pressure rocket.

He was aware of another feeling, too – the flutter in his belly he got when he was about to see Kasia. This time there was fear mingled with the anticipation: would she be okay? What about the baby – their baby? The prospect of having to wait even minutes before finding out felt almost unbearable.

The rendezvous Janusz had proposed was outside the greasy spoon in one corner of the market, chosen because he knew it would be crowded with market traders grabbing a cup of tea and a bacon roll. He took up position with his back to the market's outer wall and a few anxious moments later, the short and stocky figure of the Russian materialised from his right. He appeared to be alone.

'Where is she?' growled Janusz.

'Calm down, Polak. She's not far away, she's just not feeling up to public appearances right now.'

'If you've laid a hand ...'

'Keep your fucking hair on,' there was an aggrieved note in the Russian's anger – like someone who was clearing up a mess not of his making. 'It wasn't me who had her off her tits on *narkotiki* for a week.' He lifted his chin, imperious. 'Where's the article?'

Janusz shook his head. 'Not until I've seen her.'

The Russian turned his weather-beaten face up to Janusz, his gaze suddenly murderous. 'Show it to me right now,' he said under his breath, 'or go buy your girlfriend a coffin.'

The constant traffic of porters and traders going to and

fro showed not the least interest in the odd couple standing against the wall, but Janusz had no doubt that if the Russian tried anything, he'd disappear under a scrum of well-built Cockneys before getting even halfway to the exit. He produced the oversized bullet from his inside pocket, opening his big fist briefly to allow the guy a glimpse.

The Russian gave a single nod. 'Follow me,' he said, pulling his phone out as he walked and tapping the screen.

After a beat, Janusz obeyed – *what choice did he have?* – and the pair weaved their way through the fishy scrum towards the entrance. As they emerged, a Mercedes van, brand-new, clearly a rental, pulled up to the right of the market building. Janusz was glad to see, even here, a steady trickle of porters through the market's portal, wheeling boxes to waiting vehicles.

The Russian spoke to the driver through the open passenger window. Then, standing back, he invited Janusz to look into the back with a mock-chivalrous gesture. In the driver's seat, a young guy frowned down at his iPhone, ignoring him. Tensing himself against a possible ambush, Janusz leaned in just as far as was necessary to see into the back.

His eyes took a second to adjust to the gloom. Then he saw her. She lay curled in the foetal position on a piece of foam, her eyes blindfolded with blue plastic. Her face was the colour of buttermilk, but for a grey rectangle of what looked like gaffer tape over her mouth – a sight that made him grind his teeth. Worst of all, she was utterly still. Janusz felt the sudden bloom of sweat on his upper lip.

'Kasia?' His voice cracked on the upward inflection like a pubescent boy's. There passed what seemed like a yawning aeon. Then he saw her head move, just a fraction.

Dragging his gaze from her, he turned back to the Russian, and handed him the carrier bag of cash. Then, pulling out the data stick he held it up between them. 'Open up the back and it's all yours.'

The Russian's eyes narrowed. 'Where's Fisher?' he asked.

Janusz turned away from the van, so that Kasia wouldn't hear him, and spoke under his breath. 'Sea View Caravan Park in Southend. Plot 17.'

The guy checked his watch, before leaning in the passenger window to ask the driver something in Russian. Picking up the word *aeroport* and a flight time, Janusz gathered that he was checking that they'd have time to go to Southend and still make the afternoon flight.

When the Russian held out his hand for the stick, Janusz gave it up.

He juggled it in his palm for a moment before taking a step closer to Janusz. 'I'm curious,' he said, in a murmur. 'What's on here?'

Meeting his eyes squarely, Janusz said, 'I didn't look.'

'Come on. You must have been tempted.' The guy wore a half-smile, but his gaze was unblinking.

Janusz snorted, incredulous. 'Not remotely. I'm looking forward to collecting my old age pension.'

The Russian turned the bullet shape in his fingers. 'If this thing has been opened, I'm told it's child's play to find out.'

282

Janusz gave an unworried shrug. But inside he was praying that Stefan was right when he promised that the data stick's memory would bear no trace of it having been accessed.

A barely perceptible move of the guy's head was followed by the soft but unmistakable clunk of the boot release mechanism.

Janusz strode to the van's rear doors. Within seconds, Kasia was in his arms. Holding her up, he peeled the tape from her mouth, all the time murmuring words of reassurance – but this time there was no response. He pressed his lips to her hair: she smelled musty, unwashed – with a chemical undertone – *but she smelled of Kasia*.

As he chafed her pale cheeks, trying to rouse her, the driver appeared and, after slamming the rear doors, disappeared again. Next thing Janusz knew, the van was slewing around in reverse, bringing him face-to-face with the Russian through his open window. It took Janusz a beat to realise that the guy had a gun levelled at his chest.

He felt his insides plummet like a broken lift. The weapon was a .22 pistol with a silencer screwed onto the barrel, the type of thing it was easy enough to pick up in an East End boozer. He had to fight the instinct to hold Kasia closer – as if that could protect her from a bullet.

'I hope you've got plenty of time to decontaminate yourself,' he told the guy, his voice sounding way cooler than he felt.

The Russian's face creased, uncomprehending.

'Didn't you know? All UK airports have gunshot residue sensors now,' Janusz went on. 'If you try to board a flight after firing that thing, you'll set off alarms all over the place.'

Janusz could see the cogs whirring behind the man's eyes as he weighed up this information, wondering whether it was for real.

Suddenly, his deliberations were interrupted.

'Oi! You!' – the angry shout came from the other side of the van.

The Russian slipped the hand holding the gun inside his jacket just as a big round face loomed in the driver's open window. 'You can't park here, sunshine, not without a permit.' The fat man, who was wearing porter's overalls, took no notice of Janusz on the other side of the van, and his vantage point wouldn't allow him to see Kasia.

There was an agonising moment of silence during which Janusz could sense the Russian recalculating the risk-and-reward equation of the evolving situation. As he leaned across the driver towards the porter, his gun hand still hidden, Janusz held his breath.

'Sorry, friend,' he told him. 'We're just leaving.'

The guy grunted and crossed his arms, evidently planning to stay put until the van departed.

The Russian turned his pockmarked face back to Janusz. 'You and your lady friend just got lucky, Polak,' he said under his breath. He seemed unperturbed – amused, almost – by the turn of events. 'But you owe me. Next time I'm in London, I'll be calling in the favour.' Without waiting for an answer, he nodded to the driver and the van sped away.

'What the fuck ...?' This from the porter who had just taken in the scene revealed by the van's departure – a big bastard in a military coat holding an unconscious woman in his arms.

Janusz ignored him: Kasia's eyes had just drifted open. As they looked at one another, he saw recognition crystallise in her green-amber gaze. *Dzieki Bogu!* A great wave of relief enveloped him.

Seeing her cracked lips moving, he bent his head to hers. 'What is it, *kochanie*?'

It took him a moment to make out her slurred words: 'I'm so sorry, Janusz.'

Forty-One

At Whitechapel Hospital, doctors whisked Kasia – who was still drifting in and out of consciousness – into resus.

Janusz found himself consigned to the 'relatives room' along with Jim, the Billingsgate porter, who had insisted on coming in the cab with them, no doubt because – initially, at least – he was suspicious of the big Pole who claimed to be the boyfriend. Now they sat in companionable silence, waiting for news, Jim reading his copy of *The Sun*, his overalls smelling like a fishing smack.

Finally, a doctor arrived carrying a clipboard, wanting to ask Janusz some questions.

'I'll make myself scarce, mate,' said Jim the porter, getting to his feet. 'Let you talk in private.' Janusz stood, too, and shook his hand in grateful farewell.

'You're her boyfriend, is that right, Mr Kiss-zaka?' asked the doctor – who appeared to Janusz to be about five years older than Bobek. 'You told the nurses you have no idea what drugs she took?'

'She didn't *take* them, they were given to her against her will.'

He made a note. 'And you don't have any idea what they were?'

'No. She was kidnapped. It would have been something to keep her knocked out, I guess.'

The teenage doctor nodded. 'Only toxicology tests will tell us for sure, but from her symptoms I'd say she's most likely suffering from a Rohypnol overdose.'

'The rape drug?'

'Yes, but I wouldn't read anything into that. She's had a few bumps and grazes, but no injuries of the kind we usually see in cases of sexual assault.'

'She is going to be all right, isn't she?' Janusz had to make an effort not to make it sound like a threat.

'I'd say she's out of immediate danger,' said the doctor, eyeing the unkempt-looking boyfriend: the police would be wanting to question him. 'But we will need to monitor her breathing and blood pressure over the next couple of days, while she detoxifies.'

Janusz leaned back in the chair, feeling the weight of a small planet lift from his shoulders, and passed a hand over his face. 'Can I see her?'

'She's sleeping now, but if you'd like to leave your number we'll let you know when she's well enough for visitors.'

'What about the baby?'

'We examined her after you told us. There's nothing to suggest that the pregnancy is at risk.'

The doctor was touched to see the smile that spread across the boyfriend's jaw, transforming his stern expression.

After he'd left, Janusz just sat there, feeling his muscles unknot themselves as the mental torment of the last nine days began to dissipate. There was only one thing clouding his sense of relief: the words Kasia had said to him that morning, in her brief moment of consciousness – words that he'd been puzzling over ever since.

What could she possibly have to be sorry about?

Forty-Two

Some forty miles from Whitechapel Hospital, on the Essex coast, the skies were brightening, promising a fine and dry spring day, although the bitterly cold east wind that shrieked in off the North Sea was bending and battering the trees behind the beach into submission.

In the centre of Southend, a gleaming Mercedes van slowed as it approached a junction on the A13. The older of the two men inside consulted his phone – apparently checking the route. After a brief exchange with the driver, the van rejoined the stream of traffic, its indicator flashing, and slid into the right-hand lane for the turnoff to the coast road.

Steve Fisher rolled a cigarette using the contents of a couple of discarded dog ends retrieved from the bin. He'd smoked his last fag in the early hours, but with Kiszka making such a big deal of him staying in the caravan, he hadn't dared to risk the fifteen-minute walk to the petrol station in case he missed him. He wasn't even sure whether Kiszka was going to call the old bat in the office with news, or turn up in person.

As he poured boiling water onto a teabag, he wondered whether sending his phone to Glasgow, to put the mockers on anyone tracing the signal, had been the right thing to do. After getting on for two weeks with only a crappy old radio for company, he was going stir crazy. Settling himself at the table with his brew, he lit his roll-up. *Yeah*, he decided, you couldn't be too careful – not with some fucking nutter going round knocking off his mates. Thinking for a moment about Jared, and poor old Bill, he felt a rush of self-pity: no matter how hard he tried, everything he did always seemed to turn to shit.

He'd given up trying to work out why they'd died and why he might be next. All he could do now was to rely on Kiszka to do the business. The big ugly bastard might have a seriously high opinion of himself – not to mention a nasty temper – but even Steve had to admit that if anyone was going to rescue Kasia, it would be him.

The Mercedes van carrying the two men came down the B-road that ran northeast out of town – its dawdling speed suggesting they were on the lookout for something. A few minutes later, the van pulled up at the side of the road, just beyond the entrance to a driveway. The older man, solidly built and with a reddened, weather-beaten face, climbed down from the van and walked back towards the driveway. He went over to a faded sign, his boots crunching on the gravel. Reading the words 'Sea View Caravan Park', he turned to the driver and gave a single nod. Apparently, they had found their destination.

Steve chucked half his brew undrunk down the tiny sink in the kitchen – he hated tea without sugar, another thing he'd run out of – and started fiddling with the tuning knob on the radio, trying to get a decent signal. After a few moments of nothing but shash, he picked it up and threw it at the wall. Staring at the wreckage, he felt a twinge of regret – it probably just needed new batteries. Then his expression brightened as he remembered the porn mag he'd bought a few days ago at the garage. He was about to head for the bedroom to retrieve it, when he froze. He stood stock-still, ears cocked.

He could've sworn he'd heard something in the distance. Something that sounded a lot like the distinctive crackle of tyres on gravel, driving slowly and cautiously. But now he couldn't hear anything except the wind howling up from the beach, rattling the branches of the trees.

Seven minutes later, Steve had barely started in on his porn mag when it happened.

Crack-crack! Two bangs from the caravan's door. *Fuck!* Next thing he knew he was cowering on the floor, cradling his head, half deafened. He pressed his eyes tight closed, the skin on his neck crawling, expecting a bullet in the back of the head. Through the ringing in his ears he became dimly aware of shouting, and then someone kicked him in the leg. His hearing recovered enough for him to make out what was being shouted.

'Armed Police! Spread your legs and put your hands out to the sides. Do it *now*!'

And he felt his mouth curve into a stupid grin.

After examining the sign, the weather-beaten man started to turn, about to head back to the van, when something caught his attention. Tensing, he appeared to squint down the tree-lined drive. At the farthest end stood a parked car. As he watched, a dark-clad figure reached in and switched on its blue flashing light. He stared for a long moment, making out the fluttering tape across the road beyond the car, the dark shapes of other figures moving purposefully to and fro in the distance.

Cursing, he opened the van door and in one efficient movement swung himself up into the seat.

Forty-Three

Kershaw stood on the Southend seafront, mobile pressed to her ear, looking out over the North Sea. Across the bay, she could see the fat finger of the power station chimney on the Isle of Grain – its lazy skein of smoke looking almost romantic against the milky blue of the sky. She suddenly remembered, on a day out here when she was little, her dad telling her it was where they harvested rainbows, turning them into the bright pinks, yellows and greens of seaside rock.

'Thanks for that,' she said, when Adam Ackroyd, her former colleague from murder squad, came back on the line. She scribbled a note on her pad. 'Yeah, he's a bit busy at the moment,' she glanced back to see the Sarge emerging from the fish and chip shop carrying a carrier bag and hot drinks. 'But I'll give him the update.'

After hanging up, she lingered for a moment, listening to the sound of the incoming tide and the seagulls complaining overhead – and realised something. She wasn't going back to SCO19 – even if she did get signed off to carry a weapon again. It wasn't anything to do with the Kyle Furnell shooting, nor the fallout that followed it. *No.* It struck her that Paula the shrink had been right all along: the appeal of carrying a firearm had been a direct outcome of getting stabbed. Up until that point, she'd always felt invulnerable, somehow – but wherever her imaginary suit of armour had come from, she'd lost it along with her spleen.

Now though, having put herself – unarmed – into some dangerous situations on the Duff investigation, albeit with Streaky close at hand – she'd finally climbed back on the bike. Hard on the heels of this insight came a whole new worry: by chopping and changing at a crucial stage of her career, had she completely screwed her chances of becoming a detective again?

By the time she'd walked back along the promenade, Streaky had taken possession of a bench, his fish and chips already spread out on his ample lap. 'Rock eel,' he told her, handing over a fat, off-white package as if presenting the crown jewels. 'You don't see that very often these days.' The rich smell of the fat and the vinegar tang rising from the food made her stomach gurgle, making her realise it would be the first thing she'd eaten all day. The surprise call that had sent her and Streaky racing eastward to the seaside caravan park had come around 7 a.m., just as she'd been getting out of the shower.

'So did you get hold of your Polish boyfriend?' he asked, before folding three or four fat chips into his mouth.

'If you mean Kiszka, yes I did.'

'How does he explain this Billingsgate business then?' In the aftermath of the armed operation at Steve's caravan, Kershaw had got a text from Kiszka saying that Kasia was safe, and recovering from her ordeal in Whitechapel Hospital.

'He doesn't, well not believably, anyway.' Kershaw made a sardonic face. 'The way he tells it, he gets a call in the middle of the night from someone he's never met nor spoken to before, who tells him to go to Billingsgate Market at 0600 hours to collect Kasia.'

'Just like that.'

'Just like that.'

A seagull that had been inching closer flapped up onto the arm of the bench to make a cheeky grab for Streaky's chips, before he shooed it away with a sweep of his arm. 'And he says no money changed hands?'

'He claims not.'

'Do you believe him?'

She shook her head. 'He must have given them *something* in return. If they just wanted shot of her, then why not just dump her somewhere? Why would they risk handing over a kidnap victim in public?'

Streaky grunted his agreement. 'And of course, it didn't occur to him to share this dawn rendezvous with us?'

'He said his priority was getting Kasia back.' This was actually the diplomatic version. What Kiszka had *actually* said was that he'd had no intention of entrusting his girl-friend's rescue to a load of 'pumped up, trigger-happy cops', as he wanted to get her back without any holes in her.

Streaky conveyed a wedge of battered fish to his mouth and chewed thoughtfully. 'Does the handover story check out?'

'Yep. Adam got hold of some porter down there who saw it all.'

'Did he see anything change hands?'

'No.'

'I don't suppose he got a number plate?'

''Fraid not.'

Streaky sighed. 'So Kiszka did some kind of deal with the villain who strung up Joey Duff and took Kasia. What are the chances of persuading him to provide us with an identity, would you say?'

Her dry look was answer enough.

He pointed a chip at her. 'Did Adam get anywhere on the mysterious anonymous phone call?'

Early that morning, Walthamstow Police had received a call from a man who wouldn't give his name. He'd reported seeing 'a guy waving a gun around' in one of the caravans at the Sea View site. The caller had helpfully added that the man's name was Steve Fisher and that the information should be passed to Detective Sergeant Bacon without delay.

'Apparently, the operator said the caller sounded English,' she flicked through her notebook, 'but she also said the way he spoke was quite posh – "*like someone out of a black and white war movie*".'

They looked at each other.

'Kiszka denies making the call, of course?'

'Yep.'

'Has it been traced yet?'

'Call was made from a phone box in East London. At 0642.'

Streaky's chuckle held a tinge of admiration. 'Right after he'd got his girlfriend to the hospital.' He paused to take a draught of orange-coloured tea. 'Strictly speaking, of course, we should be looking to nail Kiszka on a charge of withholding and obstructing.'

'Uh-huh.'

'But the alternative view is that he's done us a favour.' Kershaw raised an enquiring eyebrow. 'Handing us a fugitive criminal who might just have the goods on Joey Duff. Not to mention his part in resolving a nasty abduction. How's Kasia doing, anyway?'

'Stable. I'm going down there later, see if the docs will let me talk to her.'

'Any chance of her being able to pick Joey Duff out of a lineup?' Streaky pulled out a bright yellow handkerchief to wipe his greasy lips.

'I wouldn't hold your breath. She was probably blindfolded most of the time and one of the main side effects of Rohypnol is memory loss.'

Streaky gave a snort of disgust. 'Hence its popularity with scumbags who don't mind their lady friends unconscious and drooling.'

'Yeah. Still, at least we've got Fisher.'

Setting her fish and chips aside half-finished, Kershaw wiped her fingers on the paper. That morning's raid on Fisher's caravan had been textbook. Cops from the armed unit at Boreham had used Hatton rounds to blow the front door off: known in the Job as 'Avon Calling', they were faster than a ram. By the time Kershaw and the Sarge got inside, Fisher had been on the deck, handcuffed to the leg of his dining table, shivering like a wet dog. He'd clearly been expecting a visit from the Grim Reaper, which made him unusually compliant – not to say grateful – at least to begin with. Once they'd started throwing questions at him – *What was he doing there? Who was he hiding from? Was Joey Duff after him?* – his responses became more and more monosyllabic, finally stuttering to a halt like a car running out of petrol.

'I'll be giving him a proper going-over this afternoon,' said Streaky. 'His brief's coming down the nick.'

'Can I attend the interview?'

'Yes, okay,' he sighed. 'I suppose one way or another, you know more about this clusterfuck than anyone.'

She folded her grease-stained paper into a neat package and slotted it into the litterbin next to the bench. 'Sarge?'

'Hmm?' Streaky had spread-eagled himself across the bench-back, eyes closed. He looked like an overweight ginger reptile basking in the sunshine.

'I know you were disappointed, when I left murder squad to go into firearms.' She paused, waiting for a response, but he appeared so immobile she wondered if he'd fallen asleep. 'Anyway, helping out on this case, it's made me reassess what I want to do. So I wanted to ask – I know I'd have to do some retraining – but in principle, would you ever consider having me back in the squad, as a detective?'

Opening one somnolent eye, he surveyed her, before closing it again. 'I don't know. I'd have to think about it.'

Kershaw swallowed, taken aback by the sudden burning sensation behind her eyes and nose.

Streaky opened the eye again and yawned. 'I've thought about it. The answer's yes.'

'The time is 5.45 p.m. and this is Detective Sergeant Bacon interviewing Steven Fisher. Also present is PC Natalie Kershaw ...'

Once the formalities were over, Streaky fixed Steve with his matiest grin.

'So, Steven. That must have been a nasty shock for you, getting your caravan door blown off its hinges by armed officers?'

He shrugged.

'*Boom!!*' Streaky clapped his hands together.

Steve flinched and his brief, a young guy in a tightly fitting suit, looked up from the iPad on which he was making notes to give Streaky a meaningful look.

'Sorry. I didn't mean to make you jump,' Streaky told Steve. 'Of course, if I was you I'd be pretty jumpy, too.' He widened his eyes for emphasis. 'Especially now your seaside hideout's been blown.'

Steve just stared at the ceiling.

'You know the phrase "between the Devil and the deep blue sea"?' Streaky mused. 'It just occurred to me that it describes your position perfectly.'

Steve shot his brief an uneasy look. He'd been all set to go straight 'no comment' on everything – but no one – not the gingernut Sergeant nor the little blonde bird had asked him anything yet.

'Either you're a prime suspect in the torture and murder of your close associates, Jared Bateman and Bill Boyce' – Streaky gave an inappropriate chuckle – 'or, they were killed by someone else, which means you're next on the list!'

'I never ...' Steve clamped his lips shut. 'No comment.'

Streaky paused to pull a rogue hair from one nostril, staring at it for a moment, before flicking it away. 'Would you say you have a fulfilling life, Steve?'

Steve's mouth opened, about to go 'no comment', but instead he stuck out his chin and said, 'Yeah, I do.'

'Will you miss it?'

The brief leaned forward. 'Are you planning to get onto the substantive matters, Sergeant? Or just play pointless games?'

'Oh, I think your client's survival *is* a substantive matter. Once he leaves these four walls, I'm afraid he's likely to become what our American friends call a "dead man walking".'

Steve's right knee started to jig up and down – a tic the Sarge always called '*the scumbag boogie*'.

'Here are the facts,' Streaky told him, suddenly deadly serious. 'You and your chums have upset some very nasty people – people capable of doing this,' he pushed a selection of close-up post-mortem photos across the table. 'For the benefit of the tape, I am showing Steven Fisher photographs of injuries sustained by his friends Jared Bateman and Bill Boyce.'

Steve pretended to examine his fingernails, but Kershaw could see his eyes flickering towards the snaps. His right knee was still doing its guilty dance, but faster now.

Kershaw piped up now, as planned. 'Steve, I don't need to tell you that Joey Duff is a very dangerous man. A man who we expect soon to be charging with the abduction of your wife.'

'Kasia?' Steve's head shot up. 'You've found her? Is she okay?'

The brief tried to catch Steve's gaze, but Kershaw had his full attention. 'He kept her tied up and drugged for nine days. Rohypnol. But she's recovering.'

'Thank God!' Steve pressed his hands together before his face, as though in devout prayer.

Aye aye, thought Kershaw. The marriage might be done and dusted from Kasia's point of view, but it was clear that Steve was still very much in love with his wife.

'Would you like to take a break?' the brief murmured to Steve – but getting no response.

'The trouble is,' Kershaw went on, 'the drugs mean she's unlikely to make a good witness. We want to see the man who hurt your wife put away for a very long time, Steve, and for that we need your help.'

Now Streaky pitched back in: 'You were in Duff's gang when they pulled the Felixstowe job – maybe only on the fringes, shifting the goods, but close enough to know he was the boss. Tell us what you know about his involvement.' As they watched, Steve's expression congealed into sullen prisoner mode. 'Did he ever phone you about it or talk to you directly?'

'No comment.'

Kershaw took over. 'You know the lorry driver Duff shot in that raid? He's got to have an operation next week, to have a colostomy bag fitted. It's pretty common, apparently, when you've been paralysed.'

Steve's shrug said *Life's a bitch*.

Kershaw leaned towards him. 'If we don't put Duff away, do you really think he'll let you just waltz back into your old life? After he kidnapped your wife?'

His eyes went from side to side, something in his expression shifting, as if inwardly, he conceded the point.

'Listen, Steve. We know you did some kind of job for him – and whatever it was kicked off all the killings. We're not looking to charge you with anything – we just want to stop anyone else dying.' He was looking at her now, taking in what she was saying. 'He's decided you're a loose end, Steve. And we all know how people like Duff deal with loose ends.'

'If you play ball with us, we can protect you,' said Streaky. 'Give us quality information to connect Duff to the Felixstowe job, and I'm confident we can get you into witness protection. Give you a fresh start, somewhere far away from the Duffs.'

Eyes narrowed, Steve appeared to be thinking it over.

Finally he said, 'Nah. I can look after myself.' His attempt at a cocky leer was lame, thought Kershaw, like something he'd practised in the mirror.

'What about Kasia's safety?'

'What about it?' he said sulkily. 'She's leaving me for that Polak.' He looked away but not before Kershaw caught a flicker of something in his expression.

Kasia was evidently Steve's weak spot. Now she just had to work out how to lean on it.

Forty-Four

The next day, Janusz was on his way to visit Kasia when he glimpsed the compact outline of Natalie Kershaw – a blonde guided missile – beetling down the hospital corridor towards him. Seeing that she had yet to notice him, he was gripped by a sudden urge to duck into one of the wards. He knew he couldn't avoid the inevitable grilling indefinitely, but in this place, preoccupied with Kasia's recovery, he felt *obnazony* – raw – less able to fend off her questions.

'Janusz!'

Too late. He raised a hand in reluctant acknowledgement: maybe it would be better to get it over with before visiting Kasia.

In the hospital canteen, Janusz asked her to find a table while he went to order the drinks, buying himself a bit of time to prepare for the interrogation. But when she took the cup of tea from him, the look in her grey-blue eyes seemed almost playful. It struck him that she looked much more relaxed – and healthier – than she had when he'd first asked for her help finding Kasia. That was what, just eight, nine days ago? It felt more like nine months.

He put his head on one side 'You look good. *Piekna*. New boyfriend?'

'Er, no-o,' said Kershaw, feeling a blush creep up her cheeks. She had no clue what *pee-ek-nah* might mean but she knew a compliment when she heard it. 'Maybe I'm just living a blameless life.' There was some truth in that, she realised: as well as cutting down on the booze, she'd even been back to the climbing wall – something she hadn't done in years. 'Anyway, never mind me – how's Kasia doing?'

He smiled into his tea. 'The medics say she's on the mend.' According to the nurse he'd spoken to, Kasia was conscious, if still drowsy, and coping well with the withdrawal from the Rohypnol.

'I'd like to have a chat with her today,' said Kershaw, 'see what she can remember while it's still fresh.'

'You can try – but the docs say she has almost no memory of who took her, if that's what you were hoping for.' He picked up on her troubled look. 'You said on the phone you've got DNA evidence, though? To prove that Kasia was in Duff's hideout?'

She half shrugged. 'We got a match off the water bottle, but the CPS say it might not be enough. Duff's brief is bound to argue that simply putting his client and Kasia in the same location doesn't prove beyond doubt that he kidnapped her.'

They sat in silence for a moment. 'You must know that we don't buy your handover story for a nanosecond,' she told him.

'What story?'

304

'The mystery call from the mysterious Mr X offering to deliver Kasia at the fish market – and asking for nothing in return.'

He shrugged. 'It's how it happened, darling.'

He always called her 'darling', Kershaw noticed, when he had something to hide.

'What about this call alerting us to where Steve Fisher was holed up?'

He shrugged. 'I wouldn't know anything about that.'

'It came from a call box in East London – a five-minute walk from Whitechapel Hospital, funnily enough.'

'It's a small world.'

Kershaw folded her arms. 'Just in theory, why do you think the person who gave us that tip-off made such a big deal of him having a firearm? Especially since he didn't have one.'

'Hypothetically?'

'Yes.'

He frowned. 'I suppose the mention of a gun would ensure the cops got there fast.'

'My conclusion exactly – but why the urgency?'

To stop Steve Fisher getting assassinated by a Russian psychol, thought Janusz.

'I wouldn't know,' he said.

After much soul-searching, Janusz had decided that tipping off the cops about Steve's whereabouts before the Russian could reach him was the only course of action that would allow him to preserve a sense of human decency. More selfishly, it meant that he'd be able to look Kasia in the eye without having to hide a terrible secret – a secret that would have cast a shadow over their future life together. Double-crossing the Russian had been a

305

risk, of course, but the guy did already know the cops were looking for Steve; and anyway, the idea that Janusz might tip off the police in order to protect his love rival would be a concept he'd find impossible to compute.

Kershaw scanned Janusz's face but found his expression about as readable as a granite cliff-face. It was clear from the timing of the tip-off, just after Kasia's release, that the two events were linked – but she couldn't for the life of her work out how.

'Come on, Janusz. Kasia's safe now. Can't you tell me a bit more about what's been going on?'

The plaintive note in her voice tugged at Janusz's conscience – she had risked her job to help him, after all, when he'd had nowhere else to turn.

'Look, Natalia. I'd love to,' he told her. 'But you need to take my word for it when I say that there are some people you'll never be able to reach.' Fingering the scab on his upper lip, he visualised the Russian, no doubt happily ensconced back home with his Siberian Forest Cat by now, enjoying the proceeds of his London mission.

She chewed at the side of a fingernail. 'What about the mysterious job that Steve did for Joey Duff? The one that led to his friends getting murdered?'

'What about it?'

'We can't find anything that fits the bill – there are no reports of armed robberies just before Steve went missing. Have you got any idea what it might have been?'

'How would that help?'

She lowered her voice. 'Joey Duff doesn't know it yet, but he's our prime suspect for shooting that lorry driver in Felixstowe. Anything that gives us an insight into his activities might help us put him away.' Leaning across the table, she fixed him with an intent look. 'Don't you want to see that bastard behind bars, after what he did to Kasia?'

Janusz had pulled out his cigar tin, and was turning it over and over in his fist. He had to admit that the idea of seeing the *skurwysyn* Duff punished for what he'd done to Kasia was a compelling prospect. 'Okay,' he said, finally. 'Off the record. Although I doubt it'll be much use.'

He laid it out for her as he saw it. How Joey Duff had returned from Australia to take control of the family firm – only to find Russian gangsters parking their tanks on the Duff family's lawn, muscling in on its criminal interests around Stratford. 'The way I see it, Joey Duff got word that the Russians were using a local flat as their stash house,' said Janusz. 'I think he decided enough was enough, and came up with a plan to turn the place over – to send the Russians a message that they weren't welcome.'

'*Foreigners go home.*'

He raised an eyebrow. 'A perennially popular sentiment.'

'Okay, I'm with you so far. But why would Duff hire a couple of low-level fences like Steve and Jared to do the job?'

Janusz pulled a sardonic grin. 'Because Russian gangsters have a certain reputation, and Joey Duff wasn't sure how they might respond.'

'So rather than risk using his usual crew, with its links to him, he sends in Steve and Jared like, like ... human minesweepers.'

'Yeah. He's hoping that the Russians will get the message and choose a less troublesome area.' Janusz lifted massive shoulders. 'But if the worst comes to the worst, Steve and Jared are dispensable.'

'So the stash – money, drugs, whatever – wasn't the main objective. This was about Joey Duff marking his territory.'

'A tactic which badly backfires. The Russians respond by sending an enforcer to find out who's behind the raid. He finds Jared and Bill and tortures them – but Jared pegs it before he talks, Bill doesn't know anything – and Steve's already done a runner.'

Kershaw's expression cleared as she pieced it together. 'Duff is frantic that Steve might put him in the frame with the Russians? So he abducts Kasia in a desperate attempt to reach him.'

'Yeah. Steve is the last thread linking Duff to the job and he wants it snapped – fast. But Steve's dumped his mobile and disappeared off the face of the earth.'

Kershaw nodded to herself. 'Do you have any clue what kind of racket the Russians were muscling in on? Prostitution? Drugs?'

Janusz frowned, recalling the carrier bag Steve had stolen from the flat above the launderette, the envelopes of cash with the scribbled first names and mysterious initials. Pulling out his mobile, he opened the memo he'd made, before handing it over to her. 'Do these initials mean anything to you?'

Kershaw read aloud: 'LB, M, ML, BH, CL ... I dunno. What context was this in?' – he gave her what her dad would have called an old-fashioned look – 'Well, LB is the abbreviation for a pound. Could ML be milli-litre, CL centi-litre? But BH doesn't sound like any measurement I can think of.'

Janusz was no more than mildly curious as to the nature of the racket – he knew it was irrelevant to the bigger picture. The thing that had turned a simple stash raid into something more murderous and far-reaching was the bullet-shaped data stick – or rather, its contents.

She handed him back his phone. 'If you're right, then these Russians of yours went to a shedload of trouble trying to find out who robbed them.' She bit her lip, frustrated. 'Whatever Steve stole from them, it must have been really valuable – but we didn't find anything when we searched his caravan.'

Time to change the subject. 'I nearly forgot,' he said, consulting his phone again. 'You might want to get DVLA to check out this registration number. U-A-5 I-L-Y.' He spelled out the number plate for the custard-yellow Porsche, which was no doubt still gathering dust in the car park under the flat in Stratford. 'I'm pretty sure the owner will turn out to be the unidentified dead guy your colleagues found in Victoria Park.' Had Vasily Vetrov not worked for some very nasty gangsters, his personalised number plate might have struck Janusz as almost poignant – an object lesson in human vanity rendered pointless by death.

'You mean the guy who was blowtorched and shot in the back of the neck?' Her eyes widened as she recalled something Nathan had said. 'He had Russian dental work!'

Janusz was enjoying the look on the girl *detektyw*'s face. 'So where does he fit in?' she asked.

'He was the Russians' accountant – he lived in the flat that got rolled. There's a lady in a Polish grocery shop nearby who can confirm his ID.'

'So he was the guy looking after the stash for the Russian crims?'

'Yeah.'

'And he paid the price for losing it.'

Not exactly, thought Janusz. But what he said was: 'That's certainly how it looks, isn't it?' After knocking back the last of his tea – now stone-cold – he tapped his cigar tin on the table. 'Listen, Natalia. I'm afraid I must go. I want to grab a smoke before I see Kasia.'

'Yeah, sure.' Then she stared at him.

'What?'

'Show me those initials again.'

He handed her the phone.

A moment later she raised her head to shoot him a triumphant grin.

'It's not BH. It's B *and* H.'

'Sorry?'

'B and H – Benson & Hedges. My Auntie Carol used to send me down the shop to buy them for her. Look,' she turned the phone's screen round so he could read it. 'LB – that's gotta be Lambert & Butler. M ...'

'Marlboro.'

'Yeah, of course. So ML must be Marlboro Lights. And CL – Camel Lights. The Russians were selling smuggled cigarettes.'

She was right, Janusz realised. Sky-high UK duty had made tobacco London's number one contraband item. He himself had bought Kasia cartons of Silk Cut in Asian corner shops and Polski *skleps* where he was known and trusted – even, a couple of times, from shady guys cruising the car park at Asda in Leyton.

'*Brawo*, Natalia,' said Janusz, clapping his hands softly in a round of solo applause.

'Incredible.' She shook her head. 'Three people dead because of a turf war over who gets to sell cheap fags to East Enders.'

'It's big business,' shrugged Janusz, getting to his feet, but Kershaw wasn't finished with him.

'Hang on a sec. We're hoping Steve might help us to nail Joey Duff for the Felixstowe job, shooting that lorry driver. Any idea how we might get him to talk?'

He looked down at her, a single line of worry stitched between her brows, and shook his head. 'Sorry, Natalia.'

'The Sarge is talking to the Home Office about giving him a new identity in exchange for turning witness. Do you think he might go for that?'

Janusz recalled Steve's twisted code of honour, the pride he took in having declined to turn grass when he'd been caught selling the stolen iPads. Then he tried to imagine him starting over, on his own, out of his East End comfort zone. Steve might have contemplated escaping to a new life in Spain, running a beach bar, but that plan had included Kasia, who possessed the necessary skills to make it work – skills that he lacked.

'No chance.'

'Could you talk to him?'

He let out a woof of laughter that turned heads at nearby tables. 'You're kidding! What makes you think he'd listen to the bastard who's setting up house with his wife?'

311

Forty-Five

Entering the ward, Janusz saw Kasia sitting up in bed, a sight which made him pause to cross himself and send up a prayer of thanks, something he'd done countless times since she'd been returned to him.

'*Czesc*, Janek.'

Although her words came in a rusty whisper, he couldn't help but grin – wan complexion and red-rimmed eyes aside, this was the first time that he'd seen her looking anything like her old self again. After he perched himself on the edge of the bedside armchair, an awkward silence fell, but that was hardly surprising given the presence of a nurse who was adding something to Kasia's drip. 'I'll be out of your way in a moment, sweetheart,' she told him with a wink.

Once the nurse had gone, he took a good look at her, as if committing her face to memory all over again. He noticed a tiny scar he'd never seen before at her hairline, too old to be the result of her recent trauma, but then she didn't usually wear her hair scraped back this way.

'How are you feeling?' he asked, at a loss for what else to say.

'*Fantastycznie*,' she said, pulling that lop-sided smile of hers – the first thing he'd noticed about her at their initial encounter, three years earlier.

'You'll be fine once you get out of this place,' he said, taking her little hand into his big mitt.

'Maybe.' Defocusing, her gaze drifted over his shoulder.

'You're freezing!' He chafed her hand between his, feeling the bones beneath the skin, the result of her enforced crash diet. 'When we get you home I'm going to make you a big pile of *kopytka* with wild mushroom sauce' – the tiny potato dumplings were her favourite comfort food – 'and Oskar's been helping me with getting the bathroom tiled and painted, so everything will be ready for you.'

'You are a good man, Janek. The best man I ever knew.'

He was alarmed to see tears fill her eyes. 'Kasiulka, don't! I know you've had a terrible time, but … it's over now.' He dropped his eyes to the hospital-blue coverlet, grasping for the right words: he'd always been hopeless at this kind of conversation. 'The rest … well, it's true what they say, you know. Time will heal it.'

Janusz stared, appalled and helpless, as Kasia's tears overflowed, two tracks running down her lovely face.

'Shhh,' he told her. 'It's my fault. I shouldn't have talked about you coming home when you're still not properly recovered.' He couldn't recall ever having seen Kasia in less than full control of herself. Of course, one heard about people suffering PTSD after terrible experiences, but he'd never have said she was the type.

313

'Did … something happen to you that you haven't told anyone about?' he asked, struck by a sudden intimation of what might be causing her such distress. 'You do know you could tell me, don't you?'

A silent but definite shake of the head.

Going to sit beside her on the bed, he put an arm around her narrow shoulders and pulling her closer, brushed away the tears dripping from her jawline. She leaned fiercely into him, pressing her wet cheek against his bristled one, but his efforts to console her only seemed to make things worse. He let her cry, then, making the kind of soothing noises he remembered making to Bobek when the boy had woken howling from some nightmare.

Minutes passed before Kasia peeled her face from his. Breathing deeply to still her tears, she wiped her cheeks flat-handed with a trace of her usual determination. 'Janusz, darling, there's something I have to tell you.' She met his gaze, her eyes bottomless wells of sorrow. 'I can't come home with you.'

'What?' He stared at her, a silly half-smile on his face.

'I won't be … I can't come to live with you. I'm so sorry, *moje kochanie.*'

All this was surely just some artefact of the drugs combined with the terrible ordeal she'd been through, Janusz told himself. 'Listen,' he said, 'there's no rush – I know you're still in a bad way …'

'… It's nothing to do with that.' She drew a shaky breath. 'I have to stay with Steve.'

'You're not making any sense, Kasiulka. You said you were dead set on leaving him this time.' He spun through his memory, recalling that even Steve had appeared to be convinced of her departure, at the caravan.

314

'I know. And I was. Nothing would have made me happier.'

'We'll still be happy!' Although Janusz managed a reassuring grin, he was aware of a dim roar starting up at the back of his head.

'*Nie*, Janek. You don't understand.' Her next words, when they came, fell like stones. 'I took an oath.'

Kurwa mac! The roar in Janusz's head grew louder. 'Was it that old fool Pietruski? Did he threaten you with hellfire and damnation? You know there are other priests, ones who will still give you communion – especially in London. I've heard of them.'

'He did speak to me, it's true – I ran into him on Highbury Fields after I left your apartment, the last time we saw each other.'

He must have been waiting for her there, the old bastard, thought Janusz with a surge of murderous rage.

'And?'

'And I told him I was leaving Steve.'

'Good for you. So why ...?'

'The promise that I made, it wasn't to him. It was to God.'

It came pouring out of her then. How she'd surfaced briefly from her Rohypnol stupor, tied hand and foot, being jolted around in the back of the kidnapper's van, and felt a tugging pain in her lower abdomen. How it had come to her with a terrible clarity that she was losing the baby.

'*Our baby*, Janusz,' she said fiercely, gripping his hand. 'I was going to lose our child.'

'But even if you had, we could still have had another!'

A single, sorrowing shake of her head. 'I haven't told you this before, but I already lost a little girl, years ago.'

315

The stillborn child Steve had mentioned at the caravan.

'You must see, Janek. I couldn't risk losing this one.'

'So what exactly did you promise the Almighty?'

'That I'd stay with Steve, try to make my marriage work. Please try to understand, Janek. I'm forty years old. It's probably my last chance.'

'Right. And you believe that God will keep his side of the deal.' Janusz made no effort to keep the ugly edge from his voice.

She lifted her chin. 'I'm still pregnant – the doctors say everything is all right.'

Janusz gave way then to a deluge of cold rage. 'And your God would prefer our child to be brought up in a loveless marriage, would he? By a man who isn't even his father? Let alone a pointless waste of oxygen like *Steve*?'

Kasia shook her head, mouth twisting to one side, a look that said there was no point explaining the nature of her faith to him: he might call himself a Catholic, but they both knew he'd always been more fellow traveller than true believer.

They sat side by side, no longer touching, the ten centimetres of coverlet between them seeming to Janusz's miserable gaze like an endless icy wasteland.

He was the first to break the silence. 'Kasia, *moj kotku*. Are you seriously telling me that you'd give up everything we have – our future happiness, raising our child together – for the sake of some superstitious promise?'

Her nod was barely discernible, but there was something so final in her expression, that he felt the last thread of hope snap inside him.

The woman who spoke to him next was no longer Kasia his lover, his life partner and hope of future happiness, but a kindly friend. 'This baby we made between us, Janek. That's the important thing. And I promise you this, on the soul of our child. One day, when she's old enough, I will tell her all about her wonderful father, so she can come and find you.'

As she reached out and took his hand, a gesture intended to fortify and comfort him, something struck Janusz with renewed and poignant force: the utter wrongheadedness of those who claimed that men were the unromantic sex.

Kasia

The dragging pain in her abdomen she'd felt in the back of her captor's van that day was far worse than anything else she'd had to endure. Not the pain itself, but the memories it stirred – and the searing knowledge of the loss it promised.

It pitched her back to that other, terrible day, seven years and seven months ago. The one that had ended with her gazing into the utterly still, serene face of her little girl, framed by a hospital blanket. Angelika. Named for the angels she was joining. The nurses had let her keep the baby for a while. She had combed her fine hair, rocked her and sung to her, before dressing her in the cardigan she'd bought to take her home in – the one with the bunny rabbits. Terrible, yes. And yet those last precious moments with her baby were still Kasia's most cherished memory.

The noise of the traffic outside had receded and the jolting became rougher – the van must have turned off the main road.

The thought of losing this child … Nie. That was something she could not contemplate. 'I will protect you, maluszku,' she told her. 'I swear it.'

Now they were coming to a stop. The man would give her another injection. Before that dark oblivion, Kasia knew what she had to do. Behind the blindfold, her eyes filled with tears.

'Father in Heaven,' she prayed. 'Ever-living source of all that is good. Help me to do your will …'

Forty-Six

Twelve days and what felt like a lifetime later, Janusz found himself at an airport in the depths of Kent – if a steel shed with a single runway even merited the term. He'd been met at reception by a guy with thinning hair and a purple birthmark like a thumbprint under one eye – presumably one of the witness protection cops – who'd shown him up to a private waiting room on the first floor. Now he stood at the floor to ceiling window, staring out over the airfield, a plastic cup of machine-made tea burning his fingers.

He'd rather be anywhere else in the world than here. The prospect of seeing Kasia leaving for a life God-knew-where felt as unbearable as it was pointless, gravel ground into a fresh wound. But the girl *detektyw* had been insistent – had said that Kasia's safety was at stake.

A moment later, Natalia came through the door.

'Is that the plane?' he asked, gesturing towards a Cessna parked on the apron, which was taking on fuel from a pocket-sized tanker. It had been raining off and on all morning but now the clouds were clearing and the plane's white paintwork, spot-lit in a shaft of sunshine, dazzled.

'Yeah.' She shot him a warning look. 'There's no point asking me where it's going, though: only their handlers know that.'

He snorted. 'I couldn't care less.'

She studied him out of the corner of her eye. He looked thinner, with new lines either side of his mouth, and even more rumpled than usual, but it was his tone of voice – roughened by a new bitterness – that caught her attention. He could be a grumpy old bastard, for sure, but there had always been a streak of wry humour never far beneath the scowl.

'I know this must be really difficult for you,' she said. 'But we both know Joey Duff will have people working 24/7 to find Steve, and at least this way you can be sure that Kasia will be safe.'

She'd be even safer if I'd let the Russian kill her husband when I had the chance, thought Janusz.

'What is it you want from me, exactly?' he asked.

'Tell Steve he's doing the right thing, turning Queen's Evidence against Joey Duff, and that going into witness protection is the only way to ensure their safety.'

'You said on the phone that he'd already informed on Duff – for shooting that lorry driver.'

She grimaced. 'He's given us enough to charge Duff with attempted murder and put him on remand, yes. But we've still got to get a conviction.'

Kasia's decision to stay with Steve Fisher had been bad news for Janusz but a lucky break for the investigation, Kershaw reflected. After Kasia left hospital, she and her husband had been whisked to a safe house a healthy distance from the capital. While negotiations with Fisher and his brief got underway, there were parallel meetings with the brass in London, who needed convincing that it was worth the cost of resettling the couple in order to take a ruthless armed gang off the grid.

It had finally dawned on Fisher that a fresh start somewhere far from the East End was the only safe option for him and his prodigal wife. He'd spilled the beans after one long, late night session, fingering Joey Duff as the leader of the gang who'd carried out the Felixstowe lorry heist. His statement gave a detailed account of his visit to a lock-up garage in Walthamstow where he'd overheard a man boasting about shooting the lorry driver – a man he'd gone on to positively identify as Joey Duff from a digital identity parade.

'So Steve's statement is the only evidence you've got?' asked Janusz.

'Not entirely. Luckily for us Duff was too stupid, or more likely, too arrogant, to have his secret lock-up properly cleared out,' Kershaw told Janusz. 'The crime scene guys found the remains of discarded packaging from the stolen shipment with his prints all over them.'

'It sounds as if you've got him over a barrel.'

She puffed out her cheeks in exasperation. 'You'd think so. But he'll have a shit-hot barrister, and without Steve's testimony, he'll probably get off with handling stolen goods.'

Janusz frowned. 'And you're worried that Steve's going to get cold feet, and change his story when it comes to trial.'

'I'm worried he'll change his mind *today*, and refuse to get on that plane,' she said, nodding out the window.

'Apparently he's been getting twitchy in the last few days, whingeing to his handler about being sent to "the sticks".'

'Isn't it his *wife* you should be talking to?' Janusz shook the last drops of cold tea into his mouth, before crushing the plastic cup in his fist. 'She's no idiot. She'll know it makes sense to keep his side of the bargain.'

'I have done, and she's on-side, especially with a baby on the way' – Kershaw rushed on, aware that this was dangerous territory – 'but well, actually it was Steve who asked to see you today.'

'What? Why?'

'I don't know. I got the impression that he feels the need to talk to someone who ... who inhabits his world.'

'Thank you very much.'

She rolled her eyes at him. 'Come on, Janusz. You know what I mean.'

On the face of it, Kiszka seemed like the last person Steve Fisher would listen to – but whenever his name came up, Kershaw sensed that, despite their history, Fisher viewed the big Pole with a wary respect.

'Okay,' said Janusz. 'But I need you to do me a favour.' Reaching into his inside coat pocket, he produced a large white envelope.

'What's in it?' she said, taking it from him somewhat reluctantly.

'Five grand. For Kasia. I want to make sure she has enough money of her own.'

After checking the envelope's contents, Kershaw nodded. 'No problem.'

They both fell silent. 'You know, I really appreciate you coming here today,' she told him. 'I'm sure the last couple of weeks must have been … awful for you.' Reaching out, she set her hand lightly on his shoulder. He flinched, apparently surprised, but didn't – as she'd half-expected – shake it off. 'Listen, Janusz. I want you to know that if you need someone to talk to, have a jar with – I'm there, okay?' His muscles felt tense under her hand, like that of some wild animal at bay. 'I'm not saying that as a cop – I'm saying it … as a mate.'

His profile gave nothing away, but he did give one of his grunts in which she thought she detected an acknowledgement – maybe even a hint of appreciation – for her offer of friendship. But a moment later, he turned to throw his destroyed cup into a nearby bin. 'Can we get this over with?' he said.

A couple of minutes later, Janusz heard the door open behind him.

'All right?' said Steve.

He didn't turn round.

A moment later, Steve joined him at the window. 'Christ,' he said nodding at the Cessna. 'They never said we was going on a toy plane.'

'Well, they're hardly likely to send you on Ryanair, are they?' said Janusz.

'Nah. Thank Christ for that!' Steve tried a matey chuckle: it wasn't convincing.

Janusz threw him an icy glance. Steve had shaved off his irritating demi-beard and was dressed respectably in a jacket and freshly pressed shirt – no doubt at his wife's insistence. Janusz was waylaid by a sudden image, pin-sharp: *Kasia ironing, in his living room – dressed only in a white slip*. He pushed it away.

'You wanted to see me,' he said flatly.

'Yeah. It's just, I wanted to thank you. For everything you did, for finding Kasia.'

Janusz clenched his jaw for a long moment before replying. 'Well, make sure you look after her this time, wherever it is you're going.'

'I wish I knew,' said Steve, his tone suddenly aggrieved. 'They won't even tell us what continent we're going to. I'm hardly likely to blab it to anyone, am I?'

Thank God they had the good sense not to tell him, thought Janusz. 'Look ... Steve,' he said, keeping his voice as civil as he could manage. 'This deal you've done with the cops, taking Kasia someplace where you'll both be safe – it's your only option, you know.'

'Maybe.' Steve fidgeted for a moment before bursting out: 'I still say we could go up north. I've got friends in Sheff ... *aargh!*'

Janusz had grabbed him by the lapels and had him pressed against the window. 'Listen to me,' he said, abandoning all attempts at diplomacy. 'The cops don't know this, but you pissed off some very serious people when you raided that flat. If you don't disappear, they will find you. Then they'll rip your head off and piss in the hole – if Joey Duff's goons don't get there first.'

'Okay, okay!'

'So don't delude yourself for a second that you can duck and dive your way out of this one. Personally? I couldn't give a shit if Duff or anyone else puts you in the morgue, but I do care about Kasia.'

Janusz fell silent, the subject of the child she was expecting hanging between them. He let go of Steve's jacket but held his gaze. 'Go where the cops tell you,' he said quietly. 'Be good to Kasia. Work hard. Be somebody the child can respect.' Their eyes flickered apart. 'You're getting a second chance you don't deserve – don't fuck it up.'

Steve straightened his jacket with a certain amount of dignity. 'I know you don't think much of me,' he said. 'Which is fair enough, I suppose. But I'm going to do things right this time. I'm not going to let anyone down.'

Janusz turned to look out the window at the Cessna; the fuel tanker had disappeared and a man in black trousers and a white shirt with epaulettes, presumably the pilot, was giving the plane the once over.

'Good,' he told Steve out of the side of his mouth. 'Because if you do, I'll find you and kill you myself.'

After Steve left, Janusz knew he ought to go, too. No possible good could come of watching Kasia climb aboard that plane. He willed himself to leave. But five minutes passed and he was still standing at the window.

All of a sudden, she was there below him, a slender figure in long boots and her favourite black coat, walking out across the apron a step or two behind Steve. His heart lurched in his chest as he recalled the time he'd watched her crossing Highbury Fields from the window of his apartment. Then, her lilting step had spoken of optimism and hope for the future; now, although she was still the most graceful woman he'd ever seen, there hung about her the air of someone embarking on an unwished-for duty.

It occurred to Janusz that if he leaned forward and rapped on the glass, she'd still be close enough to hear him. He had to thrust his bunched fists into his coat pockets in order to stop himself. *What would be the point?*

The plane door closed silently behind her, and still Janusz found he couldn't walk away. He closed his eyes and, seconds later, heard the low whirr of the engine as the plane taxied to its take-off position, then the hike in engine pitch as the pilot throttled up and started to speed down the runway.

When he opened his eyes again it was already a distant white dot in the vastness of a pale-grey English sky.

Forty-Seven

At 0900 hours the following day, Kershaw settled herself in her usual armchair opposite Paula the shrink.

'I've decided something,' she said. 'I'm not going back to SCO19.'

Paula made one of her trademark noises to indicate moderate interest but it was clear to Kershaw that she'd been caught unawares.

'I've surprised you,' she said with a grin.

'Perhaps a little. You've always seemed so determined to go back to firearms.'

'I know. And I was, to start with. But I think it was more about being told I couldn't carry a gun any more, rather than any real commitment to it as a career.' Kershaw pulled a rueful grin. 'I hate being told I can't do something.' She had a flashback to a room not unlike this one, and a conversation with her school's career officer in which he'd tried to put her off joining the police. The Met was a hotbed of misogyny, he'd told her – an impossibly tough place for a woman to make a career in. She'd been livid at the time, but now it occurred to her that his negativity had only spurred her on to pursue her ambition.

'And you're feeling comfortable with this decision?'

'Yeah, I think so. I probably never should have gone into firearms in the first place.' She took a breath, let it out. 'You were right. I think, after I … got stabbed, I wanted a gun. I wanted to feel safe.'

'And you don't feel that way any more?'

'No. That is, not so much that I'm gonna stay in a job that's ninety per cent false alarms and ten per cent real action.' She shrugged. 'I'm a good shot and I think I could have made a competent firearms officer, but, truthfully? I think I'm a much better detective.'

Paula nodded. 'So what are your plans?'

'My old Sarge is pleased with the work I've done on a kidnapping case, and he's got a vacancy coming up on his squad in a couple of months, so fingers crossed.'

'Of course, even as a detective, you'll be required to go into potentially dangerous situations from time to time. How will you feel, do you think, doing that without a weapon?'

'Scared, probably.' She gave a shrug. 'But maybe that's no bad thing. It might make me approach things a bit more cautiously? My Sarge would say about chuffing time.'

They smiled at each other.

'You were sent to me as a result of the Kyle Furnell incident,' said Paula. 'What's your thinking on that now?'

'I'm not ashamed of it. I had to shoot him to save my life.' She waited for Paula to say something – as usual, in vain. 'But I do wish … I wish I could go back and do things differently.' Again she saw the image from the TV report, of Kyle's mum on the courtroom steps, defiant in her fake fur – a woman from a background not unlike hers. A woman whose life had been ripped apart, through no fault of her own.

It struck Kershaw that while she could walk away from that day, from SCO19, and make a fresh start – Kyle Furnell's mum never could.

'I'm going to go and see Tanya Furnell,' she said suddenly.

'Really? What on earth for?'

It amused Kershaw to see Paula jolted out of her Zen-like professional calm.

'To try and explain what happened, why I had to shoot that day – or be killed. To … tell her I'm sorry that she lost her son.'

'And if she doesn't want to see you?'

A shrug. 'She can tell me to piss off.'

There was a moment of silence before Paula spoke. 'Such a visit would be … highly irregular. Especially since the coroner found no fault with the Met's actions.' The light reflecting off her specs made it difficult to read her expression, but to Kershaw it sounded like she was reading from the manual, trotting out what the brass would expect her to say. 'And I'm sure you're aware that it wouldn't go down well with your superiors.'

Kershaw suddenly heard something that made her face split in a grin. Something she hadn't heard in over a year. Her dad's voice, piping up in her ear.

Sue me, it said.

Forty-Eight

'What do you fancy for lunch, Janek?' asked Oskar, peering into an empty fridge.

'How should I know?' said Janusz, testily. 'It's only eleven o'clock – I'm not hungry.' Since Kasia had dumped him and disappeared to another country, eleven days earlier, Oskar had more or less moved in, kipping down on the sofa at night. He'd given some story about needing a place to stay, due to unspecified building work at his place in Walthamstow, but Janusz suspected that in truth, his mate wanted to keep an eye on him – something that managed to touch and enrage him at the same time.

He reached past Oskar's barrel-like figure to retrieve a can of Tyskie from the fridge door. Popping the ring pull, he took a deep draught, welcoming the way the chill fizzy liquid stung his throat.

'*Kurwa*, Oskar! Don't look at me like that,' he growled. 'You're not my mother.' So what if it was his third or fourth beer of the morning? It was nowhere near enough to get him drunk, just the right amount to tip him into that slightly fuzzy zone which took the edge off his mood.

'Why don't I make us some *bigos*?' said Oskar, his chubby face lighting up.

Janusz snorted. 'If it's anything like the *barszcz* you served up yesterday, I'll pass.' Oskar's cack-handed attempt at making the classic beetroot soup had left the kitchen looking like the scene of a chainsaw accident.

Seeing his mate's face fall, Janusz felt like a heel. He knew Oskar was only trying to look out for him, but all he really wanted was to be left alone.

When his phone buzzed, he was tempted to ignore it but seeing Stefan's name come up on the screen, he changed his mind. Whatever the old rogue might want, any distraction from his mind's endless circling around the subject of Kasia, the child, what might have been, *should* have been … was to be welcomed.

'Easter Greetings!' said Stefan. Janusz had almost forgotten it was Good Friday. Last year he'd gone to church for evening Mass and to pay his respects to the tableau of Christ's tomb. No chance he'd been doing that this year – *nor ever again*, he swore silently.

'Stefan. What can I do for you?'

'It's about the cat.'

'The cat?'

'I left a message offering you good money to find him, and you haven't even had the decency to come and get the details!'

Two possibilities went through Janusz's head: either Stefan was losing his marbles, or he couldn't discuss whatever was on his mind over the phone.

'I'm sorry about that – I've been a bit busy.' He checked the time. 'I can be there in an hour.'

Draining his can of beer, he went to collect his coat from the sofa. As he picked it up, his gaze snagged on a ladder of paint stripes on the wall behind – the legacy of Kasia's deliberations over what colour to paint the living room.

'I'm off out for a bit,' he told Oskar, who was at the draining board drying up some plates. 'Leave that,' he told him, guilt and exasperation vying in his voice, 'we're only going to use them again later.'

'*Dobrze*,' said Oskar, his gaze flickering anxiously over Janusz's face. 'Will you be back by three?'

'How should I know?' he growled. 'Anyway, what's happening at three?'

'Nothing.'

It was a relief to be striding across the Fields, beyond the reach of Oskar's well-meaning ministrations, although even here there lurked memories ready to trip him up. There was the lime tree under which he and Kasia had sat one hot and humid day last summer, sharing a chilly rectangle of cheesecake from the local *sklep*. He could still smell the blossom-honeyed air and picture Kasia, long legs scissored neatly before her, cheeks flushed from the sticky embrace of a London heatwave.

Janusz had agreed to meet Stefan at a pub in Wanstead. The old boy had chosen it because it had a van selling seafood in the car park – once a common sight through-out the East End. After getting the drinks in, Janusz joined Stefan in the beer garden, where he sat under a gas-fired heater, a styrofoam tray piled with rollmops and shellfish in front of him.

The old man rubbed his hands together, producing a sound like balsa wood being sanded. 'Fish on Friday. A happy conjunction of East End and Catholic traditions,' he pronounced. Using a cocktail stick, he dragged a whelk from its shell, before chewing it with the air of a connoisseur sampling the finest beluga.

'Are you sure you won't help me out?' he asked Janusz, waving at his fishy cornucopia. 'No? When you reach my age, you'll discover that food is one of life's great consolations. My father – God rest his Soul – used to say there weren't many things you could look forward to doing three times a day until you die.'

Having first asked permission, Janusz lit a cigar, holding it out to one side so his smoke wouldn't disturb the old man's meal. 'So, what's all this about a cat?'

'You'll forgive the fabrication, I hope,' said Stefan. 'Excessive caution on my part, no doubt, but the kind of people you've come close to have a discourteous habit of eavesdropping on people's phone calls.'

Janusz lowered his voice. 'We're talking about the Russians? The ones the data stick belonged to.'

'Quite so.'

'I thought we'd agreed that subject was closed,' said Janusz, casting a casual look around: luckily, this early in the day theirs was the only occupied table. 'They got back what they were looking for and, as far as I'm concerned, that's the end of it.'

Over the lip of his glass of Guinness, Stefan's blackcurrant eyes danced. 'I'm guessing that the person behind the financial transactions detailed on that stick has no desire to see it entering the public domain.'

A mouthful of Janusz's lager went down the wrong way, provoking a coughing fit. After many hours pondering the chain of events that had led to the murder of the hapless Vasily Vetrov, he could find only one possible explanation of why the gang's own accountant would risk keeping a private record of such incriminating documents. His conclusion: that Vetrov had decided they might come in useful one day, either as some sort of leverage against his masters, or as an insurance policy in case the cops ever came knocking. In the event, it was Steve and Jared who'd turned up on his doorstep, and he'd had no alternative but to report the robbery to his Russian masters. The Spetsnaz enforcer had been dispatched to investigate, and after Vetrov's tongue had been loosened, he'd confessed that the robbers had made off with more than just a carrier bag full of cash.

Janusz was sure of one thing: he had no desire to share Vetrov's fate. Leaning forward, he spoke in a murmur. 'Look, Stefan: I have no idea who these people are, but I do know they're completely ruthless. They killed three men, one of them an innocent bystander, to keep that information under wraps.'

If Stefan was surprised, he showed no sign of it. 'Which is precisely why I wondered whether you mightn't share my desire to see justice done.'

'Justice?' Janusz stared at him. 'We can hardly phone up the cops and say, by the way, here's some info on a Russian criminal gang we found on a data stick.'

'I agree it wouldn't be safe to share it with the police.' Stefan speared a couple of brown shrimp. 'But there may be another way. I don't know how much you gathered about the documents I decoded?'

335

Janusz blew cigar smoke out the side of his mouth. 'This Brunswick Entertainment is obviously a shell company the gang uses to launder dirty money through a string of accounts. The cash mostly gets turned into assets, but one time, somebody needed some cash urgently. Hence the email asking for the transfer of the two hundred thousand euros from the Cyprus bank to a Moscow account.'

Stefan nodded. 'Direct routes are usually avoided, in case the authorities should ever try to "follow the money", but on that single occasion, they broke their own rules.' He locked his penetrating gaze on Janusz. 'Remember where the email came from? *SBelyakov@MinskTel.com.*'

Janusz nodded.

'Well, I've done a little research,' said Stefan. 'MinskTel is a telecoms company based in Belarus, owned by one Nikolai Belyakov. The email address belongs to his younger brother, Sacha, one of the directors.'

'So this Belyakov, he's a gangster as well as a businessman?'

Stefan made an eloquent gesture suggesting the imprecision of such distinctions in the Russian context. 'Organised criminals have been infiltrating the business sector for decades: companies are a useful cover for their extra-curricular activities. You know, in his youth, Nikolai Belyakov fought in Afghanistan' – he paused to send Janusz a meaningful look – 'as a member of Spetsnaz.'

The old boy evidently hadn't forgotten Janusz quizzing him about Russia's elite special forces. Janusz sensed another piece of the puzzle slipping into place: who else would this Belyakov character call on to sort out a difficult situation but a trusted former comrade in arms?

'But Stefan, where's the point in discussing all this?' he waved his cigar. 'Even if I wanted to go to the cops – which I don't – people like Belyakov never get punished.'

'Certainly, there's little chance of putting him behind bars.' Stefan paused, his brown eyes alight with mischief. 'Except perhaps figuratively.'

Janusz winced – realising he'd let his cigar burn down to his fingers. 'What do you mean?'

'Belyakov has been spending a lot of time, not to mention money, in London lately. In the last year, he's acquired a club in Mayfair and a whole street of Georgian terraces in Ladbroke Grove. His wife *adores* Harvey Nicks and I hear he's put his six-year-old, Alexei, down for Harrow School.'

'How the hell do you know all this?'

Stefan ignored the question. 'For a man like Belyakov, I suspect being barred from coming here would constitute a cruel and unusual punishment. But he has managed to stay off the list of sanctioned individuals … so far.'

Janusz's brain scrabbled to catch up. The list imposed on Russia by the international community to dissuade Putin from his covert military activity in Eastern Ukraine had blacklisted hundreds of people close to the regime, freezing their overseas assets and bank accounts, and denying them and their families entry to the USA and Europe.

'Are you saying that proving he's a money launderer would be enough to put him on the list?'

'Yes. And freezing his interests in London would put him in a very tight spot. With the Russian economy in freefall, it might even be the finish of him.'

337

Janusz grinned. 'It's a nice idea, Stefan, but how the hell do you propose pulling it off?'

Stefan removed the paper napkin tucked into his collar and wiped his hands clean. 'I have friends in high places. Or perhaps I should say, shady places.'

Janusz suddenly remembered where Stefan had worked for sixteen years after the war. 'You mean ... in the intelligence services?'

Stefan opened a gnarled hand in assent. 'I have a contact, a senior operative in the Russian section, whom I see from time to time. He knows I keep my ear to the ground. And now that relations with the Kremlin are back in the deep freeze, he's just asked me down to Vauxhall for lunch.'

After studying the old boy's expression, Janusz decided he was telling the truth. 'Why are you even telling me all this? Why not simply pass the information on to this contact of yours?'

'I thought it prudent to speak to you first, to ensure there were no potential repercussions of which I might be unaware.'

Setting his elbows on the tabletop, Janusz massaged his temples, thinking it over. 'I suppose this Belyakov would never suspect some small-time private eye of having him put on an international blacklist,' he said, finally.

Stefan nodded. 'My thoughts exactly. Your name wouldn't even be mentioned, of course, and the real reasons behind the sanctions would remain entirely secret.'

Getting Belyakov onto the sanctions list would still be a long way short of proper retribution for the mayhem he'd unleashed on the streets of East London, thought Janusz – not to mention the devastation the episode had wrought on his private life. He felt the corners of his mouth start to curl upward. *But it would be better than nothing.*

'Stefan?' He pulled a sudden, savage grin. 'Be my guest. Give your contact the information. Sanction the *skurwysyn.*'

Stefan nodded approvingly. 'A toast then,' he said, raising his Guinness. 'Goodbye, Harvey Nicks.'

Raising his pint in response, Janusz pulled a grin. 'Farewell, Harrow School.'

Forty-Nine

The surge of vengeful elation sparked by Stefan's proposal had all but dissipated by the time Janusz got back to Highbury.

Opening the door to the apartment, he found the place empty but for Copetka. The cat lay fast asleep, curled into a ginger apostrophe against the dark leather of the IKEA sofa, the one he and Kasia had picked out together just a few weeks ago.

He stood in the silent living room, holding his breath, picturing again the life that they'd planned together; the feelings of loss as sharp today as they had been when he saw her walk up the stairs and onto that plane – and out of his life. He understood for the first time what amputees experienced, when they felt the pain of a lost limb.

Going to the fridge, only to find they were out of beer, he heard the downstairs doorbell. Two long rings and one short one. *Oskar.*

He cursed out loud: he had hoped to have a couple of hours to himself, getting gently soused as the living room darkened around him, enfolded in the cloak of his own misery.

Through the intercom, Oskar said: 'Sorry, Janek. I forgot my key.'

A minute later, there came a tap at the apartment door. Janusz half opened it, but as he was turning away, he realised something wasn't right. It wasn't the stocky outline of Oskar he'd glimpsed silhouetted in the doorway, but that of a tall young man – a stranger.

Nie! Not a stranger. *Bobek.*

He came in cautiously, gaze lowered, as if unsure of his welcome. For a beat, they stood facing each other. Then Janusz enveloped his son in a bear hug, gripping him so tight he could feel the bony wings of his shoulder blades. For the first time in years, the boy submitted without complaint.

'*Kurwa*, Bobek! What are you doing here? Why didn't you tell me you were coming?'

The boy looked at the floor, wearing an embarrassed half-smile. 'Mum's been driving me nuts, so I used my Christmas money to buy a flight. I called Uncle Oskar this morning and he picked me up from Stansted.'

Janusz registered Oskar hovering in the background, a carrier bag of shopping hanging from each fist.

'You said I could come and stay for Easter,' the boy said. 'Is it okay?'

'Sure, of course. It's ... fine.' Janusz couldn't take his eyes off him. *When did he get so tall?* 'We'd better phone home to let your mum know you're safe.'

Bobek shrugged. Dropping his rucksack on the floor, he threw himself down on the sofa. 'You've got Sky!

Mega!' he said, scooping up the remote control. 'Is there any food, Tato? I'm starving.'

'Sure,' said Janusz: there was something bracing about the selfishness of youth. His eyes met Oskar's and they shared an eloquent grin. 'Uncle Oskar is threatening to make *bigos.'*

Epilogue

The air was so veiled in vapour that the only sign a second man had entered the steam room was the soft thunk of the heavy glass door closing.

The man, who wore only a white towel fastened round his waist, hesitated before stepping into the hot wet fog. Making out the outline of a stocky, dark-haired man, completely naked, sitting on the bench lining the wall, he chose a spot at right angles to him. For a long moment, the only sound was the burble of the steam machine and the *tink tink* of water dripping from the granite-lined ceiling.

'Simeon, right?' he murmured.

'Towel,' replied the stocky man.

Lifting his butt, he slipped off his towel and rolled it up, before handing it over.

'That's better,' said Simeon, setting it to one side.

'How do I know … it's you?'

'Because I'm the one who left the present for you in locker 101.' For someone so well built, he had a surprisingly high-pitched voice. 'You did remember the combination for the padlock?'

'Yeah. Thanks.'

The steam cleared a little, and Simeon sized up the second man: early thirties, hair thinning at the temples, with a purple birthmark shaped like a thumbprint beneath his right eye.

'Good. So where can we find what we're looking for?'

The younger man's naked knee started to dance up and down. 'I don't make a habit of this, you know,' he said. 'It's just I've had some bad luck lately.'

Simeon just folded his arms. There came the low hissing sound of the steam machine starting up.

The guy murmured something, his voice so low that Simeon had to shuffle along the bench towards him. 'Come again?'

'He's in Chicago ... working for a construction company.'

'Really. You'd better have more than that for thirty fucking grand.' His tone was reasonable, but somehow that only made it sound more menacing.

'I left the address and the GPS coordinates in the locker, like you said.'

'Good. And what's the new name?'

There was a long pause. 'Terry Markham. Terry and Angelika Markham.'

A smile started to spread across Simeon's face, before it was obscured by a cloud of steam. Getting to his feet, he picked up the wet balled towel and plopped it into the younger man's lap.

'Nice doing business with you.'

344

Glossary

To save bamboozling the English reader, the many Polish words and phrases scattered through this book have been anglicised by the removal of unfamiliar characters and accent marks – for which, apologies to Polish speakers. I hope the meanings are largely self-explanatory from their context, but readers have told me a glossary is helpful, too. So below is a basic guide to pronunciation, a list of translations from the text, and some Polish swearwords – not to be used in polite company ...

Please note that Polish words take many alternative endings according to the number and gender of the addresser/addressee, to name just two of a long list of varying factors, so any apparent inconsistencies are (I hope) not typos, but a glimpse into the complexity of the language.

Pronunciation pointers

Janusz (Yan-ush) – 'j' is always a 'y' sound; 'sz' is 'sh'

czesc (chesh) – 'hi'. Similar to the Italian *ciao*. 'Cz' gives a
  harder 'ch' sound than the 'sh' of 'sc'

Kasia (Kash-ah) – 'si' makes another very common 'sh'
  sound

Bohuslaw (Boh-hoos-wav) – in the Polish alphabet this
  version of l is written ł and pronounced 'w'

wodka (vod-ka) – 'w' is always pronounced 'v'

zurek (zhur-ek) – 'z' is often (but not always!)
  pronounced with a soft 'j' sound as in this, a kind of
  soup

makowiec (mah-koh-vee-ets) – the 'c' in 'iec' is actually
  pronounced 'ts' in this, Janusz's favourite, poppyseed
  cake

Everyday expressions

nie (nee-ay) – no

tak (tak) – yes

prosze pana/pani (prosha-pan-ah/pan-ee) – please sir/
  madam/Mr/Mrs

dobrze (dob-zha) – okay

naprawde? (na-prav-dah) – really? is that right?

to prawde (toh-prav-dah) – that's true

dzien dobry (zhin dob-ry) – good day

dziekuje (zhin koo-ya) – thank you

na zdrowie! (nazh-drovia) – cheers!

przepraszam (prruh-shuh-prasham) – sorry/excuse me
  (polite form)

Other words and phrases in the text

ani o jote – not one jot

barszcz – beetroot soup

biszkopty – biscuits

brawo – bravo, well done

dyskretny – discreet

dziadzia – grandfather

glupek – fool, idiot

honorowy – honourable

kapitulowali – capitulated; surrendered

katastrofa – disaster

kochanie; moj kochanie – beloved; my beloved

kolego – mate, buddy

komiczne – funny, humorous

kotku – diminutive of cat (*kot*) i.e. little cat; endearment

maluszku – little one

misiu – teddy bear; endearment

mniam mniam – nom nom/yum yum

naturalnie – naturally; of course

niemozliwe – impossible

okropne – terrible

piekna – pretty, cute

psychol – nutter (offensive)

sklep – shop

smaczny – delicious; tasty

solidne – solid, reliable

spoko – okay

straszny – creepy

szmalec – literally, lard; slang for cash. Probably from the
    Yiddish *schmaltz*

tato – dad

zlom – scrap metal

skomputeryzowane – computerised

moj tygrysku – my little tiger; endearment

Poles love diminutives of names and 'ek' is one of the commonest, giving something akin to Johnny, Billy etc. So Janusz becomes Janek – (Yan-ek); and Bohuslaw, Slawek (Swah-vek). There are a host of other variations: e.g. someone with the name Kasia, which is already a diminutive of Katarzyna, might also be affectionately called Kasiek, Kaska, Kasiulka and Kasiunia ...

Swearwords, insults, and exclamations

dupa blada! (dupa blah-dah) – pale arse! An exclamation that defies translation.

dupe (dupa) – literally, arse; can also mean idiot, fool, twat

dziekie – thank God!

gowno (goov-no) – shit

jaja (yah-yah) – balls

kutas (koo-tas) – prick

kurwa, (koor-vah) *kurwa mac* (koor-vah mash) – literally, 'whore' and 'whore mother' but used as an all-purpose intensifier like 'fucking'. Among Polish workmen, *kurwa* seems almost a conversational condiment ...

mega – cool

pedzio (ped-zhio) – offensive term for a gay man

skurwysyn (skoor-vis-in) – literally, 'son of a whore' or 'son of a bitch'

skurwiel (skoor-veel) – fuckhead

chuj (hoo-ey) – literally, prick, but the closest Anglo Saxon equivalent to this, the worst possible term of abuse, would be cunt.

Notes and Thanks

Many readers might be surprised to learn that it was three Polish codebreakers who first broke the German air force Enigma code in the early thirties, laying the groundwork for Turing's later breakthrough on the German Navy code – work for which they have only recently received any recognition. Hugh Sebag-Montefiore's Enigma *is excellent reading for anyone interested in the story.*

There are so many people who helped me to create this third book in the series.

Thanks go to finance veteran Paul McNamara for his advice on money laundering and the world of Russian finance; and to IT forensics whizz Jonathan Bonnick for the computer security and hacking info.

I am indebted to Anja Majek who not only checked the Polish grammar and spellings but was also an invaluable source of evocative phrases and sayings. My personal favourite: 'clean as a teardrop'. I'm sorry I'll never grasp all those Polish endings, Anja.

My dear friend DS Paula James has once again been a great help on police life and procedure, while gracefully accepting that fiction inevitably involves missing out some of the more tedious parts of the process. Many thanks, too, to a certain female firearms officer, who must remain nameless, for giving me inspiration and advice on Kershaw's latest (mis)adventures. Any departures from proper procedure are, as ever, down to me.

I am also very grateful to the Polish Cultural Institute, and its lovely head of literature, Magda Raczynska, for its unstinting and generous support of my work; to the fine folk at Merseyside Polonia; and to Theakstons Old Peculier Crime Festival – aka Harrogate – the unmissable summit of the crime writers' year.

The many friends, readers and fellow writers who've supported me, spread the word, and put up with all the moaning and angst, are too numerous to thank here, but here's a few … David Mark, Mark Billingham, Martyn Waites, Barry Forshaw, Stav Sherez, Sarah Hilary, Mari Hannah, Katherine Armstrong, Jamie Lee Nardone, Malcolm McKay, Emlyn Rees, James Craig, Lynn Roberts, Asia – aka A.M. Bakalar, and Selina O'Grady.

Huge thanks and farewell to my former publisher Scott Pack, who has now left the building, and hello to my new one, that minx Minna Fry. A heartfelt thank you to Lucy Dauman for her fine editing, and another to the tireless Cicely Aspinall.

Finally, loving thanks to my dear husband Tomasz Piotr, who, when asked whether the character of Janusz is based on him, replied that he fears he's more likely to be the inspiration for Oskar.

Connect with Anya on Facebook:
facebook.com/AnyaLipskaWriter
& Twitter @AnyaLipska
or learn more at www.anyalipska.com